SAME
DIFFERENCE

ALSO BY SIOBHAN VIVIAN

The List

Not That Kind of Girl

A Little Friendly Advice

SAME DIFFERENCE

SIOBHAN VIVIAN

SCHOLASTIC INC.

No part of this publication may be reproduced, stored in a retrieval system, or transmitted in any form or by any means, electronic, mechanical, photocopying, recording, or otherwise, without written permission of the publisher. For information regarding permission, write to Scholastic Inc., Attention: Permissions Department, 557 Broadway, New York, NY 10012.

This book was originally published in hardcover by PUSH, an imprint of Scholastic Inc., in 2009.

ISBN 978-0-545-75802-4

12 11 10 9 8 7 6 5 4 3 2   14 15 16 17 18 19/0

Printed in the U.S.A. 40

This edition first printing, December 2014

The text type was set in Electra LH.

For Nicky, xoxo

ACKNOWLEDGMENTS

David Levithan — from pep talks to mixes, from title wars to eloquent flap — you are the editor of dreams. Thanks to you, and to everyone at Scholastic, for the love.

Oh Ro Stimo. Your wisdom is invaluable (sung to the tune of "Oh Yoko").

Jenny Han, only you could turn a dungeon into a writer's paradise. JS forever!

Brian Carr and Emily RosenBerg–Big love. Seriously.

Special thanks to Erin Elman, Kristina Wyatt, Rosi Dispensa, and the University of the Arts Pre-College Summer Program faculty and students.

To the Longstockings, Emmy Widener, Morgan Matson, Amalia Ellison, Lynn Weingarten, Eamon Tobin, Brenna Heaps, Robin Drew, the entire Vivian clan, Grammy, and Miss Bridget Siobhan Charlotte Addams McLaughlin—without you, this book would not exist.

One

When I was a kid, I drew clouds that looked like the bodies of cartoon sheep. The sun was a perfect yellow circle. Birds flew in flocks of little black Vs. And I made sure there was always a rainbow.

It's too bad the sky doesn't actually look like that. In a way, the real thing is sort of a letdown.

"Emily?"

"Yeah?" I raise my head off my towel and squint away the sun. Meg is lying on her side, with dark oversized sunglasses perched on the top of her head. She's staring at me. I give her a few seconds to say something, but her lips stay pressed together tight. "What is it?"

"I'm trying to imagine you with a mohawk," she says, leaning forward.

I laugh. "Why?"

"Oh, I don't know." She pauses to retie the plaid strings on her bikini bottom. "I bet mohawks are cool in art school. But I think you'd regret it. Maybe not right away, but definitely in September."

Meg reaches for the coconut oil and gives her flat stomach a spritz, then fires one at mine to be cute. "Just remember, it's not like bangs or layers that you can hide underneath a headband until they grow out. There is no graceful way to grow out a mohawk."

I rake my fingers through the knots in my damp hair. A few dark blond strands get left behind, swirled around my fingers. It took me practically all of junior year to grow my thin hair past my shoulders. "I'm not getting a mohawk," I say, probably more serious than I need to be.

"Okay, okay." She lets a giggle slip. "Could you imagine if you did, though? You'd be the talk of Cherry Grove." Meg slides her sunglasses back in place and lies down. But she's only still for a minute before she rolls around, tugging on the corners of her towel, trying unsuccessfully to get comfortable. "Tomorrow's going to feel so weird without you here."

There's a bowl full of cut lemons between us on a green glass mosaic table. I fish around, find a juicy half, and give it a squeeze over my head. I've always wished my hair was striking platinum instead of dark honey, which is the most unexciting shade of blond, the one that some people even call brown. A bit of juice drips into my eyes and stings them like crazy. "You'll have Rick," I remind her. Though I doubt she's forgotten.

"Rick's not my best friend." Meg stands up suddenly. Red stripes run across her back from the thick rubber strips of her lounge chair. She walks over to her pool, sits down at the edge, and dips her feet in the water.

"It's not like I'm moving to Philadelphia," I say. "It's only three days a week, and I'll be home by dinner if I catch the five-thirty train."

4

June

She sighs. "Maybe I'll get a job. Maybe Starbucks is hiring."

We both know Meg isn't going to get a summer job, so neither of us says anything. I let her sit with her back to me, kicking her legs through the water in slow motion. I get what she's hinting at. Even though there've been lots of changes this year, and even though my summer art classes aren't a big deal, the reality is that we've never spent a summer apart since becoming best friends and neighbors five years ago. Meg's going to miss me.

I already miss her.

A cloud passes the sun and drops a cold shadow over the backyard. Meg takes off her sunglasses and tosses them onto her towel. "No use laying out now. Do you wanna walk to Starbucks?"

"Yeah," I say. "Sure."

We throw clothes over our still-damp bathing suits and flip-flop down the stone path that leads from the backyard to the front of Meg's house.

Meg and I live inside a gated community called Blossom Manor, which is made up of ten cul-de-sacs shaped like thermometers. Houses run up the sides in pairs, leading to the three biggest homes curved around the bulbous tip. That's where we live, directly across from each other, in identical mansions.

The homes of Blossom Manor are all posh and stately, with thick green lawns stretching to the curbs. The streets are named after pretty flowers, like Petunia and Bluebell, and paved with rich red brick in zigzag patterns. The low-pitch hum of purring central air-conditioning units only makes the chirping birds sound sweeter.

I'm suddenly overcome with an achy, sentimental feeling. Cherry Grove, New Jersey, is practically perfect, especially in the summertime. It makes me wish that I was still a kid, when summers meant I played with Meg from morning until night, pool hopping until our skin was pruned and our lips were blue, eating nothing but hot dogs from backyard grills and bomb pops from the ice cream truck. There's a weight in my stomach that doesn't usually appear until August, right before school starts up. The sadness of summer coming to an end, even though mine only just started. That's how things go when you get older, I guess. Summers matter less and less, until you turn into a grown-up and they disappear entirely.

Meg and I reach the back of the development and squeeze through a line of tall, tightly packed bushes that serve as a natural fence to keep nonresidents out of Blossom Manor. When Meg and I first discovered this passage, we felt a rush. It was like our little world had suddenly become huge.

On the other side, there's a steep sandy hill. Meg and I slip and slide as we amble our way up, clinging to each other for traction, and then again for balance as we reach Route 38 and brush away the grit that sticks to our coconut-oiled legs. Even though we live right off the highway, you wouldn't know it. The noise of the traffic gets tangled in the bushes.

The Starbucks is an oasis in the middle of the sun-baked parking lot. The heat of the blacktop burns through my flip-flops, so I run for the door. Inside, it's refreshingly frosty. My hair blows around my face in damp wisps, and goose bumps compete with mosquito bites for space on my legs and arms.

When we step up to the counter, the barista rings us up without even asking for our order, because Meg and I always get the same thing — two grande frozen peppermint mochas and one old-fashioned glazed donut, cut in half.

"My treat," Meg says, and hands me a crisp twenty from inside her woven straw purse. "And I'm sorry if I sounded like a wet blanket earlier. I mean, it'll suck not to hang out whenever we want to this summer, but we'll just make the most of the days when you don't have classes. And, like you said, you'll be around for parties and stuff at night." She smiles. "I'm so proud of you, Emily."

"For what?"

"For following your passion! Pursuing your art!" It sounds corny when Meg puts it that way, but she truly means it. She puts her hand to her chest and fiddles with the delicate M charm hanging off her silver necklace. It was my Christmas gift to her, from Tiffany's. Meg bought me an E one in gold, because she said gold looks better with my coloring. We never take them off. "It is seriously inspirational. I mean, I wish there was something that I was good at. I'm so untalented, it's ridiculous."

"Please. You have lots of talent." Meg is really pretty, she's in all honors classes, and she has a popular boyfriend. But I don't mention any of that out loud, because they only seem like talents to the people who don't have them. Instead, I grin and say, "You're double-jointed!"

Meg laughs, and my heart surges with love for her. Meg is the kind of best friend you read about in old books. She's that sweet all the time. A lot of girls in our high school think she's fake, but they're totally, totally wrong.

While I wait for the drinks, Meg drags two overstuffed armchairs to our favorite table — the checkerboard table centered at the big window. I drop into my seat and tuck my legs underneath me to keep them warm. Over Meg's shoulder, traffic whizzes along the highway. A big green sign hovers over the road. My eyes trace the reflective white letters twinkling in the sunlight.

"Can you believe Philly is only thirty miles away?" I take a small sip, because frozen peppermint mochas are too sweet to gulp and I want mine to last forever. "I mean, thirty miles is actually pretty close. We could walk thirty miles, if we had to."

Cherry Grove doesn't have a trace of city to it. A lot of people commute from here to Philadelphia for work. People who don't like the city. There are no tall buildings or high-rise apartment complexes here. Things feel very quaint — most of the buildings are old, and if they're not, they're eventually made to look that way. Like our town hall. Before the fire last summer, it was an ugly office building, with brown stucco and mirrored windows. But then it was rebuilt with fieldstone shipped in from somewhere in rural Pennsylvania, and black shutters were attached to all the windows. They even added a big clock that hammers a brass bell on the hour.

Meg uses her tongue to chase a drip of whipped cream off the side of her cup. "Do you remember freshman year, when Becky Martin came back from Easter break with those bangs she cut herself? She had to wear that floppy velvet hat to the spring dance." She closes her eyes and shakes her head. "I felt so bad for her."

I remember. Becky's bangs were so short that they stuck straight out like a visor. She cut them because she was bored. I overheard her say that when she was crying in the bathroom, trying to find someone with extra bobby pins. Boredom can be dangerous in a place like Cherry Grove. It can make you do things you'll regret.

June

But I don't get why Meg is bringing this up now. I don't need to be scared out of a hairstyle I don't even want.

Meg picks off a few crumbs from her half of the donut and pops them into her mouth. "Ooh! I almost forgot. I have a big favor to ask you."

"Yeah?"

She spins around in her chair so that her tan legs dangle off one armrest while the other supports her back. Then she twists her long chestnut hair up into a messy bun. Like clockwork, freshly snipped layers fall out the sides and frame her face. "I want to surprise Rick with a great gift for our six-month anniversary. Not like a dumb shirt or video game." She looks sad for a second, but then she brightens. "Could you help me think of something special?"

"Umm, sure," I say. But I don't have any ideas right this second, maybe because I myself have never had a boyfriend, an anniversary, or even a French kiss that didn't occur during spin the bottle or taste like beer. Before junior year, Meg hadn't either. We'd both been equal.

Meg's purse buzzes on the floor. It lies just out of Meg's reach, so I dig the cell out for her. At the bottom, I touch a chewed-up blue pen. My fingers cling to it like it's magnetized. It's almost like I can't help but pick it up.

Meg flips open her phone and starts texting. While she does, I brush the crumbs off my napkin and start to draw. The pen fits in my hand so comfortably, like an extension of my fingers. I draw a lot in moments like this. It gives me something to concentrate on while life happens to everyone else.

There's a tiny dip between Meg's nose and upper lip, and it's shaped like a perfect teardrop. I draw that pretty quickly, but it looks funny there, floating on the napkin. It needs more context. And since Meg is otherwise occupied — texting away with Rick, no doubt — I draw the flat lines of her lips. Then I add her nose and the sloping angles of her heart-shaped face. I don't try to map the couple of dark freckles she has, because the pen is leaky and the napkin only too happy to soak up the extra ink.

As Meg appears on the napkin, it makes me excited. I mean, I'm relatively new at this — drawing for real. Not cartoon-style where eyeballs are round circles with big black dots inside and feet face outward at an impossible angle. It's still surprising when I'm able to draw something that actually looks like what I want it to. Each time feels like a tiny miracle.

When I glance up from the napkin, Meg is staring at me. "Emily, are you drawing me?! Like, right now?"

I take a quick sip of my mocha and put the cup down so it blocks her view. "Sort of. Not really."

Meg rises up out of her seat, trying to peek. "Yeah, right! You never show me any of your drawings. Come on! Let me see it."

My first instinct is to crumple it up, because it's just a quick sketch and not anything I'm even trying to make good. But I know I have to get better about showing my work to people, especially considering my art classes start tomorrow. So I hand it over, and pretend I'm not nervous about what she thinks.

Meg takes the napkin carefully, cradling it in her hands. "Wow," she says slowly, like each letter is its own sentence.

"You like it?" I'm not trying to fish for compliments, but I want to make sure she's being honest. Meg definitely prefers niceness to truthfulness, and when you know that about somebody, it's practically impossible not to feel insecure, no matter what they tell you.

And then it hits me. Maybe I could draw a portrait for Meg to give to Rick for their anniversary! Nothing too colorful or big. Just a simple sketch done in pencil on a small sheet of heavy paper — the kind where you can see the spidery veins of the tree pulp. Then we could go pick out a nice frame to put the portrait in. It might seem like a girly gift for some guys, but not Rick. He's got photos of Meg all over the place — in his wallet, tucked into the visor in his truck. He even keeps one underneath the insole of his baseball cleat for good luck.

But just as I'm about to share my idea, Meg's head drops to the side and her bottom lip gets so pouty, it shows a rim of the slick pink inside.

"I would seriously rather get a nose job than a car this summer."

My stomach muscles get tight, like they don't want to do the work it's going to take for another breath. "What?" I reach for my napkin.

But Meg won't hand it back to me. She keeps staring down at it in her manicured hands, blinking a lot. "I just hate how fat the tip looks," she says quietly, and scratches the drawing with her nail, as if she could shave the pen marks down.

"Here, let me fix it," I stutter after a few awkward seconds. The thing is, Meg's nose *is* kind of round. Not in an ugly way. In a Meg way.

The door opens and the air makes a suction sound as Rick steps into Starbucks. He's wearing stiff gray coveralls, mud-caked

Timberland work boots, and a red baseball cap embroidered with the name of his family business, WILEY LANDSCAPING. Rick is so tall and broad-shouldered that he blocks out most of the sun shining through the glass behind him.

Meg and I stare at each other in a moment of panic, my napkin drawing hanging in limbo between us. I absolutely don't want Rick to see it, so I reach for it, but Meg snatches her hand back first.

Rick rests his hands on Meg's bare shoulders and plants a kiss on the top of her head. She climbs onto her knees and hugs his torso. I watch her discreetly slide my drawing into the back pocket of her red terry cloth shorts.

I guess I should feel relief that it's hidden. Only it's kind of weird, how upset it makes me to see my drawing become a lumpy wad. She should have just given it back to me.

Rick smiles at me. "Hey, Emily. I like your flip-flops."

"Hi," I say back, and then shove my straw in my mouth. My flip-flops are the same old Havaianas that everyone in town wears. But Rick always finds some random thing like that to compliment me on. Meg says Rick's afraid I don't like him. Which isn't true, exactly. He's nice, nicer than a guy of his good looks should probably be. He's just not that smart, especially compared to someone like Meg. But he understands how tight Meg and I are, close enough so that our names are always mushed together in conversations around school, like *MegandEmily*. He gets that I'm important, that I matter.

Rick stretches and yawns. His armpits are damp, but he doesn't smell stinky. He wears the spicy smell of fresh-cut grass like a too-powerful cologne. "I thought you guys would be hanging out by the pool all day. I've just got to take one last trip to the greenhouse and then I can come over and swim." Since Rick's dad owns their landscaping business, he pretty much gets to set his own hours. Which is to say, he's always around. "Do you guys want me to drop you off anywhere on my way?"

Meg turns to me. "Do you want a ride back home? Or we can walk. It's just hot out and I'm kind of tired. But whatever you want, Emily. It's your last summer afternoon." She's talking fast. Her light blue eyes sparkle. She still gets so excited about Rick driving us around, even though he's probably given us over a million rides.

"Hey, that's right!" Rick says. "Emily, are you dreading summer school or what? I was so happy when I passed my US History final so I wouldn't have to go again this year and lose out on all the money I'd make working for my dad. But don't worry. The classes are way easier than regular school."

Even though I don't want to get into it with Rick, I feel the need to defend myself. "It's not summer school," I tell him. "It's a pre-college art program." Rick looks at me blankly, like I'm speaking another language. "It's at the Philadelphia College of Fine Art." Still nothing. "I chose to go to it."

Rick takes off his ball cap, runs his hand through his matted brown hair, and puts it back on again. Thinking. Then he chuckles in a friendly, quiet way. "Okay, that makes sense. I've never heard of anyone failing Art at Cherry Grove High."

I don't know why this annoys me so much, because Rick's right. Ms. Kay's Art class is an easy A. That's why it's so popular. That's why I took it in the first place.

No one takes it seriously. In my class, all the boys ever drew were sports players or weird *Alice in Wonderland*-type drug stuff. Amy Waterman turned every project into a chance to practice her bubble letters. And the rest of the girls were obsessed with glitter pens and making origami roses for each other. Everyone but me slept during the weekly slide-show presentations. Though it *was* actually hard to pay attention, since Ms. Kay always had the projector tweaked slightly out of focus, and unless you squinted the whole time, you'd get nauseous.

But for whatever reason, I really did like it. I looked forward to tying on my musty apron, even the eggy smell of the water in the slop sink. It was a place where I didn't have to think about anything other than what I was drawing.

So when Ms. Kay offered to recommend me for the invitation-only summer program, I felt relieved. Though, honestly, I doubt anyone else in our class would have been interested. But I needed a break from it all, and taking some art classes in Philadelphia a few times a week was as good an idea as any I could think of. Meg got a boyfriend and I got a hobby. That's just the way things worked out.

"Well, don't worry, Emily. Meg's going to be lost without you." Rick shuffles backward toward the register and grabs a bottle of water. "But I'll take good care of her while you're gone. Promise."

I say "thanks" — not because I'm thankful, but because it seems like that's what I'm expected to say.

Meg pivots so Rick can't see or hear us. She pulls my napkin out of her pocket, smoothes it out against her thigh, and hands it back to me. "I'm sorry, but I didn't want Rick to see your drawing before you had a chance to fix it. You're not mad, are you?"

Meg's apology is sincere. I can tell by how her mouth refuses to close until I let her know that things are okay, that I'm not upset.

June

"It's fine," I say, and give her arm a squeeze. "And we can get a ride home with Rick."

"You sure?"

"Seriously." And I take the tray and napkin from her hands and throw everything away — including my drawing — to prove it.

Meg and Rick wait for me outside, standing closer than close. I watch as Rick twirls a piece of Meg's long hair around his finger. She stands on her tiptoes, gently picking bits of cut grass off his neck.

I make sure to put on a smile before stepping through the door.

Two

My heart is not beating in my chest. Instead it thumps a tiny beat underneath the callus on my middle finger. The skin there is white, almost translucent. It bubbled up a week after taking Ms. Kay's class, in the exact spot where I steady my pencil when I draw. I usually keep the callus covered with a Band-Aid because it's not very pretty, only I forgot to put one on this morning. Luckily, the bump has gotten smaller, softer since school ended two weeks ago. But not by much.

"Mom, can you please put the top up and turn on the AC?" Even though I blew out and then flat-ironed my hair, it is already frizzing in the humidity, and soon my only option will be a boring ponytail. I wear ponytails a lot — you can tell by all the broken little pieces of hair that have been ripped by my elastic bands. They stick straight up if I don't hair-spray them down.

Mom shakes her head. "We don't have time to pull over, Emily. You'll miss your train, and I can't drive you into Philadelphia. There's too much going on here."

June

I sigh extra loud, so she hears me over the wind. It's funny how busy my mom is, considering she doesn't have a job. I think about saying this out loud, but I keep my mouth shut, because I want Mom to concentrate on driving, not being mad at me. I don't want to be late on my first day of classes. I want to make a good impression.

"Mom," my sister Claire whines, pulling her two long black laces really tight. Her cleats dimple the tan leather on the dashboard. "If I miss warm-ups, I'm gonna get benched."

Claire rides permanent shotgun in Mom's convertible, even though she's thirteen and I'm sixteen. That's because her legs are a lot longer than mine, and the backseat has barely any room. Plus, Claire has to squeeze in extra knee stretches before she gets dropped off at soccer camp, because she's already had ACL surgery. You'd think she'd be grateful for the front-seat privilege, which should be automatically mine, but she's not.

"They're not going to bench you," I grumble. Claire is the best player in middle school. She knows it, too. The high school coaches have come to see her play a few times. And her room is full of satiny ribbons stamped WINNER in gold and trophies, some so tall they have to sit on the floor.

"No one is going to be late," Mom says, gunning through a yellow light in exactly the way my Driver's Ed teacher told us not to. She eyes me in her rearview mirror. "But, Emily, you're going to have to get up earlier from now on, so the rest of us aren't in a panic every morning. That means no late nights before summer school."

"It's not summer school," I say. "And I didn't go anywhere last night." Rick and Meg invited me out with them for pizza and then to Putt Putt Palace, but I didn't feel like tagging along. I'm no good

17

at sports. Neither is Meg, but without a boyfriend, there's no one to laugh or tell me I'm cute when I swing and completely miss the golf ball. I just feel like I suck.

Mom shakes her head, disappointed. "Dad saw the light underneath your door after two in the morning, Emily."

The thing was, I had a hard time falling asleep. I lay in bed for the longest time with my eyes closed and my television off, hoping it would happen. But it didn't. So I got up and laid out my clothes for today on my club chair. That took about five seconds, because Meg and I had already discussed in detail what I should wear — my white capris, a tan and white striped cami, and a pair of pale gold leather skimmers that Meg let me borrow. I turned on my laptop, but no one else was online, so I shut it back down. I threw out some old makeup that I didn't use anymore. And then, when I couldn't think of anything else to do, I randomly decided to lay my new art supplies out on my floor in neat little piles.

A few weeks ago, Philadelphia College of Fine Art sent a list of materials that I'd need, like paint and brushes and charcoal and Strathmore drawing pads. It took Mom and me over an hour at Pearl to find everything.

When you're a kid, colors have obvious names. Green is grass, red is cherry, and yellow is lemon. That changes when you grow out of markers that can be washed off the kitchen walls. How was I supposed to know that Sanguine is a fancy word for red? And what kind of purple was Dioxazine? It sounded like something I should have learned in Chemistry. Mars Black didn't make much sense to me, either. Wasn't Mars the Red Planet? It kind of freaked me out.

June

Mom felt bad for me, so she made this big show of buying the most expensive stuff they had, insisting that all my brushes be sable, and not the synthetic ones that are way cheaper. I didn't complain because they were really nice, as soft as my makeup brushes from Bloomingdale's.

I'd never owned real art supplies before, and seeing my whole floor covered in them felt luxurious. The materials in Ms. Kay's classroom were old and gross. We only had big jugs of primary colors, like the ones a preschooler would finger paint with. And the brushes were frayed and fanned out and sometimes left strands behind in your strokes. We stopped using the clay because it was hard and flaky, even if you let it soak overnight inside a wet paper towel. I guess that's why it felt like the possibilities of things I could do with my new supplies were limitless. It lit me up inside. I couldn't sleep after touching everything. I was too excited for today.

"So all you're going to do is art? Like, for the whole day?" Claire turns around in her seat. "That sounds kind of boring."

Sometimes, it takes me a minute to recognize Claire as my sister. She's tall, taller than all the boys in her class. Her hair is dark brown like my dad's, and it's a lot thicker than mine. She's awkward now — a teenager's body paired up with a kid's face. But you can already tell that she's going to be somebody when she gets to high school this fall. Maybe even as soon as her braces come off.

"Right, Claire. And running up and down a field a million times sounds so fun."

"It is. And at least I'll be with my friends. How are you going to survive a whole day away from Meg?"

Claire always makes jokes about how close Meg and I are, but it's only because she doesn't have a real best friend. She just has a big group of girls who she plays sports with.

"You're just jealous. I heard you crying to Mom yesterday because I wouldn't let you come swim with us. Maybe I'd let you if you weren't so freaking annoying!"

Her face flushes deep red, like it does by the halftime of her soccer games. "Geez, Emily." She turns back around and sinks low in her seat.

"Emily, be nice to your sister," Mom scolds.

"She started it," I say.

"But you're older," Mom says. "You're supposed to be more mature."

Whatever.

We turn into the parking lot of the Cherry Grove train station. It's as crowded as the mall at Christmas.

"Just drop me off," I say, unbuckling my seat belt.

"I want to make sure you're on the right train," she says, getting out with me.

I don't understand why my mom thinks this is such a big deal. This won't be the first time I've been to Philly — there have been plenty of family drives and school trips there. It's just the first time I'll be going alone.

The track that goes to Philadelphia is easy to find because everyone's crowding together on it. The station doesn't have any windows or service people there to buy tickets. The three automated ticket machines are completely surrounded.

"I've still got to buy a ticket!"

June

"Don't worry. You can buy them on the train," Mom says. "Do you have enough cash?"

"Yeah. And I've got my credit card, too."

"What about your cell phone? Is it all charged up? Keep your wallet on you at all times. Don't talk to strangers. You need to appear street-smart, so always walk with a purpose." The train chugs into the station, and Mom yells over the noise. "And please don't forget to call me when you get there." Her bottom lip quivers.

I feel like such a baby. Luckily, no one pays me any attention, except to jostle me out of their way.

Everyone on the train is the same age as my parents. A few people watch with interest as I squish down the aisle with my big bags of art supplies. I feel confident, even a bit mysterious. I wonder if they wonder what I'm doing here all by myself.

It takes two cars before I find an empty seat. Well, it's not exactly empty. A pair of super high heels pokes out of a black leather bag on the seat next to a lady in a business suit and spotless white running sneakers.

I wait a few seconds for the lady to notice me, but she never looks up from her newspaper. I'd keep searching, but my bags are heavy and the plastic handles are starting to rip. Finally I fake cough. The woman glances at me and grudgingly moves her bag to the floor so I can sit down.

A bell rings and "Tickets!" is shouted out in a rough, gravelly voice, like you'd expect in an old movie. The passengers slide their paper tickets into shallow pockets on the seats in front of them. I take out my wallet.

Eventually, a man steps up to my row. He's got on a white button-up with a light gray tie, and his navy jacket is covered in brass buttons. I can't see the hair on his head because of his cap, but his beard has a bunch of different shades of red and blond and white in it. "Where you going, miss?"

"Round-trip to Philadelphia," I say proudly, and maybe a bit louder than necessary. And I hold out a crisp fifty-dollar bill.

He frowns and doesn't take it. "I can't break a fifty."

"Oh, sorry." I hand over a ten instead.

He still doesn't take it. And he looks annoyed. "Your ticket's thirteen dollars."

"I thought tickets were ten," I say, my voice squeaking so loud the man in front of me turns around to stare. That's what I'd read on the transit website last night.

"There's a three-dollar surcharge for buying on the train during peak hours," he explains to me. "You need to use the ticket machines on the platform."

I search through my change pocket, hoping for some quarters to make up the difference, but all I have are a few pennies and a dime. "Can I use my credit card?" I ask, yanking the silver square out of my wallet, dropping some receipts and my change on the floor.

The man laughs, not like I've said something funny, but because I've said something incredibly stupid. He points to his book of paper tickets and his hole puncher and shakes his head.

I panic. Are they going to make me get off the train at the next stop? I glance at the lady next to me. Maybe she'd help? Lend me three bucks? I'm obviously not some kind of homeless beggar.

June

But her newspaper is a shield. She doesn't want to see what's going on.

The last thing in the world I want is to cry here and now, in front of all these people. I take a couple deep breaths.

The conductor looks at me, then quickly over each shoulder. "Listen," he whispers, "just give me the ten and remember to buy your ticket on the platform next time."

I thank him, but too quietly for him to hear, as I hand over the money. He punches a bunch of holes in my ticket, sending bits of yellow confetti cascading onto the floor.

I settle back into my seat with a deep exhale. The fake leather sticks to the skin on my back and it's hard to get comfortable with my bags of supplies taking up all my legroom. The lady next to me drops her paper, gives me a flat smile, as if she were completely unaware of what happened right next to her a few seconds ago, and then flaps it open to another page.

I smile back, because what else am I going to do?

A few seconds later, my cell jingles. I think it might be Meg. But it's my dad.

good luck today picasso

Dad is the only adult I know who can text. That's how he and his secretary communicate while he's showing real estate properties and taking bids. He was the one who filled all the homes in Blossom Manor, who sold Meg's family their house. He also brought in the Starbucks and leased the stores in the strip mall across the highway. He's the real estate king of Cherry Grove.

SAME DIFFERENCE

Thirty minutes later, the train rolls over the steely blue Ben Franklin Bridge, the gray water of the Delaware River splashing in white-capped waves below us. At the end of the bridge, there's a huge sculpture of a lightning bolt crashing into an oversized metal key, which I guess represents Ben Franklin's discovery of electricity. It's like I've been struck by lightning, too, the way the hairs suddenly prickle up on my arms.

I am really doing this. It's kind of funny, how far thirty miles can be. How much bigger than myself I feel already.

As we pull into the station, everyone stands up even though we can't walk off the train yet. Someone behind me pushes into the small of my back with a briefcase. The train comes to a stop and everyone files out the small doors. I don't really know where to go so I follow the flow of the masses up to the street.

I try to find the map that came with my orientation packet, but there are too many old school papers in my bag that I forgot to throw out. A huge clock behind me chimes 9:00 a.m. Orientation will be starting.

I take off and run . . . even though I'm still not sure if I'm going in the right direction.

Three

If you're lost and trying to find an art school, you might as well forget about asking anyone who looks normal. Like moms pushing their babies in expensive-looking strollers, people in suits, groups of old ladies on their way to have brunch, or even police officers. That's gotten me nothing but confused looks and indifferent shoulder shrugs, and now I'm twenty minutes late for orientation and completely disoriented. You can't see for long distances when you're lost in the middle of a city. There's no horizon — just stacks of buildings interrupting your sight line. It's like running through a maze with tall, tall walls.

I kneel down on the sidewalk and open up my bag to try to find something with the exact address printed on it. The salty smell of bacon drifts over and makes my stomach growl. I wish I hadn't skipped breakfast.

I'm a couple feet away from a shiny metal food truck parked next to a fire hydrant. A few people are in line — two construction workers and an old lady with a dog. There's also a very, very cute guy who's watching me. He's tall and lean, in a loose pair of dirty jeans and a VACATION RHODE ISLAND! tee that looks real . . . not like one you'd buy new in the mall. His hair locks in thick curls that look like rollatini pasta, and are almost the very same color of his skin — a rich, chocolaty brown.

I smile quickly at him and go back to looking through my papers. But as I shift my weight up off my knees and the rough pavement, the breeze catches the papers and a couple of them flutter out of my bag and into the air.

Luckily, the cute boy steps off the line and grabs them for me. He actually has to jump in the air for one, and his shirt lifts up from his waistband, revealing a very flat stomach, a stretch of gray elastic band from his Calvins, and a couple of star tattoos across his hip bones.

"I'm sorry," I say, heated. "I made you lose your place in line."

"No problem," he says with a smile. "Coffee can wait." But I'm not so sure. He looks half asleep, and a bit of toothpaste flakes off the left corner of his mouth. "Are you lost?"

"Is it that obvious?" I say, still digging frantically. "Ow!" My fingertip gets sliced on the edge of a paper. I squeeze the tip to stop the burn, and it bleeds a deep red drop.

"Maybe you just need coffee. I'm always lost without coffee." He looks down at his sneakers. "Can I buy you a cup?"

It's sweet how awkward he is. I can tell by his refusal to make eye contact and the worried look on his face that this is probably the first time he's ever done something like this. And it's painfully clear that it's the first time I've ever been asked by a cute stranger if I want some coffee, since I'm so surprised by the question that my answer comes out as "Yes?"

June

"It's okay if you'd rather have tea," he says. "I mean, I'll still want to buy you a cup if you prefer tea. Even if I don't personally understand it."

I personally don't understand drinking a hot beverage on a humid summer morning, but I seriously doubt this silver cart makes anything close to a frozen peppermint mocha. Whatever. Suffering through a few sips will be totally worth it for this guy. "Coffee would be great," I say. "Milk and sugar, please."

He acts like he's a waiter writing on a pad. "Milk and sugar, coming up."

While he returns to the silver truck and my heart skips all over my body, I finally find my orientation packet. "Thank goodness!" I say, and when he returns with two steaming cups, I triumphantly show him the bunch of red papers with the words PHILADELPHIA COLLEGE OF FINE ART printed on them in a big bold font. "Can you tell me how to get here?"

"Oh, sorry!" The boy takes a step back, and suddenly notices the bags of art supplies at my feet. "You're a summer student?" His eyebrows pop up, like that wasn't at all what he was expecting. He is now very much awake.

I nod, though I don't get what he has to be sorry for. "Do you know where the university is? I'm so late." Then my cell phone rings loud in my bag. It's a lame beeping version of Madonna's "Like a Virgin" that Meg downloaded for me as a joke one time when I was in the bathroom. We've always laughed at it, but now, in front of this boy, it makes me feel incredibly lame.

I fumble to ignore the call. "My mom," I tell him. I don't know why. "She's checking in on me. I think she's nervous because I'm in the city all by myself." And then I laugh, but it sounds so

27

uncomfortable, I close my mouth and decide never to speak again.

"Interesting," he says, with a teasing sort of grin. "No need to stress. It's just around the corner on your left."

He hands over my coffee, and I'm not sure what to do. I'd really love to stay. But I really have to go.

He makes up my mind for me.

"Maybe I'll see you around sometime," he says. "After all, you know where I get my coffee in the morning. That's practically like knowing where I live."

I point to the intersection. "I guess that makes us neighbors," I say, and take off, grinning. A cute boy was just interested in me. That never, ever happens in Cherry Grove. People know each other too well there, so much so that surprises never really happen.

As soon as I step into the crosswalk and glance to my right, I see the Philadelphia College of Fine Art, all massive and stone and old like a castle, occupying almost an entire city block. It's not what I imagined at all. When I had pictured a college, I thought about a big green lawn, kids outside playing Frisbee, a real campus. It's a bit jarring, seeing it sandwiched between the sleek architecture of the surrounding silvery skyscrapers.

A bunch of signs lead the way through a set of red wooden doors. I have to push on them a couple times before they open into a huge atrium, with a glass ceiling and three levels of catwalks running along the sides.

The noise inside is deafening. High school kids are everywhere, bright flashes of color and personality, meandering from registration table to registration table, filling out permission slips, getting their temporary IDs laminated, picking up the keys to their

June

dorm rooms, and not-so-subtly sizing each other up. Rows and rows of metal folding chairs are set up in the middle of the atrium, facing a low stage and podium. The seats are almost all filled.

A few older kids — students who are actually enrolled in this college, I guess — stare down from the catwalks, underneath a big WELCOME PRE-COLLEGE STUDENTS banner, and laugh at the whole crazy scene.

And it is crazy.

Two boys in striped shirts like Bert and Ernie are hugging and crying. They look like they are mid-good-bye. One boy fishes a red marker out of his pocket and draws a heart inside the other boy's palm. It makes them both cry harder.

Next to them, a chubby Asian girl with blue-black hair, dressed in a high-neck beige lace dress that looks incredibly out of season for the last week of June, allows her mom to wipe some tomato-y lipstick from the corners of her mouth with a tissue while she taps away on her mini video game player.

A couple of feet ahead, a tall boy with an asymmetrical haircut and swollen acne awkwardly navigates the crowd toting three canvases — one under each arm and one strapped to his back. He swats people with the corners, unintentionally branding them with touches of wet pink paint.

I take small steps backward until I'm pressed against the wall. The place is crawling with the types of people you find huddled in groups of two or three at a typical high school. I don't see anyone here who looks like me, and that feels strange. There are always people like me around. We are everywhere.

A hand squeezes my shoulder. It's a slender lady wearing a white lab coat and carrying a clipboard marked STUDENT HEALTH

SERVICES. She seems like a regular nurse, except for her orange Afro and the lei of hibiscus tattoos ringing her collarbone. "Sweetie, do you have your schedule and your ID? We're about to get started."

I shake my head. "I — my train — "

"Do you know who your roommate is?"

"No. I mean, I'm a commuter. I'm not staying in the dorms."

"Breathe. Breathe. Breathe," she chants in a warm, friendly voice. "Come with me."

I follow the nurse down through the crowds. She leads me to several tables, helps me get checked in, and fills my arms with even more papers and information. I'm glad she's taking charge of the situation, because I can't seem to concentrate on anything. There's too much to look at.

There are way more kids here than I expected, at least two hundred total. Everyone seems to have at least one creative detail on them, something that shows that they belong here. I'm plain by comparison. It's embarrassing, how much effort it took for me to wear something that looks exactly like a blank piece of paper. No wonder no one makes eye contact with me.

Though it's not like the other students are mingling all that much, either. Everyone seems cautious and careful around each other. The only people who are enjoying themselves are the parents. They talk and laugh in little groups, an *Aha!* look on their faces, like suddenly, in this context, their weird kids make sense.

"Please take a seat, everyone, and we'll get you off to classes as soon as possible," a low female voice booms out of a microphone I can't see from where I'm standing.

June

"What's your name?" a boy asks me from behind a table. He's wearing a T-shirt that says STAFF, and his black hair pokes out like carpet fringe from underneath a plaid yarmulke, covered in crudely sewn yellow lightning bolt patches.

"Emily Thompson." A flashbulb pops in my face.

He thumbs through a file box. "Okay, here's your schedule, Emily. And here's your ID." He hands me a stack of papers and a warm, plastic square. My eyes are closed in the picture, like I'm sleeping. "Go ahead and find a seat."

There are not many empty chairs. The ones that are vacant seem uncomfortably sandwiched between people who lean across them to whisper to each other. I get a hollow feeling in my chest. If I had gotten here earlier, maybe I would have met some people already.

Maybe.

I walk toward the back of the atrium and take the very last chair in the row. The section reserved for parents.

A short woman with stringy black hair and burgundy lipstick stands behind the podium on the stage. She beams a smile out into the crowd. Even from this distance, her teeth look gray and dull, like she is definitely a smoker. Of cigars.

"Hello, students. My name is Dr. Tobin, and I am the Program Director of the Pre-College Summer Art Institute. I want to welcome you to Philadelphia and to six weeks filled with personal growth and artistic discovery!" She's leaning in too close to the microphone, and her deep voice vibrates along my metal chair. "I want to begin by going over the housing rules for the summer for those of you staying in the dorms."

The funny thing is, there are very few rules for her to go over. Obviously, no drugs or alcohol are allowed, but students who live in the dorms can come and go from the campus as they please until 1:00 a.m., when curfew begins. It sounds pretty good, considering the new strict summer curfew Mom's imposed.

I actually considered living on campus when Ms. Kay first gave me the brochure, but now I'm glad I decided against it. The dorms don't have air-conditioning, and the beds are probably not nearly as comfortable as mine. And what would I actually do here all by myself at night? I'd miss home too much.

Dr. Tobin asks everyone to look at their schedules. Mine is damp and wrinkled from being squeezed in my hand. I have Drawing on Tuesdays and Mixed Media on Thursdays. Those were my first-choice classes, which is pretty nice.

"Classes will run from nine until four-thirty Tuesdays and Thursdays. Wednesdays are reserved for program-wide field trips to museums and creative destinations all over the city. Everyone will be assigned designated studio space where you can store your supplies, and you should feel free to use the campus on non-program days to continue working on your projects."

I'm relieved to hear we get studio space, because the muscle between my shoulder blades is throbbing from carrying all my bags and I definitely don't want to lug this stuff in for every class. But I doubt I'll be coming into Philadelphia on the days I don't have class.

"Finally, the summer program will culminate in a gallery reception, where student work will be displayed for faculty, friends, and family. There will be a special section where the best student work will be displayed, juried by faculty consensus." Dr. Tobin clears her throat dramatically. "But I want to remind you all that art is not about competition. It's about self-expression and discovery. I hope you will allow yourself the opportunity to explore your own creativity, to strip yourself of the hesitations and insecurities that might have limited you in your high school, and create in an environment free of judgments and established social mores. Here, you are among your true peers, people who value originality."

It's sort of nice, what Dr. Tobin is saying. From the looks of everyone around me, you can tell these kids take art seriously. It's not a joke like Ms. Kay's class. These kids actually care. They want to be here. And, honestly, I do, too.

"Now, please welcome Joe Farker, our Director of Campus Security. . . ."

Two parents want to get into my row. When I stand up to let them pass, I notice something outside the glass doors behind me. There's a girl lying flat on the ground, like she's dead.

Weird.

Her sea-foam jellies have bits of glitter on them, casting small rainbows on the concrete. She's wearing a navy cap-sleeved dress, and the elastic pinches in on the flesh of her upper arms, making rings much pinker than the rest of her pale body. The dress is covered in tiny white polka dots and reminds me of something I wore on the first day of school when I was a kid. The stringy, raw ends of a pair of gray shorts, probably cut from a man's suit pants, peek out from underneath the hem. The girl puts a dark brown cigarette to her lips, flashing five colorful rhinestone rings — a gaudy one for each finger, jewelry you'd find in a glass dish on an old lady's dresser. After a second or two, she lets the smoke out in a cloud.

The most striking thing about this girl is her hair — brown, blunt, and cut in a pageboy falling just past her chin, with bangs straight across her forehead. But there's also a bright streak of electric pink underneath. That thick pink strand is about five inches longer than her brown hair, and it cascades over her shoulder and onto the concrete like a Kool-Aid waterfall.

My eyes wander back to her face, only to see that the girl is now staring at me from the ground. Like, obviously staring at me. She lifts one hand and waves, a fluttering gesture, demure like a beauty queen.

I quickly turn away and lower myself back in my chair.

Dr. Tobin returns to the podium. "Okay, students. It is now ten o'clock. You will be free to finish up the registration process, say your good-byes to your parents, and get some lunch. All of you will be expected to report to your first classes by twelve-thirty. If you have questions or need any more information, please report to my office on the third floor." She claps her hands together. "Have an exhilarating first day!"

Everyone stands up and scatters. I wait a few seconds before moving, just in case that girl is still watching me. As I lean over to grab my stuff, I glance outside. I don't see her.

I walk outside to the courtyard between the east and west dorms. Everyone's looking down at the ground. Pointing. Smiling. The girl has traced shadows all over the pavement in smooth lines of colored chalk — a tree, a bush, a statue of a stone head perched on a big marble pedestal, a trash can. The sun has already shifted the shadows just outside her lines.

By the number of tracings, it's a safe bet that this girl probably didn't go to orientation at all, if she's even a student here. She was outside by herself the whole time, making art.

June

My phone rings. It's my mom again, but I still don't answer. Instead, I walk the edges of the shadow outlines the girl has drawn, careful like I'm on a tightrope. Other people around me do the same. Someone's mom asks a security guard who did this. He shrugs and calls maintenance on his radio, telling them to bring a hose. He doesn't get that the lady wasn't complaining. He doesn't get it at all.

I try to line myself up to where the girl was when she waved at me. There, her outline is traced on the ground. It's different from the kind you see police draw around dead bodies — there's detail and depth to it. I can see the wrinkles of her clothes, the fringe of her choppy hair, features I never thought possible to capture with sidewalk chalk.

When no one is looking, I step inside the lines. My shadow doesn't come close to filling it up.

Four

On my way out of the university cafeteria, I accidentally bump into a thin, frail girl hovering over the food bar. The force knocks the serving tongs out of her hand and into a nearby tray of thick, mayonnaisey tuna salad. Splats fly everywhere. One clump hits my capris, just above the knee.

"Oh! I'm sorry," I say, and then catch myself staring into the girl's take-out box with fear and concern. Strips of fake bacon are piled high. They look like plastic play food, technicolored in an entirely unconvincing way.

"The vegan entrée has been contaminated!" the girl screeches to no one in particular, but glares at me through her thick shaggy hair like I've just slaughtered a pig right in front of her. A cafeteria lady in a white apron and black hairnet rushes over and pushes me out of the way.

Oh well. So much for good first impressions.

I walk through a door, up a set of stairs, and out onto the street. Philadelphia feels huge. If I squint, I can see City Hall in the distance, dead center in the middle of Broad Street. It's a really

June

ornate building, a stone-colored wedding cake. A statue of William Penn is perched at the very top, watching over the whole city. It was probably the tallest building at one time, but now it's dwarfed by the surrounding skyscrapers.

My very first class, Drawing, is held in the main art building directly across the street from the atrium. It's a totally uninspiring location, where you might expect the office of an accountant, except that it has a huge, empty gallery space in the lobby. I walk to the corner and wait for the traffic light to change while other kids dart across the street when they see holes in the oncoming traffic.

I flash the security guard the college ID dangling around my neck, even though he's too busy talking on his cell phone to notice, and head down a long hallway to a set of elevators. There's a bunch of people already waiting. I delicately squeeze my way onto an elevator and reach out to press the button for the seventh floor, but it's already lit up. As the doors shut, a girl with a corncob blond pixie cut, tight pencil-leg jeans, and a red silk scarf knotted around her neck runs toward us. No one holds the door for her, though, and she looks annoyed as it closes right in her face.

The elevator moves incredibly slow. I'm stuck in the corner near the buttons, and can't see the people behind me. But I hear two iPods playing different songs in a musical mess, and someone smells like they haven't learned what deodorant is yet.

I think the first stop is a photography floor, because the chemicals make my eyes water as soon as the doors open. That, and one of the kids who steps off the elevator turns around and, with his camera dangling mid-chest, takes a picture of us.

"Idiot," a boy next to me mutters as the doors close. His long hair is split in two pigtails. Fake white plastic flowers are tucked into each elastic.

I try not to stare. Maybe he's sweet or secretly good at sports, but I can't help but wonder how exactly a boy like that survives in high school.

By the time we stop on the seventh floor, there are three kids left in the elevator beside me. I smile at one freckly girl with thick tentacles of auburn dreadlocks. She nods her head at me, not exactly in a friendly way, but not meanly either.

It's slightly encouraging.

Room 713 is a large studio that smells of turpentine. There are twelve sets of easels and stools arranged in a circle, surrounding a tall pedestal made out of stacked white plywood boxes in the very center. The long tables across the back of the room are covered with half-finished assignments from the undergrad students — heads carved out of clay, wooden sculptures, plaster casings.

Shadow Girl is near the window, sitting on a stool. She scrapes her purple nail polish off with her teeth. Her shorts are dusted in chalk powder of all different colors, like the clouds in a summer sunset.

I wonder if Shadow Girl knows how many people were looking at her tracings in the courtyard. But I'm not going to tell her. I don't want her to remember that I was staring, so I put my head down and walk quickly past her.

She grabs my arm and pulls me to stop.

"I love your shoes," she tells me. "They're like . . . princess slippers or something."

June

"They're not mine," I admit. Though as soon as the words leave my mouth, I regret it. I should have said they were. After all, I do have practically the same pair.

She presses her lips together. "Umm, all right then," she says, followed by an awkward laugh, because I didn't leave much room to expand the conversation. "Well . . . make sure you pass along my compliment to their rightful owner."

"Okay." I stand there for a second, in case Shadow Girl says something else. Only, she doesn't, and neither do I, so we just kind of stare at each other. Then I head toward a seat on the other side of the room. It isn't until I sit that I realize I've been holding my breath.

I unload a few supplies, like a big drawing pad and the red plastic art box that holds my pencils and brushes. Glancing around the room, I notice I'm the only one with brand-new, untouched materials — paintbrushes wrapped in plastic, tubes of paint that need to be peeled open, unsharpened pencils. I'm a screaming newbie. I decide not to put on my smock, since no one else is wearing one.

Five more minutes and the classroom is practically full. Pixie Girl with the red scarf enters the room huffing and puffing, I guess because she had to take the stairs. She climbs onto a stool right next to Shadow Girl. Their eyes scan each other briefly before they nod and roll their eyes, as if they've just shared a silent joke. They are the only ones in class not wearing their IDs on the provided lanyards. They seem like they should be friends.

I'm sad that there doesn't seem to be the person like me here, the person I am so obviously supposed to hang out with while I'm here. Someone like Meg. But someone like Meg wouldn't exist in a place like this.

I grab my phone and pound out a quick text, just to tell Meg hello. I wonder what she's doing right now. Maybe lying by her pool, working on her tan. Actually, since it's Tuesday, she's probably walked to the town farmer's market to get some of that grilled summer corn we both love. Meg likes plain butter on hers, but I use paprika and garlic salt. Maybe Rick took the afternoon off to go with her. Probably.

The teacher comes in, a tall, skinny old man wearing frumpy brown linen pants and a raggedy black T-shirt. His head is full of wild white hair, jutting out from all angles like the bristles of an old toothbrush. A tall boy follows him, toting two bags of supplies — and holding a very familiar cup of coffee.

He spots me right away and stops at my easel.

"Wow," he says, shaking his head. "You're in my class."

"Yeah," I say. The realization makes my eyes go wide.

I accidentally flirted with my teacher this morning.

The boy still has toothpaste in the corner of his mouth, but it doesn't detract from his smile one bit. But when the older teacher glances back at him, the smile drops right off his face.

Shadow Girl and Pixie Girl both stare at me, shocked. I feel their eyes.

My phone twitters, a charm of beeps that sounds like glitter. A signal I've gotten a text. I'm sure it's from Meg, probably saying hi back. But it's not worth it to check, because now everyone's staring at me. The boy winces, like I'm in for it.

"Rule number one! No cell phones on in my class!" the old man barks. He's got a bit of an accent. Maybe Russian. I can't tell. "Absolutely none!"

"Sorry," I whisper and shut off my phone.

June

The old man walks in the center of our easels, climbs up on the platform, and stares at us with big dark eyes. He signals for the tall boy to shut the door. He does not smile. "I am Mr. Frank."

We murmur hello back to Mr. Frank. He still doesn't smile. In fact, he looks pained to be here.

"I will be your drawing teacher for the summer." His annoyance with us breaks as he gestures to the tall boy, warmly. "This is Yates, my teaching assistant. Yates has just completed his freshman year at this college and will also be giving you instruction and answering questions." Yates has his back turned to us, unloading Mr. Frank's supplies. "I would like to start today by going around the room. Tell me a little about yourself and your goals for this class."

It's too much to process at once. His name is Yates. And if Yates just finished his freshman year, he's probably only nineteen. I'll turn seventeen in September. Two years older than me isn't much of an age difference at all. But the fact that he's my teacher is a big difference. Huge, even.

Mr. Frank looks in my general direction and snaps me back to attention. "Who would like to go first?" he asks.

My stomach flips. I hate speaking in public. I'm way better with images than I am with words.

Shadow Girl raises her hand, the only volunteer. Everyone in the room sits up and pays attention. I know I do.

"My name's Fiona Crawford, and I'm from the glamorously named Fish Town." Her voice is drowsy and raspy, but it projects like she's used to addressing a crowd. "I'll be a senior next year and I need some traditional pieces for portfolio reviews so I can apply to art school."

41

Mr. Frank takes a sip of coffee from a Styrofoam cup. "Traditional as opposed to what?"

Fiona smirks. I can't exactly tell if she's annoyed that she has to explain herself, or happy that she gets to keep talking. "My work is mainly guerrilla meets performance, so it's impossible to document."

"You can take pictures. That's entirely acceptable for a portfolio." Mr. Frank looks for the next person to speak.

"Pictures?" Fiona's face curdles. "A picture can never be as meaningful as the actual experience." She arches her back into a stretch. It's almost flirtatious. "I'd rather not show the piece at all, if it's going to be some weak, half-assed version. So yeah, just set me up with some fruit in a bowl and maybe a ceramic pitcher, or whatever. A couple of still lifes and I'll be good to go."

Mr. Frank raises his coffee to his mouth and considers this. We all stay quiet. I don't know about anyone else here, but I've never heard a person say *assed* before in a class. When he lowers the cup, he reveals the smallest smile.

The class collectively shifts its weight. Fiona's answer is a lot to live up to.

Mr. Frank continues. "How many of you are going into your senior year of high school?" About half of our class raise their hands, including me and Pixie Girl. "Well, by the end of our six weeks together, you should all have more than a few portfolio-quality pieces. And the rest of you will have quite a jump on putting together something for admissions."

I haven't ever considered going to college for art. Meg and I are looking at Trenton State. Her grades are much better than mine, but hopefully we'll both get in. I worry that maybe this drawing class is going to be more advanced or serious than some-one like me, someone with no experience, is ready for.

Pixie Girl goes next. "I'm Robyn, and I'm from northern New Jersey. But it's practically New York City," she adds quickly, "because I can see the Empire State Building from my bedroom window. My parents own a gallery in Chelsea." Robyn's eyes stop on Mr. Frank, probably to see if he is impressed. If he is, he doesn't show it. "They travel through Europe most of the sum-mer and I get shipped off to Fine Art day care." I'm surprised to hear Robyn talk in such a blasé way, like she's already over this place. I guess when your parents actually own a real art gallery, these programs seem a lot like Ms. Kay's class. "Anyhow, I'd like to work on developing a more critical eye, so I can express my opinions about art better. I plan on running my own gallery one day."

"Well, we will be doing a lot of discussions and critiques. All of you will be expected to articulate an opinion on what your peers are producing."

Great. I imagine myself hanging up a bad drawing and stand-ing there, blindfolded, like I'm in front of a firing squad. Ms. Kay was nice about not forcing our class to show pieces we weren't happy with. I have a sneaking suspicion Mr. Frank won't be as forgiving.

We continue to go around the room. The rest of the kids in my class seem average compared to Fiona and Robyn, which puts me just the smallest bit at ease. Most are from the East Coast, but one guy is from Arizona. There's a girl from Helsinki who speaks really bad English and I don't think anyone understands her answers.

43

I notice that Fiona looks a little bored while the other people talk. Not in a mean way, but where she kind of looks over your head because she's thinking about something more interesting than what you're saying. Robyn keeps leaning in and whispering things in Fiona's ear, jokes to get her attention.

When it's my turn, it's like I can't help but want to impress them, for whatever reason. But I also already know that's not going to happen.

My mouth opens. It's so dry. "My name is Emily Thompson. I'm from Cherry Grove." That's the easy part. My smile fades and my mind goes as white as the paper up on my easel.

Mr. Frank clears his throat. "And why are you here?" He asks it not like he's interested in my answer, but more like he's feeding me lines I should already know.

Fiona glances at me, as she braids and unbraids her long pink waterfall of hair.

"Uhh . . ." All the answers that flood my head are ones I wouldn't dare speak out loud. That this is the only way I could come up with to make my summer less boring, because I don't have a boyfriend like my best friend. That art was the only high school class I got an A in. None of these seem like good enough answers, even if they are all true.

I end up shrugging my shoulders. It's the best I can do.

Almost instantly, Robyn leans into Fiona, pushing that long pink lock away from her ear so she can whisper something about me. Then Robyn laughs. Loud.

I stare at the paint splatters on the floor. Even if I'm nothing special in Cherry Grove, no one laughs at me. I do enough right to keep that from happening.

June

"We're all set, Mr. Frank," Yates tells him quietly, a much-needed break to the awkwardness. I've made a fool of myself in front of him. He slips a small black notebook into Mr. Frank's hands.

"Okay." Mr. Frank stands up. "How many of you keep a sketchbook?"

A few kids raise their hands, including Fiona, though hers seems to rise above the rest. Robyn raises hers, too, but a few seconds later. I sit on my hands and enjoy the weight of my body, the pressure on my fingers, like a punishment. I've never kept a sketchbook. I've only doodled in the margins of my lined notebooks, when I got bored in school.

"For this class, I am requiring everyone to keep a sketchbook, which I want you to think of as a visual diary," Mr. Frank continues. "Except that one entry per day will not do. Rather, I want you to catalog your life, your point of view in the pages. I want you to take pause in the small, beautiful moments where you'd otherwise push on through with your normal life." He locks eyes with Fiona. "Would you mind if I took a look?" he asks, taking careful, slow steps over to her.

"*Absolument*," Fiona says in a pitch-perfect French accent, and digs deep in her tote bag, which is covered in cartoon owls. "So long as you don't narc me out to the cops."

What?

"I don't feel comfortable sharing my sketchbook," Robyn says, even though no one asked to see it. "Mine is very personal."

"Well," Mr. Frank says, "you should begin a new one, then, because I will expect you to show me drawings each week."

Fiona pulls out a thick blue book that looks handmade, stitched together with red yarn. It's stuffed full, the way my binders

45

get by the end of the school year, with a black band wrapped around the cover to force it closed. As she opens it up and hands it over to Mr. Frank, a few pieces of ripped paper and what looks like confetti fall to the floor. She climbs down from the stool and picks them up, like they are valuable. He flips through a few pages. Inside are lots of sketchy pencil drawings, stickers, pieces of fabric. I wish I could see better, but my easel is in the way. Robyn seems especially interested. She's practically climbed on top of her stool to get a better look.

"A visual diary will help you, as artists, become more familiar and comfortable with the way you, and you alone, see things. I don't want you to just observe, I want you to obsess. Your point of view, your voice, will be what makes your art special and unique, so I hope you'll all take this assignment seriously." Mr. Frank hands the sketchbook back to Fiona and smiles. "Wonderful."

"Thanks," she says, not even the slightest bit embarrassed by his praise. More like she hears those kinds of compliments all the time.

Even though I'm totally intimidated, I'm also inspired. I've never had a special place to draw. I've never thought about capturing my world. Lately, I've only thought of escaping it.

"And now, on to our first lesson. Mastering the human form is undoubtedly the most essential part of your training as an artist. These skills will serve you in all other media, be it photography, sculpture, painting, jewelry, or what have you. Here, unlike with your sketchbooks, creative expression is not encouraged. Rather, I will push you to be as exact and accurate as you possibly can. You must know the rules before you can break them."

I bite the inside of my cheek. This is so different from Ms. Kay's art class. She was much goofier, and always encouraged us to be open to mistakes and happy accidents. Sometimes, she'd even tell us to draw with our eyes closed. Now I feel the pressure to be good. Better than good, if possible, to prove I belong here.

As Mr. Frank continues, a woman emerges from behind a canvas curtain slung in the corner of the room that I did not notice before. She's maybe my mom's age, wearing a plum satin kimono robe very loosely tied at her waist. Her silver-streaked hair is spun into two tight buns behind her ears. She has no shoes on. Her toenails are long and polished an acidic orange.

Yates moves quickly around the room, pulling down the shades.

Mr. Frank hops off the platform. "Lily, I'm looking for something not terribly difficult. Twenty minutes and then we'll have a break."

Lily nods and climbs up. In a flash, her robe falls to the floor. She's completely naked and very, very pale. You can see most of her veins, like little blue rivers and streams on a map. She sits down, twists her back and lifts her chin up to the ceiling.

A few people, including myself, giggle. For the first time I remember that I'm in a room full of teenagers. And I'm not the only one who seems to look to Fiona for her reaction. It's like everyone turns their heads her way. But she's not laughing or smiling or rolling her eyes like the rest of us. She's already drawing.

Mr. Frank takes an egg timer and spins the dial around. It starts ticking. Slowly. "For this first drawing, I'd like to get a sense of your skill level. Please just capture the form at its most basic. We shall, obviously, progress from there." He claps his hands. "Begin."

The pencils of the students around me fly over their papers. I gaze ever so slightly above the edge of my drawing pad. Just look and get the shock over with. The woman's boobs are huge and hang heavy off her slightly lumpy frame. And her nipples are erect because it's so cold in here. Is Mr. Frank going to want us to draw nipples? Because I seriously don't think I can do that.

I've never seen anyone else naked in real life, definitely not an adult, except for the time everyone went skinny-dipping in Billy Barker's hot tub after New Year's. Rick invited us to the party after he and Meg first started talking. Everyone was game for it, except for Meg and me. Luckily, it was dark and we couldn't really see anyone. Not that we were trying to look. Rick didn't try to make Meg go in or anything. Instead, he stayed with her on the chaise lounge and they talked about school and stuff. I sat high and dry at the picnic table and blacked out the teeth of the models in the J.Crew catalog.

With the way she's twisting, if I lean to my left, I can't see the model's private parts at all. The girl from Helsinki across the room probably doesn't see anything else but the private parts. The model's got a bit of a belly, round and plump, and some love handles that hide the shape of her hip bones. I have a perfect view of her butt crack, before it smashes into the base of the pedestal.

Mr. Frank is suddenly behind me, his shadow the only thing darkening my white sheet of paper. "What is your name again?"

Everyone glances my way. Of course he hasn't remembered. "Emily," I say.

"Emily, start with the spine. Always build from the spine."

I pick up one of my pencils and press it to the paper halfway up the page. I try to start drawing but the pencil point is so sharp, it pushes off the paper like it doesn't want to listen to me. So I just hold it there, without moving, until my arm prickles from lack of blood flow.

"Hey," a smooth voice comes from behind. Yates. "Which pencil are you using?" His breath smells icy, like a fresh piece of gum.

I roll it between my fingers until I see the foil stamp. "Umm . . . the HB?" I have absolutely no idea what that means.

"Use the 6B," Yates instructs. Then, before he walks away, he whispers, "The name has to do with the softness of the lead."

I am too embarrassed to say thank you, so I just take out the 6B from my art box, even though it looks absolutely the same as the pencil I was just holding. I raise my hand and position myself . . . and the point sinks right into the paper. It's soft, like butter left out on the kitchen counter.

I try to get into my drawing, but I think I am overthinking. My lines aren't smooth — they're sharp and jagged and impatient. My eyes bounce between the model and my paper so fast it makes me dizzy. I try to get everything just right. I can't shut my brain off enough to relax, especially knowing that Mr. Frank will probably make us all share our drawings at the end of the day. It's pretty much the most impossible situation.

What seems like seconds later, the egg timer rings and Lily excuses herself for a pee and a smoke break. The rest of the class gets up to stretch and walk around. Except Fiona, Robyn, and me. Fiona keeps drawing, staring at the empty space as if the model were still there. Robyn casually walks the room, peering at everyone's sketches. I bite down on my pencil until I taste wood and flip to a new sheet before she has a chance to see how bad I suck.

Not like she can't already tell.

Five

I'm not even halfway up my front steps before Meg's sing-song call trills from across the street. "Em-i-ly!"

She bounds out of her front door, shiny hair swishing from side to side. Her arms keep her lilac slip dress from flying up past her thighs and her chunky espadrilles might as well be sneakers because of how quick she is with every step.

I feel like I've been gone for months. "Hey!" I say, and hold my arms out for a hug.

"Yay! You're home!" Meg gives me a squeeze, but quickly wriggles out of it, leaving me slightly sticky from the unabsorbed cucumber-melon lotion on her skin.

"I have about a million stories to tell you," I say, laughing as flashes of the day light up my mind. Where should I start?

"And I want to hear absolutely everything about your first day, but listen." She's all eager and excited. "A bunch of people are going to Dairy Queen, and Rick will be here any minute to pick us up." She glances down. "What's all over your pants?"

My white denim capris are smudged across the thighs with

June

pencil lead. "Art class, remember?" My hands are dirty, too — not just on the palms, but in thick black stripes under my nails. I shove them in my pockets before she notices.

"Well, quick, go change!" She brushes a piece of hair out of my eyes. "Maybe wear that green polo dress with your pink flip-flops, or your red halter with your teeny jean skirt." Meg is really good with clothes and she always helps me pick things out. "I have to run home and grab my purse. Hurry!"

I charge upstairs to my bedroom and quickly change into the green polo dress, because the red halter is in my hamper. I slide on my pink flip-flops. Cherry Grove feels more like home than ever. I know the rules here. I know how I'm supposed to think and act, and all that is very comforting after the day I've had.

At least I was able to do an okay drawing. I stopped thinking about the naked lady as a lady, and instead pretended I was drawing a statue. So that made it easier. I also just drew her torso, so I could avoid the stuff I felt was too intimate to draw. Mr. Frank said I had an "interesting composition." I hoped that was a compliment. But the rest of the class stayed quiet during my crit, so who knows.

I run into my bathroom and scrub my hands hard and fast. Most of the dirt comes off, but not all. Hopefully, no one will notice once the sun goes down. I use hair spray to smooth down my ponytail. It smells like apples, so I don't need perfume. But I put a little more deodorant on, because it's really hot outside.

The *beep beep beep* of Rick's truck horn blows in my open window.

I gotta go.

Rick and Meg are waiting in his red pickup truck. I get in, close the door, and cuddle myself against it to give Meg more room. But she doesn't want it. Rick's truck is small, and Meg seizes the opportunity to cozy up next to him.

We pass through the gates, and Meg and I wave to the security guard who mans the entrance from a white-shingled booth, made to look like a small version of the Blossom Manor it protects.

Rick waves, too, and I notice that two of his fingers, the pinky and the ring, are wrapped in white tape and unable to grip the steering wheel.

"What happened to your hand?" I ask him. The edges of the tape are frayed into white strings, and the end is all jagged, like someone ripped it with their teeth.

"I was on the push mower and a rock flew up and dinged my pinky. It's probably broken, but I'm just going to buddy-tape it like coach did for me last season when my other one got hit with a curve ball." He holds up that hand and proudly flashes a crooked zigzag of a pinky like a trophy. "That was right before we met," he says, and pats Meg's thigh.

He's talking about when Meg sprained her ankle jumping the horse in gym class. I had put Meg's arm around my shoulder and tried to walk her to the nurse myself, but Meg was crying and afraid that she was going to slip and fall if she hopped on the linoleum floor. So Mrs. Lord called one of the boys out of the weight room to help support her other side. That was Rick. But instead of helping me, he scooped up Meg into his arms and carried her up three flights of stairs and all the way down the hall. He kept telling Meg how light she was. Like a feather. It was sweet, because Meg was actually on a diet then, not like she needed to be, and after that day, she went back to eating pizza. She sniffled back her tears and thanked him over and over for the help.

June

I guess I could have gone back to gym alone, but I didn't. I just walked next to them and stayed quiet. Actually, I walked a little bit behind them. I guess we've been a threesome from the very start.

"So, how was your first day of school?" Meg asks, in the same voice my mom used when she picked me up. "Tell us all about it."

I try not to get annoyed, but talking to Meg alone is much different from talking to Rick and Meg as a couple. It's like she's playing house, and I get to be their kid.

Rick pushes his hat up off his brow to the top of his hairline. "Were there a lot of freaky kids there?"

"Yeah, some, I guess." There's something about Rick's tone I don't like. Maybe what it implies about me. "Not too many people talked to me," I say, like that makes it any better.

"It's always hard on the first day." Meg touches my arm. "What did you do in class?"

"Well . . ." I think about not telling them anything, but I'm curious to see their reactions. "I had to draw a nude model." I say it like it was no big deal.

They both stare at me, mouths open. "Shut up!" they say in unison.

"Swear to God," I say, and then laugh with them. Though I was definitely caught off guard by the model, I still managed to hold it together. I bet Meg and Rick would've freaked. It makes me feel a little better.

"Like totally nude?" Meg asks. "Was it a guy or a girl?"

"It was a woman."

"Was she hot?" That's Rick.

Meg slaps him on the arm.

I shake my head. "Not at all. She was old. Like a mom."

Meg and Rick turn to each other and laugh. And then, a disturbed look crosses Rick's face. "Will you have to draw naked guys?"

"Yeah," I say casually, even though that never dawned on me before. "Probably." It's kind of funny to think that the first time I see a guy naked, it's not going to be my boyfriend. Though maybe it's better that way. Maybe I won't be as nervous when it finally happens for real.

"Art is so weird," Rick says, shaking his head. "I mean, I don't know much about it, but some of those paintings Ms. Kay showed me two years ago were just stupid. Anyone could do that stuff." He shakes his head again. "Sure some art is, like, unbelievable. Like the Mona Lisa. I can definitely appreciate that. But the other stuff. Paint splatters and colored squares and whatever. I just don't get it."

Meg laughs. "I bet half of the people who say they get that stuff actually have no clue. They just don't want to sound dumb."

I wonder what Meg and Rick would think of Fiona's shadows. Sure, any three-year-old can trace with chalk, but there *was* something amazing about them. Like she showed something I'd never noticed was there. I want to tell them about it, but I don't think I could explain it right. It's just like Fiona said, I guess — the experience is the thing. Talking about it wouldn't do it justice.

The parking lot of the Dairy Queen is packed. It's one of the meeting places for all Cherry Grove high schoolers during the summer. Everyone eats ice cream while they plot ways to get beer and a place to drink it. On most nights they come up short on both accounts.

We pull in and park. A bunch of kids from school come by while we're in line and say hello. Meg and I are friendly with most of the same people, but there are a few of Rick's friends who I don't know as well as she does. I turn and spin and nod my head and pretend to be interested in the gossip, but it's all the same sort of stuff you hear during the year.

We eat our ice cream over by the chain-link fence, where Jimmy Carr and Chad Daly are talking. Meg always says I should like Chad Daly, but I don't think he's my type. He wears too much hair gel, and he never eats ice cream, even though he's always hanging out at DQ. Instead, he orders a large Mountain Dew from the fountain and chews the straw until it barely works.

"Hey, guys," Rick says. They slap hands, all loose and relaxed.

"So, what's everyone up to?" Meg asks them. "Getting excited for the Babe Ruth opening game?"

Chad and Jimmy and Rick all play baseball together on the summer league. It's the only way for them to get practice in without breaking the high school rules. Meg asks more questions, about the lineups and their pitcher's shoulder injury. I have no idea how she learned all this stuff about baseball. I guess Rick's explained it to her. I try to nod at appropriate times so it's like I get it, too.

But eventually the conversations that I'm not actually participating in soften into whispers. I can't hear people talking, or taste the vanilla ice cream in my Blizzard. That happens to me sometimes, when I get bored. When other people zone out, it's because they're lost in the lyrics of a song or thinking of a funny story. For most people, it's all about words.

Not for me. I find it fun to look at something and reduce it to the small parts that make it up. Like Jenessa Wilson, leaning against the DQ counter. She's one long line, from the top of her head, curving down her spine and along her butt, which always seems to be sticking out, and then down her long, thin legs. Jenessa's on the cheerleading squad and a year younger than me, but I think she looks way older. She wears a lot of makeup, and you can usually see some of it, tan like caramel, smudged on the collars of her shirts. But guys love Jenessa. They throw themselves at her. Meg says that she's actually a nice girl when you get to talking to her, but I don't believe it. I've never once seen her truly smile. It always looks more like a sneer.

"Hey! Emily!" Meg says, knocking into me with an embarrassed laugh. "Come on, we're leaving."

Everything snaps back into normal focus. Rick is across the parking lot, unlocking the door to his truck. There's no one else around. Jimmy and Chad are gone. I'm standing here alone, in the middle of the parking lot, all by myself. My Blizzard is almost empty.

"What's everyone doing?"

"Nothing. Going home. You know how it is." Meg turns toward Rick's truck.

The night is slipping away. "Hey," I say, and take hold of her arm. "Let's go sneak into a movie, like we used to do."

Meg shrugs her shoulders. "Hmm . . . maybe. You know, ever since they redid the movie theater, they have people double-checking ticket stubs. I'm dying to see that new one about the florist who falls in love with her delivery guy, but it doesn't open until this weekend. We should just go next week. Maybe on Tuesday. I think it's supposed to rain on Tuesday."

June

"Well, we could go down to the fields and hang out there." Someone discovered that the back door to the football equipment room never locks. We've snuck in there to drink beers and listen to music sometimes. It's not all that much fun, but at least it's something.

Meg laughs. "Didn't you hear? Coach Heller got the locks replaced."

"Oh." I try to think of another possibility. I'm not ready for tonight to be over. Nothing's even happened yet.

Meg turns and looks back at the truck. "I think we're going to just go and watch some TV or something at Rick's house." She pauses briefly. "You can totally come if you want."

It's nice of Meg to invite me, but I will never go and watch television with her and Rick again. The last time I did that, they were either cuddled under a blanket together or disappearing upstairs to the kitchen together to get more snacks or whatever. I'd be left alone in Rick's dark basement watching some dumb show or movie, the kind of thing you decide to "watch" when you have a boyfriend because you don't plan on "watching" anything.

"That's okay." I say. "I've got class tomorrow anyhow. Oh! But I have to bring Claire a Blizzard or I'll never hear the end of it when I get home. Can you give me one second?"

"Of course," Meg says. "I'll be in the truck."

I run over to the counter and place my order. Across the parking lot, Meg talks to Rick in the truck. She's saying something to him, probably that I'm not coming. Rick smiles, and they start kissing. I hold Claire's Blizzard and walk as slow as I can. I don't care if the ice cream melts. I'm not rushing back over there. Their night is just getting started, and mine's about to end.

57

Six

The Philadelphia Museum of Art is an enormous building on top of a grassy hill. Almost a hundred steps lead up to the front entrance, carved in stone. Behind the building stretches a winding river, like one you might find in the country, but this one has skyscrapers rising from its banks. Long, skinny crew boats filled with shirtless frat guys from Penn slice through the dark water in unison, making lots of frothy splashes with their oars. Their chants of *Row, Row, Row* give it a pulse.

Four yellow buses drop us off at the base of the stairs. Robyn and Fiona are on my bus. Robyn has on gray leggings, a blousy yellow tank top that could almost be a dress, and a pair of saddle shoes. Fiona wears a pair of skinny frayed jean shorts cut at the knees, a cropped navy vest buttoned tight around her chest, and these vampy open-toe red heels. I think the vest might have come from a little boy's Catholic school uniform or something — it fits her like a corset. A tangle of long, thin gold chains hangs from her neck. It's the kind of outfit that belongs in a magazine, the sort of thing that you can't imagine anyone would wear in real life. But there she is, in real life, wearing it.

Fiona and Robyn have made a new friend. A boy I've never seen before is dragged down the aisle behind them. He mumbles "Excuse me, excuse me" to the kids they push out of their way. His voice is very Southern and sweet, and it rolls past his lips real slow. He looks quiet, shy, and freakishly skinny. He's got on a black T-shirt with a white spiderweb on it, thick black glasses that keep sliding down his nose, green army shorts, and black Converse. His floppy brown hair hangs in his eyes and he keeps thrashing his neck to fling it to the side, but it just falls back down a few seconds later. They walk past me on their way off the bus, talking about who knows what. But Fiona stops and ducks her head so she can peek out my window. Something outside has caught her attention.

"Every time I see that thing, I want to yak." Fiona swats her pink hair over her shoulder and points.

I can't help but look, too, since they are talking right over my head, but I try to make it not obvious. A large block of cast bronze perched on the top museum step reflects the sun back in our faces. Probably by a famous artist I've never heard of before.

The boy shrugs his shoulders. "Is that a Rodin?"

Fiona rustles a hand through his hair. "Are you kidding me, Adrian? You of all people should know who that is." She throws up her hands like she's going to punch him out. "Yo, Adrian! Adrian!" she calls out in a fake deep voice. "That's Rocky. Rocky Balboa. From those dumb Sylvester Stallone boxing movies that were filmed in Philly. You know, the ones they play on channel eleven on Sunday afternoons."

Robyn laughs. "Eww. What's Rocky doing at the art museum?"

"Because there's this part in the movie where Rocky is training and he runs up the steps of the museum, and throws his arms up when he gets to the top." She shakes her head. "Just watch," she says.

Sure enough, not one minute later, two touristy men start to race each other up the stairs. One of the guys is fat, in a Santa way, with a belly that shakes underneath his shirt. His taller friend passes him, even though he's smoking a cigarette, and when he reaches the top, he throws his hands up in the air and twirls around slow. Then he slings his arm proudly over the statue's neck and waits for someone to take his picture.

I guess Fiona's been here before.

Fiona shakes her head, and continues to walk off the bus. "These people don't even go inside the museum. They just pose with the statue like morons. I mean, go to Universal Studios if that's the kind of culture you care about."

I know they aren't talking about me specifically, but I let my hair hang in front of my face as if they were. My dad loves the movie *Rocky*, though I've never watched it. It won Best Picture, I think. I remember seeing the gold foil sticker on the DVD case. Not that it makes it any better.

I hang toward the back and follow the rest of the students inside the museum. Chatter instantly turns into whispers, as if we were in a library. The room is cavernous, dark brown stone and lit low and soft. It's cool, very cool inside, like a tomb.

Yates comes up next to me. "Do you have your sketchbook, Emily?"

June

"Umm . . . don't I have until next Tuesday?" I keep blowing every opportunity to look cool in front of Yates. I sound like I don't care.

Yates shakes his head and *tsks* me. "Here," he says, and carefully rips some pages out of his own book. "Make sure you get your own today. You don't want to make Mr. Frank think you're slacking. He takes these summer classes very seriously, and if he decides that you don't, there's no changing his mind."

I appreciate how nice Yates is to me, even if it's his job. "Thanks."

"Don't forget," he warns.

"Okay, students," Dr. Tobin says. "We're going to enter into the main wing as a group. The professors will all engage you in discussion, but you should for the most part use this time to sketch and to contemplate the pieces. Please do not wander off."

Everyone shuffles up a wide staircase into the main hall. On the landing, there's a big iron statue of Diana, goddess of the hunt, with bow and arrow pointed directly at us. It's like she's guarding the museum. I catch myself ducking out of her aim.

We enter into the first gallery room, full of colorful paintings in gilded frames. Dr. Tobin gathers us around van Gogh's *Vase with Twelve Sunflowers*. I recognize it right away. Ms. Kay has a poster of it hanging by the slop sink.

"So who can tell me the artist of this painting?"

I check to see if anyone raises their hands. But no one does. Could I possibly know something the rest of the kids here don't? My hand tentatively leaves my pocket.

"Who painted this picture?" Dr. Tobin repeats, frustrated.

My arm is just about over my head when the entire room says "Van Gogh" in the most bored, tired voices.

It's not that I was the only one who knew the answer. It's the obvious one *everyone* knows. I run my hand through my hair to play it off, but I'm sure my red cheeks give me away.

"Now, let's talk quickly about the Expressionist movement. Who can explain it?"

Robyn's hand shoots up. "That's when artists play with color and texture to express emotions in personal ways."

"Exactly," Dr. Tobin says. "I want you all to please look at the textures of this piece up close as we move along. Van Gogh was famous for his impasto style. Can anyone tell me what that is?"

At least five kids raise their hands.

I feel so completely ignorant. I have no idea what these words and terms mean.

Once everyone moves to the next room, I stop and stare at *Sunflowers*. I get close enough that my nose almost touches the canvas, so I can see the brush strokes and the energy, stuff you could never ever see on a stupid poster. Instead of feeling inspired, I feel daunted. I'll never be this good. Why even try?

After looking at a bunch more nineteenth-century paintings, we make our way into the modern art wing.

Mr. Frank holds a hand high, calling for everyone's attention. "We're about to enter the Duchamp gallery."

"This is the best freaking part of this whole museum!" Fiona says, bouncing up and down. She pulls Robyn's arm and Robyn pulls Adrian's arm and they weave together through the crowd.

I'm almost the last one in the gallery. I don't know exactly what to expect with that kind of buildup, but I'm curious to know what someone like Fiona finds inspiring. All the spotlights in the room are pointed at three pedestals. There's a bicycle wheel perched on a stool. A white porcelain urinal. Something metal and spiky that looks like a coatrack. I double-check that the walls around me are white, that there are no paintings hanging up. That this is really the stuff I should be looking at.

This gallery looks like the curbs of Blossom Manor on heavy trash day.

Mr. Frank steps forward. "These pieces are some of the most important in the history of art. These readymades were assembled between 1913 and 1917, and were a sensation at the Armory Show in New York. And see how modern, how artistically striking they still are today."

Is this art Mr. Frank would really value, considering how intent he is on making his students produce perfect, calculated drawings?

"Would anyone like to comment?" His eyes seek me out. "Emily, what is your response to these pieces?"

My ears fill with the imagined voices of Meg and Rick, making fun of this kind of art. How Rick could go to Home Depot and buy a white toilet and put it on a block and call it art. I shift my weight. I look down into the ripped blank sketchbook pages in my hands, hoping an answer will appear.

"Emily? Do you feel like this art is meaningful?"

I don't know what to say. I definitely don't want to look stupid in front of everyone. My heart pounds. I search the crowd. And there's Fiona, watching me, waiting to hear what I have to say about her favorite pieces in the whole museum.

"I'm sorry" is all I can manage. "I don't get it."

Mr. Frank laughs, amused. "But that's the point, don't you think?" A few other chuckles come from the crowd.

I shake my head. "Wait. What's the point? That I don't get it?"

"Exactly."

"Well . . . what's the point of us not getting it?" I ask.

Mr. Frank's grin spreads even wider across his face. "Duchamp was playing right into this kind of thinking, questioning the notion of what can be classified as art. Thank you, Emily, for illustrating my point so beautifully."

My face burns. Mr. Frank is basically making fun of the fact that I don't know anything. That's probably why he called on me in the first place. When I meet eyes with Yates, his gaze falls to the floor, no doubt wondering why he ever spent his money on a cup of coffee for me.

The attention shifts off me, and I take the opportunity to step backward into a dark doorway. I prop myself up against the wall and wait for the students to move to another section. The rest of my energy is spent fighting back tears.

The cool shadows of this room are a stark contrast to the brightly lit galleries we've circled through. Nothing's hanging on the walls in this space. Have I stepped into somewhere I shouldn't be?

I turn my head to the side and stare down a long dark corridor.

At the other end of the room is a huge barn door, made of rustic, splintered wood. Big black metal hinges bolt it to the wall. Light streams through two small knotty holes, just at eye level, tempting me to come closer.

June

I take a few steps but then I stop. It's hard to explain the feelings that suddenly overwhelm me. My hands get sweaty and my heart races. It's like I'm at home alone, and I've just heard a noise in the basement and I have to decide whether or not to explore. Even though I know there's nothing to be afraid of, I still can't will myself to move forward. I'm still scared.

"This is my favorite piece in the whole museum." Someone struts past me. Fiona.

She walks straight up to the barn door, presses her face to the wood, and looks through the little hole. "It's called *The Waterfall*. Duchamp didn't tell anyone about it. Not his assistants, or the museum directors. He didn't want to spoil the surprise. It took me, like, three times before I had the guts to look."

She stands there for a few seconds, taking in whatever she's seeing. Then she pulls away and spins to face me. "It sucks, though. As soon as you know what's behind the door, it changes the whole experience. Once you see it, you can never go back."

I still don't quite have a hold of myself, and I'm sure it's obvious. But Fiona looks at me with this sort of delighted smile, like she's relishing my discomfort. I'm afraid she's going to stand here and watch me sweat it out, but then Robyn and Adrian crane their heads around the wall. "You coming?" Robyn asks.

"Yeah," Fiona says. And then she walks right past me like I'm not even there, like I've turned invisible.

Seven

I make sure to be the first person off the bus when we get back to the college. The other students laugh and talk behind me, discussing another night of adventures away from home. I walk until I can't hear them, keeping my eyes locked on the William Penn statue at the top of City Hall.

Even though I'm in a rush to get to the train station, I stop in the art supply store and buy myself a sketchbook. I don't want to be caught without it again.

Then I head toward the train, passing the people who window-shop the boutiques or contemplate the menus posted outside the restaurants. I try to be as mindless as they are, with no worries except will they buy this skirt, these pants, this blazer, or if they want a salad with walnuts. Except I can't. I have bigger problems. Like the fact that I've been humiliated in front of everyone.

As I shuffle through the crowds, I come upon Fiona. I know it's her, even from a distance, by the pink hair falling over her shoulder in a stripe. She's got earbuds in and the music is so loud

June

I can hear it, even though I make sure to stay two full sidewalk squares behind her.

Fiona's ID hangs from a metal clip off her belt loop. It is red plastic like mine, which means she is also a commuter student and not living in the dorms. Which surprises me.

I take advantage of the situation and creep behind her, close. I notice things that I didn't before. Like how the insides of Fiona's forearms are covered in thin red scratches and scrapes. There seem to be hundreds. But they are all too small to do any kind of real damage. They're more like tiny paper cuts.

When we both reach the train station, I let her loose in the crowd.

I sit down on a bench and wait for my train. So far, the summer program hasn't been such a great experience. I had the opportunity to reinvent myself in Philadelphia, but it feels wasted. Maybe it's stupid to think that was possible in the first place. You are who you are, for better or worse. That's why there are Fionas and there are Megs and there are Emilys. Someone has to be me.

"Howdy."

I look up. It's Fiona. One earbud is still tucked inside her ear, one dangles down with her necklaces. The music is still on.

"Hi," I say.

She crashes next to me. "I saw you following me before."

"Umm . . . what?"

"Before. Like five minutes ago before. On the way to the train station. The sun was behind you. Your shadow gave you away."

"I was just walking to the train station." Fiona must think I am a complete weirdo. "So . . ." I say. "Sorry if you thought that."

"Riiiiight," she says. "Well, did you look through the door?"

I think about lying, but she'd catch me right away. "No."

Fiona slides a black marker out of her tote bag and starts drawing candy-cane stripes on the red high heel of her shoe. "I feel bad that I left you freaking out in the gallery like that. That was kind of a bitch move."

"I was fine," I stress.

"Where are you from again?"

"Cherry Grove."

"So you're a Jersey girl, huh? I never would have guessed."

I know this kind of joking from pretty much every bad movie and television show. New Jersey is the state everyone makes fun of. "Yeah, but Cherry Grove is actually a pretty cool place. I mean, we've got a Starbucks."

"Congratulations." I can almost hear her eyes rolling.

It's hard, when you realize someone is trying to lead you in a conversation, but you don't know where she wants you to go. "I'm just saying, it's not some hick place in the middle of nowhere. It's only thirty miles away." I don't know why I am defending it to her. Just to keep the conversation going, I guess.

"Don't get defensive! I'm just saying that coming from a place like Cherry Grove to Philadelphia can be a bit of a shock to someone like you, is all."

I'm not quite sure why Fiona cares. Or what that *like you* was supposed to imply. If she's trying to say that I'm not like her, that I'm somehow different from the other people here, I already know that.

"Seriously," I say, "I was fine."

Fiona looks up from coloring her shoe. Her eyes bounce all over, taking me in small details. Then she shakes her head, sad, and says, "I bet you have no idea how fake your smile looks." She's not mean or anything. Just matter-of-fact.

It's as if my face freezes, and my brain inside, too. And before I can thaw and answer her, say anything to her, my train rolls into the station.

"You'd better go," Fiona announces, and she sighs when she stands back up. She's disappointed. I'm not what she hoped I'd be.

"Okay," I say, still smiling because it's all I can do to keep it together. Then I take off from Fiona and walk fast to an open train door.

My train car is only half full and I have a two-seater to myself. Once we start moving, I take out my new sketchbook and a pencil, but a man across the aisle is watching me, so I put them back in the plastic bag. I'm too shy to draw here. And plus, my mind is all blurry. So I stare at my reflection in the grimy passenger window for the entire ride home.

I smile a few times. I try to figure out what it is that Fiona meant. But it just looks like me. I don't see anything else but me.

Eight

The sunset is the same color as the thick cheese drowning Meg's nachos — a deep, zesty orange. It burns my eyes when I stare into left field. That's where Rick is crouched with his mitt on his knee, in a white uniform and gray baseball stirrups, haloed by a fuzz of brightness and gnats.

I lean back against the row of metal bleachers behind me. There's just a few people at the game, mainly parents watching their sons. It isn't like the spring, when you have rivalries with other high schools and pep rallies and everyone comes out to cheer the team on. Summer leagues are more sloppy and casual, and if you go to watch the game or even play on the team, it's because there's nothing else to do.

But the ball field is a welcome change from that claustrophobic Duchamp gallery. The quick flash of yesterday makes me hot with embarrassment all over again, as does my whole conversation with Fiona at the train station. I've been thinking a lot about what she said, trying to figure out what she wanted to hear. But I'm still clueless.

June

Thankfully, Fiona wasn't in my Mixed Media class today. I don't know how I am ever going to go back to my drawing classes on Tuesdays and face her.

The teams switch sides and everyone claps as they jog to the bench. I move my hands like a zombie along with them.

Meg taps me on the shoulder. "Okay, so let me finish my story." She takes a deep, dramatic breath. "I'm sitting at home totally bored today. I mean, it's just about lunch and Rick hasn't called me once, even though I've texted him a million times to complain about how I had nothing to do. Then the doorbell rings and it's Rick, with two Subway sandwiches and a huge bouquet of wildflowers that he cut from the golf course while he was working! And they just so happened to be mostly pink daisies, even though I never told him they were my favorite kind of flowers! He's, like, psychic. And then we had a picnic right on my front lawn. Your mom saw us from across the street and was cracking up, like 'Awww, young love!'" Meg rocks back with laughter, and the pale pink flower she has tucked behind her ear falls out onto her bare legs. She scoops it up and puts it back in place. "But seriously, isn't that just like something a guy in a movie would do?"

Rick jogs over from the bench, steals a chip, and kisses Meg quickly on the cheek. "I actually did see that in a movie." He smiles with pride as he chews. "A trailer actually, for that florist movie you want to see."

Meg laughs. She doesn't seem to mind Rick's lack of original thought. Romance is romance, I guess.

Someone on our team strikes out. I think it's Chad, but I can't tell with his helmet on. A round lightbulb on the scoreboard flickers on. Two outs to go.

"I'm thinking about quitting the summer program," I tell Meg, when Rick returns to the bench.

"What?" Meg pulls out a nacho and a dribble of cheese slides down her fingers. She looks for a napkin. "Why?"

I hand her one and think a second, searching for a way to save face. "It's just not like how I thought it would be."

"What do you mean? How did you think it would be?"

"Oh, I don't know. A little less . . . intense. It's like all these kids are really sure that they want to be artists. I don't think I'm cut out for it." I grin. "Like you said, a mohawk wouldn't look too good on me."

Meg doesn't laugh at my joke. Instead, she takes a long sip of Coke. "Well, I'll support you no matter what you decide, but I'd hate to see all your talent go to waste."

That catches me off guard. I thought Meg would have been happy to have me back home with her. I thought she missed having me around. But maybe not. Maybe she's doing just fine without me. "So you don't think I should quit?"

"Do what you want, Emily. I just think you end up talking yourself out of things."

I give her a dirty look. I can't help it. "What?"

Meg sighs like I'm dense. "You're, like, afraid to be good at something."

"Umm, no." It's more like I desperately want to be good at something. "Meg, you don't get it because you've never had to work for something you wanted."

Her face turns pink, and her mouth puffs out like it's full of angry words. But she must realize that I'm right, because she lets all the air out and starts over, this time with a much softer voice.

June

"You haven't even given the program a real shot. This is only the first week. Don't you like any of your classes?"

I actually did like the Mixed Media class today. It was taught by two girls, Hanna and Charlotte, who had just graduated from the college last year. They seemed superexcited as they explained how many different techniques can go into a mixed media collage — painting, sculpture, screen printing — and we'd get basic instruction on all of it. It was definitely going to be more freeing than Drawing, and the rest of the kids in the class weren't judgy or full of bravado. We all seemed like beginners.

But I was still conscious of dodging Fiona. I took a later train, so I'd arrive once classes had already started. And I sat alone in the Starbucks on the corner of school for the lunch period. Just sat there and did nothing.

Meg shrugs her shoulders. "Well, it's up to you. Just give it some thought, is all I'm saying."

I stare down at my bare legs and trace lines with my finger, connecting the dots of my freckles. I guess it's stupid to ask someone for her opinion when you just want her to agree with you.

Rick comes back over. He looks sad that there are no more nachos. "Meg, I'm starving. Can we go to the diner after the game?"

"Sure. Emily, you'll come, too, right?"

"Yeah, okay." Then I think about it, just like Meg said. If I quit my art classes, something here is going to have to change. I can't let things go back to how they used to be. I can't be the third wheel anymore. "Maybe I'll ask Chad if he wants to come with us." I mean, who knows. Maybe I was wrong to judge him. After all, I don't really know Chad. But he seems more like me, more in my league than someone like Yates. And Meg's always saying what a nice guy Chad is and that it would be so fun if we all double-dated. I could at least give it a try.

Meg beams an excited smile at Rick. "That's a great idea!"

When I stand up, I feel a bit shaky. "Do I look okay?" I wish I had worn something cuter than my plaid shorts and a plain peach tank, but I can't do anything about that now.

Meg takes her pink flower and slides it behind my ear. "You look better than okay."

I feel silly with the flower, considering it was part of Rick's bouquet to Meg, but I wear it anyway.

The crowd claps for the last out. I walk up to the chain-link fence near the dugout. Chad sits on the team bench, untying his cleats. His white baseball socks are stained from the dirt.

"Hi, Chad," I say. "Great game."

He looks up at me. Kind of surprised. "It was okay," Chad says. "But thanks. I didn't think you liked baseball."

"Oh yeah. I definitely do. Meg and I came to cheer you all on." There's an awkward moment of silence, as I stand there and watch him pull off his shoes. He doesn't loosen the laces to make it less difficult. He just wrestles them off. I take a deep breath, then a deeper one. "Listen . . . Rick and Meg and I are going to go to the diner to get some food. Do you want to come with us?"

He looks up at me and smiles, like he's been waiting for me to ask him that very question his whole life. My heart jumps. And then I realize Chad's gaze is a little off to the left. He's not actually looking at me, but just past me instead.

A tiny body struts up next to me.

Chad says, "Hey, Jenessa."

June

I take a step back.

Jenessa loops two fingers into the chain-link fence and hangs off seductively. Her white tube top is lower than low and her bottom lip, dewy with strawberry gloss, pouts. "Can we leave now?"

"Sure," Chad says, and looks at me apologetically. I'm grateful that he doesn't decline my invitation out loud.

"I'll wait at the car," Jenessa says pointedly. She spins on her toe.

"Umm, okay," I say, and take a few unsure steps backward, until it hits me that there's nothing else to say.

I rush back over to Meg and Rick. Meg's flower falls out from behind my ear, but I don't even care. Meg is waiting with a huge smile on her face, but it quickly falls.

"He's hooking up with Jenessa!" I hiss.

"What?" Meg turns toward Rick, accusatory. "Chad is hooking up with Jenessa? Since when?"

"He is?" Rick smiles for a second, then thinks better of it. "Weird."

Meg hands Rick her trash. "Did he ever say anything to you about Jenessa?"

Rick stutters for words. He doesn't know why he's in trouble, but he knows he's in trouble. "No! I mean, nothing. Just that he thought she was hot and—"

"Shhhh!" I practically scream.

"Sorry, Emily," Rick says, truly apologetic and quiet. But he and Meg get into it, like she blames Rick for the fact that Chad likes Jenessa and not me. I know Meg really wanted this for me. It would have been the easy solution to all our problems. But nothing easy ever seems to happen for me.

"Can we please just go?" I beg them.

"Do you still want to come with us to the diner?" Meg asks.

I shoot her a look. Of course I don't want to go to the diner. I'd rather die than go to the diner.

I try not to watch Jenessa and Chad kiss on the hood of his car as we walk past to Rick's truck. I worry how many people saw me get shot down, or if Chad will tell Jenessa and then Jenessa will tell everyone. Like I'm some big joke.

"Maybe we should have a sleepover tonight," Meg says, looping her arm through mine. "I mean, it's not like you have class tomorrow. It'll be like old times. We can make brownies and then go for a midnight swim and have diving contests for quarters like we used to." Meg tries to skip, but it's like I've got sandbags strapped to my sneakers.

"I just want to go home." It's nothing personal. I wouldn't be any fun tonight. And, anyhow, Rick is hungry. Meg shouldn't break her dinner plans just because I'm all depressed.

"Okay," Meg says, glancing up at Rick with a sad face.

Rick fumbles for the keys, and Meg strokes my arm. The funny thing is, I don't even care about Chad. It's just . . . everything.

I drop my chin to my chest. The shadows bloom all around in the parking lot from the trees overhead. I stare at them. Hard. They are the only beautiful things about tonight, and I am so grateful that I see them because I really, really need them right now.

Nine

ig surprise, I can't sleep. The fact that it's only nine o'clock on a Friday night doesn't help me feel any better about it.

My room is dark except for the lamp with the grosgrain ribbon shade on my night table. I sit up in bed, braced by a mountain of pillows, and stare down at the first blank page in my new sketchbook. I try not to be afraid of it.

I tell myself that drawing will make me feel better, give me something to focus on, like it always does. I don't worry about an egg timer or a teacher circling the room. I sit quietly, force my eyes to move as slowly as possible across my bedroom, and let my pencil follow.

I quickly discover, as I peer down at my comforter, that fabric is just about the hardest thing to draw, especially in this kind of light. There are so many little peaks and valleys, where the cloth buckles and wrinkles over my legs. It seems impossible.

But I take some of Mr. Frank's advice and just capture the basic lines and folds and shadows, like an outline. I start from the bottom corner of the left side of the page and make half a rectangle that finishes on the bottom right side.

I fill that shape with the tiny rosebud pattern of my bedspread. My hand picks up a rhythm of a small spiral, the letter U, and two oblong leaves, until the entire thing is covered. That pattern continues on the two sets of window curtains to my left. Those are way easier to draw than the bedspread. They hang in long, crisp folds that pool on the wood floor.

It's creepy, how clean my room always is. I bet Fiona's room is covered in dirty clothes and half-finished art projects, and has spots of hair dye on the carpet. We have a cleaning lady who comes twice a week to straighten up and do laundry. Even if I were messy, it wouldn't have a chance to actually stay that way. I mean, I like having a neat room, but tonight it looks sterile. And cold. And boring.

My eyes follow the thick white baseboards over to the tall white bookcase near my bedroom door. There are a few books on each shelf, stories I don't remember reading, artfully arranged in pyramids and clusters. And then, on the top shelf are my ballerina figurines — white ceramic, their glaze reflecting the light from the streetlamps outside. The long-legged girls twirl gracefully, wearing bristly tutus and huge smiles.

I put down my pencil and rub my hand.

I've never taken a dance class. I've never wanted to. But here these ballerinas are on my shelf, displayed like Claire's soccer trophies, like something earned or reflective of who I am.

The ballerinas are from my mom. She picked them out for me.

She picked out the bedroom furniture, too.

June

And the rosebud comforter.

My room has always looked like this. No one bothered to ask how I wanted it to look or what my favorite color was.

Fiona's words circle through my brain. I can't stop thinking about what she said about me, about my smile. Fiona saw right through me.

This room, the one down on the page, might as well be a stranger's. There's nothing to make me recognize that it's mine. It's as blank as a piece of notebook paper, and not in that good, full of possibilities way — just in a nothing kind of way.

But the thing is, I'm seeing it now. I'm seeing it, and, like Fiona said, once you do, you can't turn back.

You have to move forward.

Ten

When I wake up Tuesday morning, I hate my closet. All my clothes are so plain, so personality-less. Just because you can buy J.Crew tank tops in every color they sell, it doesn't mean you should. It's practically a uniform. I need . . . I don't know. Something.

Before I even know what I'm doing, I grab a felt-tip marker and a lemon-yellow J.Crew tank. Then I turn seven years old and draw a doodle of my old cat Meowie, really big, right across the chest. I draw her crooked ear and her long, long whiskers. I draw her with a set of angel wings, and I put the years she lived underneath. It feels weird, and totally not me, but I do it anyway.

It doesn't look that great, because my pen keeps slipping over the fabric, breaking the lines. And some of the ink seeps through, leaving a bunch of polka dots on the backside of the tank and on my comforter. I flip the comforter over so Mom doesn't notice.

It's funny, how clothes can make you feel so different. But when I slide the tank over my head, I'm someone else. Someone more interesting than me.

I'm a bit nervous when I get into the car, but Mom doesn't notice my tank. She's too busy talking on her cell.

Claire spots it when I get out of the backseat at the train station. Her head drops to the side for a better look, kind of like she can't believe it. I thought she might have been too young to remember Meowie, but she just smiles. Like it's cool.

It's exactly the reaction I want.

When I get onto the train, I make my way to an open seat. I wonder what people would say if they saw me wearing this at DQ. They'd probably think I went crazy, because it's so not me. I feel like a spy, or someone with two identities. I've got a secret. A secret I can't wait to show to Fiona, to Yates, to everyone in my drawing class.

A hand touches mine.

"Emily!" Meg's dad motions to the empty seat. "Wait until I tell Meg about my new commuter buddy. She's going to be so jealous. You know how much she's been missing you while you're at your classes."

"Mr. Mundy." I fall into the seat and cover my chest with my bag. "Hi." I know it's stupid, that Meg's dad won't say anything to her about my tank, but I keep myself covered anyway.

"Come on in, Emily," Yates says when I get to class, gesturing like there's a big comfy couch in the center of the studio, instead of a tangled clump of paint-splattered easels. He sees my Meowie tank and double-takes with a wry smile.

I shoot him one back, and squeeze past him as he drapes a white sheet along a long table at the head of the room.

July

Two boys are in the back of the class, perched on another table, legs swinging in unison. Their skateboards are lined up against the cabinets. A couple of girls walk in together. They look tired, like they've all had a long, fun night.

Fiona's still in the hallway. She's wearing a black T-shirt that scoops low on her shoulders, a hot-pink-and-black striped miniskirt, and slouchy brown canvas boots that graze her calves. The pink in her skirt is the exact shade of her hair, and I know that's no accident.

I kind of want to tell her about the shadows that night at the ball field, and how I figured out what she meant about my smile. How everything she's been saying to me suddenly makes sense now. I hope I get a chance.

Yates looks spacey. He keeps putting his hands over his head and squinting his eyes, like he's trying to remember something. Then he takes a couple of big aluminum clip lights from out of a supply closet. He plugs one in and clicks the switch, but it doesn't turn on.

"Hey, Emily," he says. "Can you set up these pears while I find some new lightbulbs?" He lays some lumpy plastic bags on the table. I guess I don't move quickly enough, because he laughs and says, "I'll give you extra credit."

"Sure," I say. "Do you want them in a specific order?"

Yates laughs and shakes his head. I'm hilarious to him. Or I make him really nervous. "However you want."

I take out three green pears, two red pears, and two yellow pears. I peel off the supermarket stickers and set them all up in a row, in color order because it just seems right. One doesn't want to stand up, so I let it lie down on its side. I hope that's okay.

Yates comes back in with a package of new lightbulbs. "Guys, Mr. Frank is running late today," he tells us. "I'm going to get things started." He drags over two easels, clips lights to them, and clicks them on. "Okay! Now we're getting somewhere!"

It's weird, how random fruit from inside a dirty shopping bag can look elevated underneath those lights. Like a museum painting come to life. Some are lumpy and fat, some are tall and slender. Some still have delicate green leaves attached to their stems. No two look exactly alike, but all the colors seem brighter. Suddenly, I'm excited to get to work.

"Everyone position your easel so you're perpendicular to the still life, like in archery. If you're left-handed, you should be looking over your right shoulder, and vice versa."

The noise of everyone moving around lures Fiona and Robyn into the room. Fiona spots the pears on the sheet and rolls her eyes at Robyn, like this is going to be the most boring class ever.

"Drawing is about fooling your viewer to see a three-dimensional object on a two-dimensional surface. That is accomplished by the use of light and shadow." Yates goes on to explain a style of drawing called charcoal reduction, in which you cover your paper in charcoal and then use an eraser to wipe away your image. Instead of drawing the object, you carve out the light. So I cover my paper with three layers of dark charcoal, unwrap a fresh eraser, and start to clean small sections of it off to make the biggest, fattest red pear rolling on its side at the edge of the table.

I know there is a learning curve with any new thing, but I wish I were doing better than I am. I've got the roundness of the base okay, but it just looks like a circle. It doesn't look three-dimensional at all. How can I work backward, when I'm not even confident working forward?

Yates puts his hands on my shoulders and gently ushers me away from my easel. He stands in my place then, stares at my paper, and then at the view I have of the still life.

"Is this the green one on the right?" he asks.

I rub the back of my hand across my forehead. "No. The fat red one on the left."

"Ahh." He claps his hands together. "Okay. I'm going to teach you a trick. When doing these kinds of reduction drawings, you should always start with the brightest spot. An easy way to find the brightest spot of your subject is to squint your eyes." And he squints his eyes so tight at me that I'm not even sure he can still see me at all. His hand reaches out and touches my cheek really softly. "Yours is right here."

I get the chills. I hope he doesn't notice.

It seems more like a joke than a real technique. But I try it. I turn toward the pears and squint. Suddenly, I see a big white dot on the curve of the pear's belly and I know exactly where to start. It's kind of amazing. "Wow." I face Yates, still squinting. His brightest spot is at the side of his forehead, right near his hairline. Maybe I shouldn't reach out and touch him, but that's what I do.

His skin is so soft.

Yates reaches like he's going to take my hand, and I think my heart might lift me off the ground. But he just removes the piece of charcoal from my grip and fills back in all the white space I've erased. I think I actually make a gasping sound, as all the work I've done so far disappears.

"Don't worry." Yates puts a hand on my shoulder. "You'll draw at least ninety-nine bad pears before you draw one good one." Which isn't exactly comforting.

He moves on to Fiona's easel and looks around, curious, for her eraser.

"I'm more of a fingers kind of girl," Fiona says, matter-of-fact. She rubs her thumb across her paper, then wipes her hand with a paper towel that's already covered in dark smudges. Her hands look like they'll never get clean.

"But you can't get pure whites without an eraser," Yates reasons. "I'd be happy to lend you mine if you don't have one."

Fiona blinks a few times. "I always use my fingers with charcoal," she repeats again, totally unapologetic. "It's just how I do it." Fiona's not being mean or rude. Just confident, if not a little stubborn.

I wait for Yates to challenge her, but he seems to respect Fiona's answer enough to let it go. The two of them look perfect together, staring at Fiona's piece and discussing their artistic processes. Like two real artists. Exactly the opposite of how it is with me . . . a kid who needs dumbed-down tricks to help me get it together.

When Yates steps away, Fiona looks at Robyn, but Robyn's working diligently on her pears with her iPod on, unaware of the power struggle that just took place. Fiona's eyes scan the rest of the room, searching for her audience. They meet mine, just like that first day at orientation. She gives me a hard look, and it takes me by surprise. If she notices my Meowie tank, she doesn't let on.

It's like I lost my chance with her, too. And it's going to take more than my fake smile to earn another one.

Eleven

I'm not hungry when it's time for lunch, but I walk to the Starbucks on the corner and order a frozen peppermint mocha and an old-fashioned glazed donut anyhow. There's a couple open tables I could sit at, but instead I walk back outside and stare in through the smudgy glass window.

This Starbucks looks the same as the one in Cherry Grove. At least, it does at first glance. They both have the same mustard-colored walls. They have identical coffee cups for sale arranged in neat rows on a mahogany shelf. They even play the same music. But after you sit here for long enough, passing your lunch hour without anyone to talk to, you start to notice the differences.

I switch the mocha from my hand to the crook of my arm and make note of them with quick pencil drawings on a fresh page in my sketchbook. Mr. Frank said he wanted to see our personalities come through in our sketchbooks. Well, as lame as it might be, this is the kind of stuff I notice.

Like the fact that there are no plush upholstered chairs to curl up in, only the hard wooden seats that make your butt numb if you sit for too long. That's probably why people hustle in and out of here, instead of reading a book or talking for a while, like Meg and I do back home.

After I'm done, I have at least another thirty minutes to kill before Mr. Frank's class starts up again. Philadelphia is huge, but I've only seen three blocks of it. It's like I'm tethered to a rope stretching between the train station and the school. I decide to walk to the newsstand on the corner and flip through the magazines.

I'm only about a half block from the Starbucks before I notice something on the ground. Every couple of cement squares, there are tiny markings drawn on the sidewalk — each one a different color and the size of a quarter. I look around, but the other people walking along don't seem to notice them. They are too small to be noticed. I crouch down and lean in close. They are arrows, pointing off down the street. I touch a green one with my finger. It smudges.

Chalk.

I follow the arrows past the school, past the newsstand, and around the corner. Even though I've felt self-conscious today, I let it all go and follow where they lead me, because it's fun and unexpected. In a weird way, I'm proud of myself for finding them.

Four blocks later, I lose the trail. No more arrows, just the sidewalk buckling to make room for the tree roots underneath. I look hard, because there has to be a payoff. Fiona is all about the payoff. As I backtrack to the last one, I pass an alley. It's adjacent to a hospital, and has been turned into a serene little park, with trees and flowers and tufts of grass sprouting between the cobblestones. Fiona is alone, about halfway down the stretch, tracing the shadows of trees on the ground. Her colored lines are thicker and bolder than the ones at orientation, and they drip over curbs and across the pavement, into the gutters.

She must hear my footsteps because she looks up and smiles. But I guess she was expecting someone else to find her, because this surprised look washes over Fiona's face when she realizes it's me.

I think a second about turning around and walking back to school, but the idea of talking to Fiona takes hold of my brain. This is my chance.

I want to explain what's been going on with me. In a way, I owe it to her, especially since I shut down so bad in the train station. So I head down the alley toward her, making sure to step over any chalk scribbles I pass along the way.

"Hey, Fiona," I say, trying desperately to sound casual.

"Well, this is a shock," she says, and rocks back on her heels.

"I saw your arrows."

"You did?"

"Yeah. And I knew you were the one who drew them." There's a long, awkward pause as I muster up some courage. I thought this would have felt easier, since I chose to approach her instead of the other way around. "Listen, I wanted to talk to you about what happened in the museum last week. And about what you said to me in the train station."

She stares up at me from the ground, like she's trying to figure out if this is a joke or something. "Oh?"

"About how once you figure something out, it's impossible to go backward."

"What about it?"

"I just think you're right, is all."

"Of course I'm right," she says, kind of bitchy.

I look down at my flip-flops. This was a mistake.

"Are you afraid of me?" she asks.

My first instinct is to lie, but it would probably be pointless.

"Honestly? Kind of." I shiver, despite the fact that it's really warm. Nerves. I fight them by twisting my arms around each other and squeezing as hard as I can.

Fiona takes two steps away from me, over to the curb where her owl tote bag sits. I think she's just going to grab her stuff and leave me standing here like she did in the museum, but she stays put, her eyes on the ground.

"Hold still," she says, and fishes a thick, bright yellow piece of chalk out of her tote bag. "I mean, you can keep talking, but try not to move much." She starts to trace the darkened patch of cement in front of me.

If not for the shadow anchoring the tips of my flip-flops to the ground, I just might float away. Neither of us talks. We're quiet, listening as the chalk scrapes against the ground into the shape of me. Fiona's hand moves so deliberately and slow, like she's carving out the pavement with an X-Acto knife.

"Hold it right there!" An overweight security guard runs toward us. He clings to the waist of his pants with one hand, combating the weight of the huge key ring threaded through his belt loop. "You girls are going to need to come with me."

Fiona keeps drawing, totally unconcerned. "I highly doubt that."

"It's against the law to deface private property," he says. Fiona laughs, and the guard's fat, damp face goes red. "Graffiti is a crime."

July

"How can this be graffiti if it's chalk? Chalk isn't permanent." Fiona says it real slow, like the guy's got a learning disability.

He reaches for his crackling radio. "I said, put down the chalk!"

Fiona doesn't even blink. She just keeps drawing.

She's escalating the situation, not making it better. I want to help, but I don't want to ruin the project either. I want her to finish my shadow.

I say, "Excuse me, sir. We're students at the art school. And this is a special project we're working on."

His eyes narrow. "You both look young to be college students." Luckily, I have my ID on my lanyard. Trying not to move too much, I pull it out. He checks it skeptically. "Well, college students or not, this is private property. I'm sorry, but you're going to have to go."

I raise my hands to plead with him, but then quickly line them back up with my tracing on the ground. "We're almost finished —"

"Either you leave now, or I'm calling the police. The choice is yours."

"Riiiight. You'd have to call the real cops because you're just a man playing dress up." Fiona sneers. "Come on, Emily. We'd better hurry before he citizen-arrests us!"

She puts her chalk back in her tote. I'm still hesitant to move . . . my shadow's only half finished. But Fiona storms down the alleyway. So I follow her.

"What a douche," Fiona mutters. She fumbles to get a cigarette to her lips.

"He doesn't get what you're doing."

She stops to light it, sucking in a few times into the flame of her cheap plastic lighter. "And you do?"

"I'm not sure," I mumble. But there is one thing I do know, so that's what I say. "Ever since I saw your shadow drawings in the courtyard on that first day of school, everything started to change for me."

The beginnings of a smile break across Fiona's face, but she catches herself. Then she anchors her cigarette between her teeth, laces my hand inside hers, and pulls me along. "Explanation, *por favor.*"

I stretch out an "Ummm," as long as the air in my lungs will let me, and collect my thoughts. I wish I could be eloquent like the kids in the museum discussing a Picasso, but everything feels too messy and overwhelming, like a million puzzle pieces dumped on the floor of my brain. All I can do is search for straight edges and start trying to piece the big picture together. "So if I were to try and explain what a shadow is, I think I'd call it a shell."

"A shell?" Fiona asks, her face wrinkled and confused.

"Not like a seashell . . ." While I search for the right words, we pass the shadow of a parking meter. I tug on Fiona to make her stop. "So this shadow represents this parking meter," I say, and glide my hands around the dark spot like a game-show hostess. "Everyone knows what a parking meter is, so when we see its shadow, a picture of a real parking meter appears in our minds."

"Rightrightrightright." She nods, trying to hurry me along. "Abstract representation."

I suck in a deep breath and picture my half-finished shadow on the ground in that alley. When people pass that, what will they

94

think of me? "It's like . . . all I know about myself is the shadow, what I'm supposed to be."

Fiona leans against the parking meter, genuinely confused. "What are you supposed to be?"

I shrug my shoulders. "You know, like everyone else."

Fiona throws her hands up, exasperated. "Most everyone else sucks, Emily. Do you honestly not know that? And not just the drones, either. Even the artsy kids here, like Yates. Sure, he dresses the part, but what does he find inspiring? Pears!" She cracks herself up. "I mean, come on."

There's sharpness to her words that I recognize as the Big Sister voice — wisdom blended with annoyance. I talk the same way to Claire. Like the time she got all upset about the boys calling her flat-chested and I had to tell her that none of it mattered. I'm sure I sounded irritated with her. But the truth was, I wanted her to know she was better than what those stupid boys thought of her.

It's exciting to think Fiona might feel that way about me, too.

"Let me get this straight. My shadow drawings started this whole mental avalanche for you?"

First I nod. And then I shake my head, because it's way bigger than that. "What I'm saying is that I've never met anyone like you before."

I wait for Fiona to gloat, but she actually softens. "Here's the thing, Emily." She sucks in deep from her cigarette, then pushes the smoke out her nose in two thick streams. "You are a very confusing person."

I try to swallow, but my mouth is too dry. "I don't mean to be."

She takes another drag. "I've tried to talk to you a couple of times now, and even though you've seemed interested, you always revert back to this pretend person who's on autopilot or something."

"I just didn't know what to say. How to talk to someone like you."

"Yeah, but now you're trying to get my attention! Acting all smiley, finding me in the park, and showing up to class in this weird dead kitty outfit." She flicks off some ash and points at my tank top with the cigarette's glowing orange tip. "Which I love, by the way."

Her compliment heats up my face. "Thanks."

"I'm here, looking at you, trying to figure out just who you are. Because it seems like you might be this secret cool person wrapped up inside this whole other uncool person. Only you don't know it yet."

"Really?" The word is couched in an uncomfortable laugh, like I'm afraid that Fiona's wrong and afraid that she's right at the very same time. The truth is, I hardly recognize myself.

Fiona's quiet for a second, rolling the cigarette between her thumb and pointer finger. Her mouth opens like she's going to say something else, but her eyes shift from my face to over my shoulder.

I turn and see Robyn and Adrian walking toward us.

"Fiona!" Robyn calls out. "Where have you been?" As she gets closer, her face gets tighter, like she's thinking, *What's she doing with you?*

"I got you some food," Adrian says, handing Fiona a white paper bag.

96

July

"My lunch angel!" She opens it and peeks inside. "My sandwich prince!" Fiona plants a big kiss on Adrian's cheek. He smiles from ear to ear. And underneath the surface, his veins pump blood faster, spreading pink all over his face and arms.

He is in love with her.

Robyn stands right next to Fiona, and Adrian flanks her other side. I end up directly across from the three of them, forming a triangle rather than completing their circle.

"Seriously, where did you go?" Robyn says, looping her arm over Fiona's shoulder. "You went to the bathroom and never came back. We've been looking for you everywhere."

"I left you losers a bunch of clues." Fiona turns to me and smiles. It's surprisingly warm. "You just missed them." She walks over to a fire hydrant, leans against it, and opens up her sandwich. "Now, both of you be nice and say hello to Emily!"

"Hello, Emily," they say in unison.

"Hi," I say back.

"Isn't she the cutest thing ever?" Fiona takes a huge bite. "We make her so nervous!"

Robyn and Adrian share a quick look. I'm sure they're wondering why Fiona took an interest in someone like me. Or how long it might last.

I scratch a mosquito bite on my arm and just keep smiling, even though I kind of wonder that, too.

Twelve

I look for the three of them before our field trip the next day. Fiona, Robyn, and Adrian are huddled together on the steps of the university, a few above where the rest of the summer students sit and wait for the buses to arrive. Those kids have whispered conversations, or nibble on their breakfast, or sketch with their headphones on and their heads down, purpose-fully withdrawn. But the three of them are unapologetically loud, laughing like crazy as they give each other marker tattoos with black Sharpies.

I stuff my hands in my pockets and linger near the railing, where the teachers sip their coffee. I try not to stare. I wonder if I can just walk up to them like we're friends. I wish I were the kind of person who could do that, with the confidence that convinces people that you belong there with them. But I don't actually believe I do, as much as I might want to. So my only choice is to stand there and hope to be noticed. My shirt isn't as cool as it was yesterday. I couldn't think of what to wear, so I stole one of Claire's Cherry Grove recreation soccer shirts from a few years back. It's a little tight, but the rainbow decal across the chest is kind of okay. I think.

Fiona draws a thick black handlebar mustache across Adrian's hairless upper lip. She's got one hand through his brown hair, gripping it tight to keep him from moving. "Hold still!" she warns. "If you keep smiling, I'm going to give you a full beard!" Adrian isn't going anywhere. He loves it right where he is, sitting in between Fiona's legs, his hands on her knees.

Robyn twists toward her floppy leather bag and digs through it. When she looks up, I swear she spots me, because of the way her top lip curls, like I'm interrupting their fun, even though I'm several feet away. She grips the cap of her blue marker in her teeth, pulls the marker free, and scribbles something on the inside of Fiona's palm, a secret I'm not supposed to know.

I look down the sidewalk and see Yates walking toward the school with a coffee in hand. As he gets closer, I make out the bulge of his sketchbook in his front pocket. I would love to flip through it, to see what kind of drawings he does. It's probably as close as a girl can come to reading a boy's diary.

I wonder where Yates would fit in if he lived in Cherry Grove. Then I realize that Yates wouldn't have a problem making friends with whomever, because he's friendly in that easy sort of way that everyone in the world likes.

"Morning, Emily," he says. I focus on the few freckles across his cheeks. They are dark and tiny, like pricks from the tip of a supersharp pencil. Like someone drew them on.

"Hi," I say. It sounds too short, so I add, "How are you?"

He laughs. "I am quite well, thank you," he says, and bows his head like we're having some stiff, formal conversation. I hope he might actually stop and talk to me for a while, so I don't have to stand here by myself, but instead he passes by and enters the circle of teachers behind me.

When I turn around, Fiona waves to me. She's got a big star drawn inside her palm. I smile and wave hello back. She rolls her eyes. Then she changes her wave, abandoning the side-to-side hello for a rolling wrist. She wants me to go up there.

As soon as I figure it out, my legs can't move fast enough.

"Hey," I say.

Adrian takes off his old-man-style news cap and bows his head. His glasses slip right off the end of his nose and into his hands.

"I like your mustache," I tell him.

"He looks half cartoon," Fiona says with a laugh.

"I hope it washes off," Adrian says, wiggling his nose.

Fiona stares down at her star-covered palm. "I wish they were real. I'm getting, like, a million tattoos the second I turn eighteen. I've got them all mapped out in my sketchbook."

"Hey, Robyn," I say, stepping down so that I'm not so on top of her.

Robyn purses her lips and gives me the slightest head nod.

Fiona pats the patch of stone step next to her. "Want a tattoo, Emily?"

"Yeah," I say, and ignore my fear because there's no way I could say no. "Okay."

The marker swirls around my arm, while Fiona's fingers clench my bicep and pull the skin tight. I don't look at what she's drawing. Instead I close my eyes and feel the excitement. Meg and I used to play a similar game as kids, when we'd draw something or spell out words with our fingers on the other person's back, and then

July

she'd have to guess what it was. Meg's were always easy to guess because she'd draw one of three things — a flower with lots of teardrop petals, a house with one long curl of chimney smoke, or the words "best friends forever" in swirly script.

But I have no idea what Fiona's drawing on me. Some lines are smooth and long, while others are short and impatient. And she keeps jumping around from spot to spot, like she wants to trick me, like she doesn't want me to catch up with her. I take deep breaths of the peppery smell of permanent marker ink.

"Nicely done," Adrian says.

The point lifts up off my skin. "Are you finished?" I ask her, eyes still closed, just in case.

Fiona pinches me awake. "You have been officially branded," she says with a grin.

I twist my arm around and check it out. She's drawn a red outline of a heart — big and thick with the side of the marker. Then, with the tip, she surrounded it with delicate doily-like scalloping and small polka dots, so it looks like an old-fashioned Valentine's Day card. Inside, she's written my name in black, in a variety of letter styles — some in capital letters, some in bubble letters, and the tail of the Y looks crooked and crazy, like lightning.

"This is your reminder to wear your heart on your sleeve more often." Fiona winks.

I like the sound of that.

Dr. Tobin paces the sidewalk in front of the stairs and claps her hands a few times to get everyone's attention. There will be no buses, because today's field trip is a sculpture walk around Center City. We set off down the sidewalk like a meandering, indifferent parade of weird kids. I am so glad I have a group of people to walk with, unlike last week. Friends just make everything more fun.

"So, tell us something about yourself, Emily," Robyn says to me, and not in the most inviting tone of voice.

It feels like an interview, a chance to prove that I'm cool enough to hang out with them. A test I want to pass. "What do you want to know?" I ask, trying to sound indifferent.

"What's your hometown like?" Robyn keeps even pace with me, but her eyes stay straight ahead. "Does it have a huge mall?"

Her question is a trick. It's obvious someone like Robyn thinks malls are stupid. And I doubt there's a store at Cherry Grove Mall that sells saddle shoes like the scuffed ones loosely covering her bare feet. "Yeah, we do. But it's not like I hang out there." I mean, I *have* hung out there, but only when I was already shopping, which doesn't seem like it should count.

Robyn smiles. It's wide and suspicious and shows all her teeth, even the ones way in back. "What about a football team? Does your school have a football team? Do you and your friends go to all the games and cheer for your boyfriends?"

Adrian rolls his eyes at Robyn. "Every high school has a football team."

My face gets hot. I know Robyn is making fun of me. Adrian and Fiona must, too. Maybe they don't really have any intention of letting me hang out with them. Maybe I'm just some big joke.

Fiona speeds up so that she's a few steps ahead of us. Then she turns around and walks backward, so she can stare right at me. "Emily doesn't have a boyfriend. Am I right?"

My eyes drop to the sidewalk. I step on all the cracks. "Yeah."

July

"Come on." The snark from Robyn's voice is replaced with genuine surprise. She actually stops walking, and Adrian almost bumps into her. "You're not, like, dating the captain or something?"

"No," I repeat. Not me. My best friend.

"Of course she's not," Fiona says. "Jocks don't date girls who draw dead kitties on tank tops or freak out over Duchamp. Unless they put out. But you don't put out, do you, Emily?"

I'd normally be embarrassed by this question, especially with Adrian around. I mean, it's hard enough for me to hear from Meg about all the makeouts she has with Rick, and though they aren't close to having sex yet, I feel like I'm years behind them. But something about the way Fiona asks makes me feel like it's okay. Or, not just okay, but the right answer. So I shake my head.

Fiona falls back into line with us. "Good. Stupid high school boys aren't worth it." She throws an arm over my shoulder. "They're trained to like a certain type of girl, with highlights and pretty nails — the kind who are good at remembering to put on lotion every morning after they shower." She smiles like she's got a dirty secret. "And let's face it . . . sluts."

I grin, because Fiona's describing Jenessa to a T, without sugarcoating it the way Meg always does.

Adrian thrashes his head so his hair lifts off his eyes for a second. "Not all high school guys like girls like that," he says.

"And that's why I love you, Mr. Mustache," Fiona says, and kisses his cheek. Adrian explodes into a blush. Fiona laughs and kisses him again, tiny pecks all over his face.

As we round the west corner of City Hall, the parkway stretches out before us — a six-lane street lined with hundreds of international flags fluttering in a summer breeze I wish I felt.

Off to the side of City Hall is a small patch of cement called Love Park. It's named that, I guess, because of this one particular sculpture — the L-O-V-E letters in a square shape that you always see printed on Valentine's Day coffee mugs.

As Dr. Tobin talks, Fiona leans into my ear and whispers: "This place used to be a big skater hangout, but the stupid mayor made it illegal." She points down to the edge of a stone bench. Streaks of silver are gouged in the pale stone where wheels and skateboard decks ground against them. "I used to hang out here, but not anymore. Now it's lame."

"What'd you just say?" Robyn sidles up next to us, looking kind of annoyed that we're talking without her.

"I said this park is lame now, since they chased all the punks and skate rats away." Fiona crouches down and does a rubbing in her sketchbook of the scratches in the stone.

"Oh." Robyn pouts. "My ex used to skate. He tried to teach me, but I have the worst balance."

"Yeah, you do," Fiona snorts. "You almost took me out in the stairwell that first day of class!"

"Shut up!" Robyn squeals and smacks Fiona on the butt. "You were the one trying to slide down the banister and almost killed that old lady with the box full of ceramics."

They laugh like old friends even though they've only known each other eight days. I can't help but feel jealous of the way they connect, and that Robyn is throwing it in my face. I look away and see Mr. Frank watching us. I am the only one who doesn't have a sketchbook out. I fish mine from my bag and open it. But the thought of drawing here, in front of all these kids and also the people just walking around, makes me feel totally embarrassed, like I'm some kind of phony.

Dr. Tobin calls for our attention and raises her hands over her head in YMCA fashion.

"Claes Oldenburg gifted this sculpture to Philadelphia in 1976."

It's a huge metal clothespin, at least seven stories high, like a mini skyscraper, and the warmest shade of rust, glistening metallic in the sunshine. It's totally bizarre and out of place, in an interesting way.

"Isn't that insane?" Fiona says. "I heart me some Claes. He made all kinds of weird crap like this, and just dropped them where they'd mess with people's heads."

I nod, silently thrilled that I recognize the name. Though not from some art textbook. From *Clueless*, which is Meg's all-time favorite movie. Whatever, though. I'll take what I can get.

"Insane," Robyn says quickly, like she was buzzing into a game show or something.

A thought pops into my mind. I think about not saying anything, but then I lean close to Fiona's ear. "This actually reminds me of Duchamp. Sort of. But instead of just putting ordinary objects in a museum, this guy took ordinary objects and made them massive. Which is kind of more special."

"Go you!" Fiona taps my sketchbook and laughs. "Seriously, though, it's so cool when artists take other people's ideas and run with them. I'm trying to soak up the entire world for my art. You should draw it in your sketchbook to celebrate this achievement in critical thought."

I look around at all the students. Even though their heads are down and sketching, I still feel like they are watching me.

Fiona laughs. "What? You think some art cop in a black beret is going to ask you for your artistic license?"

"No!" I say, laughing. Fiona bumps me with her hip. I open up a page and start drawing it as tiny as I can. The lines are all crooked, since I'm trying to steady my sketchbook in my free hand. It just might be my worst drawing ever. I rub my fingertips on the edge of the page, so that it comes up into my grip.

"Wait!" Fiona says, lunging at me. "What are you doing?"

"I'm ripping it out."

"Are you nuts?" Fiona grabs my sketchbook from my hands. "You NEVER rip pages out of your sketchbook! It's, like, sacrilegious."

I smile, remembering that Yates did exactly that for me, at the art museum last week. But there are more pressing matters at hand. "Oh God, please don't look," I plead as I try to get it back from her. But Fiona runs away from me, sits on the edge of the fountain, and flips through.

"Umm . . . these are seriously good, you idiot," she says.

Only Fiona could pair up the words *good* and *idiot* in a compliment and have it sound more sincere than anything I've ever heard. I slide next to her.

She flips through the rest of my drawings until she gets to a blank page. Then she returns it to me. "Even bad drawings are lessons. If you throw that drawing away, you won't learn anything from it."

"Really?" I'm embarrassed because I can still see the lines of my bad sketch carved into the next blank sheet. I wish I didn't press so hard. I wouldn't have to see my mistakes, and I wouldn't have the ugly callus on my hand either.

"You haven't taken many of these kinds of classes before, have you?" Robyn asks.

"Just one high school class, and that was kind of a joke." It sounds like I'm apologizing.

"Art is always a joke in high school," Fiona says.

Adrian nods. "Do you ever wonder why every single art teacher in high school is an old woman who only knows how to make potato stamps and paper snowflakes?"

I smile and think of Ms. Kay. "Yeah." Even though she's an art teacher, I never thought of her as a real artist.

"And Mr. Hack." Fiona fake-coughs. "I mean, Mr. Frank. If he were really any good, do you think he'd be spending his summer teaching high school kids?" She shakes her head. "Listen, Emily, I think you're insanely good for a beginner. You obviously have talent. But it's not like you can be a superstar right off the bat. Especially when you've only just opened your eyes. I mean, I've been doing this for years and years. My mom had me taking art classes when I was, like, two. She's an artist herself, so that kind of stuff is important to her." I can't even imagine what Fiona's mom looks like. She's probably so cool. When Fiona dyed her hair pink, her mom probably loved it. Any other mom, like my mom, would freak for sure. "Becoming an artist is a huge thing that takes over your whole life. It's not something you can shut off just because you're scared and embarrassed of what other people might think about you or say about you. You have to own it."

"Own it," Robyn says, "but not make it up. The worst thing in the world is to be a poseur."

SAME DIFFERENCE

I'm getting tired of Robyn's attacks on me, but this time, Fiona rolls her eyes and faces her down. "Actually, I think it's the best thing ever that Emily's here in Philly, that she's trying to go outside of things that she's used to. I mean, no one cares or gets shocked with what I wear, but for her, it's a big deal. So I think she's actually pretty brave." Fiona's face lights up with an idea. It's amazing, how visible it is on her face. She turns to me. "What are you doing tomorrow? For Fourth of July? You should totally come see the fireworks with us!"

I want to, but there's no way. "I can't. I have to go someplace with my family." We go to Meg's family barbecue every year. I'm not going to tell Fiona about Meg. She'd eat someone like Meg alive.

"Bummer." She thinks. "Well, do you want to go to First Friday with us instead?"

"What's First Friday?" I regret the words immediately, because Robyn laughs under her breath and walks away from us, pulling Adrian with her.

"They open all the galleries in the city to show new artwork for sale. There's wine or champagne and cheese plates and it's all free," she says, itching the red scratches on her arms. "It's suuuuuper fun and totally inspiring."

Rick is throwing a party on Friday night. His parents are going to the shore, and Jimmy's uncle said he'd buy the keg, so long as he could drink it with everyone. I already promised Meg I'd go, but maybe I can get out of it. "You sure Robyn won't mind me tagging along?" I whisper.

"Who cares what she thinks? I'm asking you. So . . . will you come?"

A swell of something builds in my chest — and fighting the current would be worthless. "Yeah. I will. Thanks."

Thirteen

"Isn't this the life?" Meg says, smiling over at me from her lounge chair.

"I don't think I've gotten any color," I say, staring down at my pasty stomach.

"That's what you get for spending all those beautiful sunny days stuck indoors." Meg gives herself a misting of coconut oil and then tosses the bottle at me. "Here. You need to catch up."

Since classes were canceled for the Fourth of July, I slept over at Meg's house last night. We went straight from our pajamas into our bikinis and lay out by the pool all morning, while Meg's parents got the backyard ready.

Every year, Meg's family throws a huge barbecue. Mr. Mundy is a pro on his big gas grill. He even has a stamp to sear his initials on the steaks he buys from the butcher. He makes his own barbecue sauce from scratch. It's the darkest, sappy color brown, rich and sticky, and it tastes sweet and sour at the same time. He brushes it on real thick and cooks the meat slowly on a low heat, so it stays juicy. They serve summer corn and homemade mustard coleslaw and burgers with sautéed mushrooms and fancy imported cheeses from Whole Foods. They set out about fifteen different bowls of flavored potato chips.

My parents and Claire come over around noon, along with a bunch of other families from Blossom Manor. Meg and I stay lazy on the lounge chairs while Claire does goofy dives into the deep end of the pool to try and make us laugh. The parents all stay on the deck, playing cards. Eventually, Meg and I go up there for some food.

"Emily, are you enjoying your art classes?" Mrs. Mundy asks me.

"Oh yeah," I say, heading over to the burger table. "They're great."

Meg hands me a crisp white paper plate, the heavy kind that you can pile food on and not worry about it seeping through. "You know, you haven't told me much about your classes since you talked about quitting," she says. She's got her bathing suit on underneath a pink terry cloth tube dress, and her long hair dangles down her back in a loose braid. "What are they like?"

"Well, Mixed Media, the class I would have had today, is my favorite, I think," I say, cracking open a cold can of Coke.

"What's Mixed Media?" Meg asks, reaching for some lettuce.

"Wait!" Mom shouts. She tosses down her hand of cards and springs up from her seat at the table. "I want to hear all about it. Emily, you've barely told me anything about your classes!"

I shake my head and Meg laughs. "It's sort of like collage," I say, and start layering the toppings on my burger. "You take images and drawings and stuff and arrange them in an interesting, thoughtful way. Last week, each of us got an envelope full of random slips of paper, and we had to paste them down in a new shape. I got all these yellow pieces — like a picture of a baby chick, some lemons from a supermarket circular, stuff like that. I ripped them all into pieces and pasted them down in the shape of a sun." My teachers really seemed to like it. And for the first time ever, I had an idea, and instead of letting myself get all worried about it not being good enough, I just went with it. That was definitely Fiona's influence.

"Emily," my dad says in a frowny way, as he chases a slippery pasta salad noodle with his fork. "Wait for your mother. You're going to hurt her feelings."

Meg bounces on the balls of her feet. "That's awesome! You and I are going to have the best friendship page in the senior year-book! I'm already collecting good pictures of us. I found one the other day of me and you jumping into the pool hand in hand, in matching bathing suits. It's so cute!" Meg smiles at me in the way you do when you're waiting for someone to take your picture. The kind you don't blink, and it hangs on your face.

"Yeah, sure," I say, even though she's got it all wrong. Mixed Media isn't about cutting pictures out and sticking them on poster board. It's more about taking things out of their normal context and giving them new meaning somewhere else.

Kind of like what's happening to me.

"So, Emily," Mom says, joining us at the food table. "Have you made any new friends in your classes?"

Meg stands up a little straighter as she picks the tomatoes out of her salad.

"Sort of," I say, dodging the question. I know that I'm going to have to tell Meg about First Friday at some point, and that I won't be able to make it to Rick's party after all. But I'm kind of dreading it.

"Come on. I'm sure you made at least one friend!" Mom says with a laugh. "A beautiful girl like you." She beams a smile at all the neighbors, like they're supposed to agree.

I hate when Mom gets like this, saying things in a backhanded way, using compliments to cover up the truth. She knows I'm not that pretty, especially standing next to Meg. She has no idea what my life is like. "There's this one girl I met who's pretty cool. And she's the best in our drawing class. Her mom's an artist, so I guess that's where she gets it from."

"Well, you come from creative parents, too," Mom says. "So don't sell yourself short. Your father has to be extremely creative in his job."

"He's a salesman, Mom." I shake my head. "Sales is not creative."

"Hey," Dad whines.

"Theater is art," Mom says. She takes the wine that Mr. Mundy offers her and clinks her fork against her glass like she's made some incredible point. "Every property requires a new performance."

How could she think that's even close to the same thing? "Dad's not on Broadway. He's selling office space to companies." I take my food back to my lounge chair.

"I agree with your mom," Meg says, joining me. She starts cutting her lettuce. I don't know anyone else who cuts their lettuce. "Rick works a 'typical' job, but he's very creative."

I laugh. I can't help it.

"Seriously!" Meg says. "Landscape design is a real thing you can study in college."

July

Rick is not a landscape designer. He's a guy who pushes a mower and runs a weed whacker for his dad. Maybe it's mean, but I ask, "Is that what Rick is going to apply to college for? *Landscape design?*"

Meg turns her attention to the rest of the party. "Rick's not going to school. He can make a lot more money right here in Cherry Grove. His dad's landscape business is going to be his someday." She's not embarrassed or apologetic, even though both our parents are insane about us both getting into good schools. She's honestly proud of him. "In fact, he's practically running the whole business already."

I bite my burger and chew like crazy to keep from saying something I can't take back. The truth is that Rick hardly works. He's over at Meg's house all the time. But by the time I swallow, I'm still angry. "You're going to date a guy who doesn't want to go to college?" I mean, doesn't Meg want to be with someone who can teach her something new? Give her a different experience?

Meg drops her head so far that her hair almost touches the plate. Maybe this isn't perfect barbecue conversation, but come on. Sometimes I wonder if Meg really likes Rick, or if she just likes him because she thinks she should. I've been guilty of that myself, but at least now I know better. "I don't mean to get you upset," I tell her. "I just think you deserve to be with someone really special."

"Thanks," she says, kind of quiet, as she pokes her way around the red onions. I think she might actually be considering what I'm saying, but when she looks up, she says, "So . . . what are you wearing tonight? What about your red halter?"

There's no way I can force Meg to see things my way. So I let it go and talk clothes. And it's back to old times again. Except, not.

SAME DIFFERENCE

After we eat, Meg and I part ways to get ready for fireworks. Every year, the whole town walks down to the Cherry Grove High School football field, home to the annual fireworks. When you're a kid, you go with your parents, but as soon as you get to high school, you go with your friends. You bring a blanket, some mosquito repellent, and snacks. And maybe beers, if you manage to steal some, or rum mixed inside a bottle of Coke. Then the town sets off fireworks and the high school band plays all these patriotic songs. They actually do it up pretty nice for a small town in New Jersey.

I step out of the tub and grab a fresh, thick white towel from the stack in the cabinet underneath my sink. I wipe the moisture off the mirror. It's still foggy, but I can see that I got some color — creamy white lines trace the shape of my bikini against skin now the color of graham crackers.

"Hey, when are you going down to the fireworks?" Claire ducks her head inside my room.

"Why?" I walk over to my mirrored vanity and start flat-ironing my hair.

Claire flops on my bed. "I don't want to sit with Mom and Dad. They're boring. Can I come with you?"

I see her reflection in the mirror. She's darker than dark, almost the color of a hot dog left on the grill too long. And she's got on a light blue ribbed tank with a pair of white jean shorts that show off how toned her legs are from all that soccer. She looks beautiful. She looks older than me.

"I don't think so." I can't find my paddle brush. "Did you steal my brush?"

July

"No." Claire climbs down from my bed and hands it to me. It was just underneath my towel. "Why can't I come with you and Meg?"

I pull it out of her hand sort of fast. "Because there's not enough room on our blanket. And also, you're thirteen. We're going to be drinking, and I don't want you telling Mom and Dad." I'm showing off to my little sister, and it makes me feel pathetic.

"I won't tell! I promise!"

"I just don't think it's a good idea."

"But I'm going to be in the high school next year, Emily. I want to make friends."

"You'll make friends. Your *own* friends." I don't mean to snap, but I don't want Claire sitting with me. Meg is bound to be all cuddly with Rick. And then what . . . are Claire and I supposed to snuggle or something? No, thanks.

"Seriously? I can't?"

"No," I say. "Seriously. You can't."

Claire groans as she gets up off my bed, like it takes some big effort. "Whatever." She pauses before closing the door. "Don't forget to flat-iron the back of your head. You never remember to do it, and it always looks lumpy."

I finish up my hair, put on some lip gloss, and meet Meg outside. Rick is late. Meg leans against the fire hydrant, staring off into the clouds. As we wait for Rick, I figure it's as good a time as ever to tell her I can't make it to his party. So I sit down next to her on the curb and say, "I have some bad news. Well, it's not bad, but —"

"What?"

"I actually have a school thing on Friday night that I have to go to. So I don't think I'll make it to Rick's party." I give her a second to say something, but when she doesn't, I keep going. "They're taking us on a big gallery trip. It's mandatory." I hate to lie, but in a way it *is* mandatory. I have to go.

"Oh." Meg is sad. Sadder than I expect her to be. She chews on her fingernail. "Is this about Chad? Because he and Jenessa might not even come."

"No. It's not about Chad. I don't care about Chad."

"Okay, okay. Well, you could come after. I mean, the school thing won't take all night, will it? I'll just wait until you get back, and then we can go together."

"You don't have to do that," I say.

Meg's cheek dimples, like she's biting the skin on the inside. "Maybe I just won't go."

"What? Why wouldn't you go?" I don't get why this is so difficult. Sure, we've always gone to parties together, but so what? It's her boyfriend's party, after all. She's practically the guest of honor.

"What if I got someone to pick you up from the train station whatever time you come back?"

"I mean . . . I guess." Maybe I should feel good that Meg wants me there so badly. But it's been pretty well established that there's no way I'm hooking up with Chad, so what's the big deal? I've let her off the hook about some romantic night with Rick a hundred times already. Is it such a huge deal that we don't go to one party together?

"Sorry. I just really want you to come tomorrow." She can't even look at me. She just wrings the hem of her navy polo dress in her hands.

I can't stand seeing her so upset, twice today, because of me. And who knows how long this First Friday thing is going to take anyway. Maybe it will be over early, and then I'll have nothing to do. "Okay, okay, I'll come." Even though I don't want to. Even though I regret the words the moment they leave my lips.

Meg brightens. "Thanks, Em. We'll have fun there, I swear."

Rick's truck finally roars down our cul-de-sac. He parks and gets out and wraps his tan arms around Meg, kissing her neck. "Sorry I'm late. I was helping my mom clean up."

Meg wriggles out from his grip. "Hey, Emily!" She smiles. "Let's ride in the back of Rick's truck."

Rick looks sore for a second, but then he takes off his light blue baseball cap and puts on a smile. "Here," he says. "Let me get my dustpan and I'll make sure there isn't any dirt back there."

"Thanks," I tell Rick. Meg doesn't say anything to Rick at all. She just puts the blankets and her picnic basket in the cab with Rick and we both climb into the bed.

"Is everything okay?" I ask her. Maybe what I said back at the barbecue is sticking in her mind.

But Meg seems almost caught off guard by my question. "Everything's fine," she says. "Why?"

"No reason," I say. "Never mind."

Rick drives slow, past all the families walking to the field, blasting Bruce Springsteen through his open windows. We wave to our parents, to our neighbors, who all walk in a big group. Claire doesn't wave back. She keeps her hands tucked in her armpits.

At the field, I see everyone from our high school. Meg and I spread out our blanket. Meg has a picnic basket all prepared for us. It's, like, perfect. Cubes of cheese, crackers, prosciutto, and melon. A few people stop by to say hello as the field continues to get darker. The band squeaks and toots and drums its way through a warm-up. Meg and I light up two gold sparklers and swirl them through the thick, muggy air. I like the way the color burns into your eyes, leaving a trail like a ghost.

When it gets too dark to see, everything settles. People find their way back to their blankets. I sit down at the edge of the blanket and pull my arms inside my halter. Rick kneels on the other side and motions for Meg to sit between his legs.

"Emily's cold," she says, shaking her head. "Let's keep her warm."

"I'm okay, really," I say.

"It's fine, Emily," Meg says and practically pushes me into the middle of her and Rick.

I'm suffocated between them. I almost wish Claire was here, or that I was on the blanket with my family.

The band kicks into "America the Beautiful" and the fireworks start. I have to say, they're less amazing than I remember them to be. Spaced out. One blossom at a time.

I shift my eyes from the sky to the ground and watch the colored light dance along the grass and against the backs of the people sitting in front of us, and fight off the loneliness. I want to memorize the way the light looks for my sketchbook. My fingers twitch. I wish I was drawing.

Fourteen

Even though Fiona technically lives in Philadelphia, her neighborhood, Fish Town, is still really far away from the part of the city where the university is. She gave me directions that included a train and two buses, but I was afraid I'd be late, so I just took a taxi once I got into the city. Mom gave me extra money, since I'd told her it was a field trip, too. Otherwise, I doubt she'd have let me come.

The cab pulls up to Fiona's address. She's standing in her driveway, rinsing her hair with a garden hose. The pink is gone. A river of electric blue water rolls off the long strip and down the divide between the driveway and the grass.

"Wow! You're dyeing your hair." I try to hide the disappointment in my voice, because I loved the pink.

"I got bored." She squeezes the water out. "My mom doesn't let me do this in the bathroom because these vegetable dyes stain the tile grout. I don't mind so much in the summertime, but it's too freaking cold to use this hose on my head in the middle of winter."

SAME DIFFERENCE

As Fiona goes to shut off the water from a spout near the stairs, I glance around. Fiona doesn't have a house but an apartment. It's a big redbrick building with a wooden steeple up on the very top, which makes me think it was some kind of factory or maybe even a church before it became an apartment building. Broken glass sparkles on the curb in front of it. Thick black wires hang slacked and sloppy across the street, and it looks so unprofessional that it makes you think it was done illegally or by someone who just didn't care.

I follow Fiona inside. We walk down a long hallway with apartment doors on either side and take a staircase up a few flights. On the walls hang black-and-white photos of the building back in the day, with lines of men and women in starched white clothes posing in front of big white trucks.

"This place was an old washhouse," Fiona explains. "All the rich people from Center City would send their laundry here." We reach the end of the hallway and stand in front of a large red door. "Our apartment used to be the president's office. It's nice because it has two floors. I hate apartments on all the same floor. They're like coffins."

We step inside the apartment, and it does seem bigger than I thought it would. But I don't get a chance to look around. We pass the kitchen and immediately charge up the stairs and into her bedroom. I'm right behind Fiona as she opens the door, because I'm so excited to see inside.

The room is like an attic, with vaulted ceilings, and two tiny, four-panel windows perched up high, with deep windowsills that act as shelves. One is full of half-burnt religious candles with Spanish names. She has Christmas lights strung around the door. The wood floor is covered in splattered paint. Japanese candies and paper lanterns are piled in the corner. Her old wooden dresser is missing both the top and bottom drawers, but clothes are crammed inside anyway. There's a big green chair in the corner. Rips in the velvet are patched by silver duct tape.

And there are tons of live animals, too. A pair of lovebirds cooing in a white wire cage. An iguana baking under a lightbulb inside a huge glass fish tank. I saw a litter box in the foyer downstairs, but I haven't seen a cat yet.

It's like the total opposite of my room. It's alive.

I step carefully around everything, like I could somehow pollute it with my plainness. I find myself standing in front of a poster of Andy Warhol, who I remember from Ms. Kay's slide shows. It's a screen-printed photograph of him, all fuzzy and orange, wearing black Ray-Ban sunglasses. Underneath is his famous quote, IN THE FUTURE, EVERYONE WILL BE WORLD-FAMOUS FOR FIFTEEN MINUTES. Only Fiona's crossed the fifteen-minute part out and replaced it with FIFTY YEARS TO LIFE! in black marker. The exclamation point has its own shadow.

Fiona crouches in front of her mirror, and in two seconds she has pinned up her hair all funky and cute. "I love your hair like that," I tell her.

I watch her eyes move from her reflection on to me. "Do you want to play beauty parlor?"

I bounce on my toes. I can't help it. "Really?"

"Here." Fiona throws some stuff off a plastic mushroom stool. "Come sit."

It's weird, actually watching myself transform. My reflection in the mirror, though partially obscured by a million random pieces of paper and stickers tucked into the edges of the black plastic frame, reminds me of the films they show in science class, where a flower grows out of the ground at warp speed.

Fiona parts a bobby pin using her free hand and her mouth. "Your hair is so healthy, I want to throw up all over you." She secures a twisty section up on the crown of my head. "I'll be lucky if I don't go bald by graduation," she says, scrunching her hair in her hand. It does sound dry. "I think I'm going to have to dye it all black in a few days. That's the best color to do. It seeps into the tiny holes and flakes in your hair strands and pumps them up and makes it strong again. It's like hair steroids."

"I love the colored stripe!"

"Yeah, I know, but I get bored of things really quick, so it's like I'm always on to something new. I think my mind speed is double that of everyone else." Fiona smiles. "Okay. You're done!"

I turn and check out the side of my head. The countless blond swirls make me look like a girl from another time. Fiona has also parted my hair on the side, pulling a big sweep across my forehead. It looks dramatic. "I wish I could do things like this to my hair," I say.

"You're so funny, Emily. I'm just pinning it up. It's not like heart surgery."

I stand up and check out the rest of me in the full-length mirror. My new hairstyle totally doesn't go with my outfit. I wanted to wear something cool for First Friday, but I also needed my outfit to work for Rick's party. I stole my dad's Villanova shirt and safety-pinned the sides of it on the train so it would fit tighter. I paired that with my white jean miniskirt, which would also work for Rick's party. But the hair is too fancy for the T-shirt. I have a purple silk cami Meg really likes me in, stuffed in my bag. I figured I'd change into that in the train station, but I guess I could wear it now. Only

July

my hair is too original for the clothes that will get me by for the second part of my night. A piece of hair uncoils and falls in front of my right eye, like it knows this isn't going to work.

Fiona steps to the rescue, and twists it back into place. "You could borrow something of mine to wear, if you wanted," she says. "In fact, you should probably dress a little more fancy. That way, no one says anything when you reach for the wine."

"Thanks," I say.

"Speaking of free booze, I was thinking we should order dinner, otherwise we're bound to get sloppy drunk. Do you like Indian food?"

"I've never had Indian food."

"Geez! It's like you're from the moon or something! I'll order you some stuff I know you'll love. And I guess I should text Robyn and Adrian about the dress code thing, too. I mean, I'm sure Robyn already knows, but Adrian is clueless. At least you grew up remotely near the city. He's almost a lost cause." She disappears, then sticks her head back in the door a second later. "Ooh. The clothes on the floor of my closet are clean. I swear."

I wait to move until I hear her feet pounding down the stairs. Then I pull open the door to Fiona's closet.

I don't know if it happens because there's almost too much to look at, patterns and shapes and colors and materials, but on the floor, at the very top of the mountain of clothes, is this bright blue dress. It's simple in shape — tight on top, with two thick straps, then it balloons to a short skirt with lots of white tulle layers underneath that puff it out.

I take off my clothes and quickly slide the dress on. It's a bit loose in the boobs, so I keep my bra on and try to line the straps up, but otherwise, it's a perfect fit. I do a twirl, right there in the middle of the room, and wonder what it would be like if I were really this person.

It feels good, even if it's just pretend for a night.

Fiona stops in the doorway. "Oh my God, Emily! You look so rad!"

"So do you," I say. Fiona's changed, too, into a black tube dress with a ruffle across the bottom hem and skinny black heels. A huge amber pendant lies on her chest. She looks sexy, older.

Fiona curtseys. "I love this dress, but I always have to dry it on high to get it tight again. Cheapie clothes are like that. You can only wear them once. By the end of the night, it'll be all bagged out."

"Well, I've never worn a dress like this."

"Guess where I got it?" She laughs. "This Halloween costume shop on South Street was going out of business and everything was a million percent off. I think it was part of an Alice in Wonderland costume, but someone stole the shoes and the little white apron."

"Oh no." I peel down the straps, embarrassed.

"Don't worry. You can't tell!" she says. "Here!" She ducks down deep into the closet. She pulls out a black cotton cardigan that smells like incense and tells me to take off my flip-flops and wear her round-toe black patent leather mary janes instead. Her feet are bigger than mine, but I can walk okay, if I scrunch up my toes.

The last thing I do is unhinge my Tiffany's necklace, the one Meg gave to me. I try not to feel guilty about it, either. It just doesn't go with the dress.

Fiona throws a couple of shirts and things into a plastic bag for me, stuff that she says won't fit her or that she's tired of.

"Wow," I say. "Are you sure you want to give all this away?"

July

"Think of these as a donation to your Cause of Cool," she says. "I seriously don't have room for any more clothes in here, anyhow."

A flash of white runs across the floor in front of me. I jump back.

"Snowflake!" Fiona chases her bunny and swoops it up into a hug. Snowflake's claws scrape her arms, leaving behind a fresh set of the little scratches and red marks. I feel silly for thinking they were something else, something dark.

Fiona and Snowflake take me on a tour of the rest of the house. In the mismatched living room, Fiona points out a collection of paintings.

"These are my mom's," she says proudly.

I lean in for a closer look.

The paintings are not what I expected them to be. Classical-looking landscapes, like the pastorals we saw at the museum. They're beautiful.

"And this is me," she says, pointing to a few strokes that suddenly take the shape of a young girl, out of focus in a grassy field. "At my grandma's house. She lived in Amish country. My mom actually hates these paintings. She does much more modern stuff now. But I think she keeps them up because she's still sad about my grandma dying." The doorbell rings. "Food!"

Fiona looks through her wallet. I can see from where I'm standing that it's empty.

"Crap. I'm sorry, Emily, but do you have any cash?" She looks embarrassed. "My mom was supposed to be home by now. She's probably working late at her studio. She always loses track of time when she's painting."

"Oh yeah! Sure!" I say, and fish for my wallet. I take out a twenty. And then, two more.

"I'll pay you back. I swear," Fiona promises as she takes them from my hand. "Wait. This is too much."

"No! Don't worry. You gave me all those clothes and everything. And you invited me out tonight."

"Really?" Shyness looks odd on someone like Fiona. It doesn't fit.

But I'm happy to do something for her. "It's no problem at all." She pays the man at the door and we take the food into her kitchen. "So, your mom is a full-time artist? That's so cool."

"Yup." Fiona rips open the bags and starts pulling out plastic containers. Lots of them. "She's been working on this new series of paintings that are totally freaking amazing. I've seen them and they blow me away! She kicks the ass of any of our professors. Well, maybe not my Performance Art teacher. She's a complete genius. But definitely Mr. Frank." She takes off the lids and suddenly the whole room smells warm and spicy. "I ordered a ton of food because I want you to try all my favorites." Fiona makes a bed of rice on my plate. Then she scoops out some red sauce on top, careful to not let the sauce seep out to where she spoons the salad. After a minute, my plate is expertly divided with six different tastes of food in the brightest colors. She hands it to me and says, "Emily, you've NEVER tasted anything like this before."

I know it's true before it hits my lips.

Fifteen

y the time we push our way inside the seventh gallery of the evening, Fiona doesn't even bother to look at what's hanging on the walls. Instead, she searches the crowds until she spots a tuxedoed waiter, twirling around the room with a tray of wineglasses. Fiona grabs two with each hand, completely oblivious of the disapproving look he shoots her.

"Cheers to art!" Fiona squeals, a little too loud, as she runs back over to us and hands out the drinks.

Fiona, Robyn, Adrian, and I all clink plastic goblets. I'm toasting what feels like the first night of my new life.

"Your hair looks cute up like that, Emily," Robyn says. "I wish mine was longer."

Robyn's been nicer to me tonight, which is a welcome change. Maybe I've finally earned her respect. "Your hair is awesome," I tell her. Not many people could pull off a cut as short as hers and not look like a boy. But Robyn always wears sparkly barrettes or headbands. And her clothes are ultrafeminine, like tonight's oversized black sequined tank and the wide-leg gray trousers that pool at her feet.

"All you girls look gorgeous," Adrian says, straightening his black skinny tie. It's probably the coolest tie I've ever seen. Up close, there doesn't seem to be a pattern to the million little colored dots, but from across the room, they form the shape of a cartoon rocket ship blasting up into the sky.

"But me most of all, right?" Fiona says, sliding up beside him.

"Fiona, you are *everything* most of all." Adrian turns his head, and I think they are going to kiss right there in front of us. Fiona leans in just next to his lips, but then pulls away at the last minute, laughing her head off. Not meanly. Flirtatious. Like the real kiss will happen, but not yet.

Tonight has been so inspiring, and not just because of the art I've seen in the galleries. It's also what's been going on right under my nose, the everyday world I've somehow missed seeing. Like the penguin drawing Fiona spotted hanging up behind the deli register, when we stopped to buy mints and a new pack of cigarettes. It was drawn by a kid on a ripped paper bag, and proclaimed itself in scribbly crayon writing to be THE BEST DRAWING OF A PENGUIN EVER.

Even though there were people waiting behind us in line, Fiona pushed the Tic Tacs and stuff on the countertop out of her way and quickly sketched it down on a blank page in her sketchbook. I stood behind her, on my tiptoes, watching as her pencil moved across the page.

In a way I could probably never explain, it *was* the best penguin drawing ever. I was so glad Fiona pointed it out.

July

In between galleries, we all draw shadows on the street. Fiona takes the lead like a conductor, and we are her hands, carving out pieces of the night in the brightest chalk colors. I feel euphoric just thinking about what I've left behind. We've given gifts to unsuspecting people all night long.

"Are you having the time of your life or what?" Fiona asks me. She pulls out a loose bobby pin in my hair and puts it back in tighter. "More fun than Cherry Grove, I bet."

"They can't even be compared," I say.

"Wait until you see the galleries in New York, Emily," Robyn says. "Openings are an even bigger deal. My parents usually hire a whole security team."

Fiona rolls her eyes at Adrian and me, and pulls us to look at some paintings on the far wall. I feel a little bad for Robyn. Fiona's obviously getting annoyed with her bragging, but I appreciate the fact that she's making an effort with me tonight, so I smile and say, "Cool."

Each gallery is like a mini museum, a plain white box with artwork hanging in even rows on the walls. Except here, the art is actually for sale. Tonight, I've seen delicate pottery that was purposefully shattered and then painstakingly reglued, a wood carving of a death certificate, paintings of pears, and dog portrait photography.

"What do the red stickers mean?" I whisper to Adrian, and point at a small dot next to a painting. I feel like I can ask Adrian these kinds of questions, knowing he's as much of an outsider here as I am. From our conversations tonight, I've learned he's from a small town in Kansas. His family actually owns two tractors. And he's not so much into fine art as he is into comic books and graphic novels. Still, he seems to know the answers.

"It's been sold," he tells me.

I try to imagine some of these pieces hanging in my home in Cherry Grove, but I can't. Maybe it's because we don't own any art, even though I guess we could afford it. Our walls are covered with framed pictures of the family. We take a new one each year at this local photo studio, each time with a new theme — red sweaters, denim shirts, white button-ups. Mom wanted to do swimsuits last year, but I told her absolutely no way.

I can't believe how much they are asking for some of this stuff — like the painting of Elvis selling for three thousand dollars. I wonder how much Fiona's mom charges for her paintings. It seems like you could easily become rich. Then again, Fiona's dad doesn't seem to be around, and they probably live off just her art.

"Ridiculous, right?" Fiona shouts between gulps. "People think that just because it's hanging in a gallery, it deserves to be bought. When I have a solo show, people are going to know it's good. And if they can't explain why a piece is good, then I'm not going to sell it to them, simple as that."

"Badass." Adrian laughs.

"You better believe it," Fiona says, resting her head on his shoulder. "I've got it all figured out. I'm going to hang up my shadow paintings on the walls, and then bring in fake trees and stuff and draw the shadows right there on the gallery walls and floors. And then I'll have someone adjusting the lights while I keep redrawing the shadows. The whole thing will be totally interactive."

July

Fiona's confidence is pretty incredible. For her, it's not a matter of IF she succeeds, but WHEN. And I have to say, I don't question it at all.

"And you're not going to sell pieces to people if they don't understand them?" Robyn asks. "Isn't that, like, self-defeating?"

"My art doesn't deserve to live in a place where it's not respected and understood. Why make things in the first place?" She's getting aggravated. Her voice is loud, and a few people turn around to look at us.

"You're right," Adrian says, running his fingers so very gently through her hair. It's incredibly sweet how much he likes her. And Fiona seems to settle down. I bet she'll kiss him at the end of the night, or something dramatic like that. She's the kind of person who makes moments happen.

"I was reading something in the *City Paper* today about a cool gallery called Space . . . something," Robyn says. "Have you ever heard of it?"

"It's Space Invaded," Fiona spits back. She drains her glass in one gulp. "And I was just going to suggest we go there." She grabs Adrian's hand. "Come on."

Our repeated pattern of bounding into an air-conditioned gallery, chugging chilled white wine, and heading back out to the steamy street has taken its toll. I step outside and feel pretty drunk. Fiona hails us a cab and we all climb in. She sits on Adrian's lap.

My bag vibrates, and I check the clock on the taxi's dashboard. "Crap!" It's already ten-thirty? I don't even know what time the trains to Cherry Grove stop running. Everyone is definitely at Rick's house by now, the party in full swing. I'm sure Meg is wondering where I am. But I don't really want to leave. Not even close.

"What's wrong, Cinderella? Have to get home to the suburbs before you turn into a pumpkin?" Robyn's voice walks the thinnest line between insulting and joking.

"No," I say, trying to play it cool. I fumble in my bag and pull out my cell phone.

I've got a text from Meg.

r u done yet? hurry!

I cuddle myself against the door, so no one can see what I text back.

almost!

Hopefully that buys me a little more time.

The cab drives through Old City, which is the section of Philadelphia that looks like something out of the history books. We actually pass the Liberty Bell, all aglow inside a glass building. I've been there on school field trips when I was a kid, and now I'm zooming past in a taxi, in a beautiful dress with a bunch of cool new friends. It's insane to think about.

A few turns later and we drive underneath a huge red Chinese gate that spans the entire width of the block. Gold lettering and colorful dragons are etched into the sides. Suddenly, none of the store signs are in English. Skinless ducks hang in the windows of butcher shops. We make a left at the fortune cookie factory. An actual fortune cookie factory! And then the cab pulls up to another big, industrial-looking building. Robyn pays the driver. I offer to split it with her, but she says no thanks.

July

"What is this place called again?" I ask, looking up. The bottom three floors are dark, but the windows of the very top are lit, and hip-hop beats rattle through the glass.

But Fiona's so excited, I don't even think she hears me. "You guys are going to die," Fiona says. "It's freaking amazing."

The stairway smells like dirty laundry. A few fluorescent lights flicker and buzz overhead. As we walk up three flights, I notice some intricate graffiti rambling up the walls — undulating words in shades of red and black. I can't make out the writing. I would stop and look for another minute or two, but there are footsteps behind us, more people coming up the stairs.

Fiona talks while we climb. "So, this place was founded by a bunch of art school graduates three years ago. They rent studio space for supercheap for struggling yet-to-be-famous artists, and their gallery showcases work that could never find a home in those stuffy galleries we were at before. It's, like, impossible to get studio space in here unless you know someone. Which totally sucks. Because I want in badly!"

She pulls open the dented metal door and we step inside.

In the middle of the gallery is a huge skate ramp. The ceilings tower high over my head, tin that reverberates all the sounds and the wheels against wood and the music pumping out of the speakers.

The other galleries had cheese — this one has bags of Cheez Doodles. Instead of wine, they have cheap beer in cans — the kind my dad's brother brings over and no one but him drinks, so it sits in the back of our pool fridge for the entire summer.

The vibe in this gallery is totally different. It's raw and passionate and intense, college kids drinking and laughing and dancing and having a ball. It's practically a house party, the wildest I've ever seen. Not like in suburbia, where they play the Grateful Dead and everyone's all mellow and some people are smoking pot. The energy is something you can feel and smell and taste.

And the art on the walls here is amazing and eclectic. Not just one artist, but several, each with his or her own wall. Someone's painted on the decks of broken, splintered skateboards. Someone's screen-printed huge posters with retro-looking slogans about voting, where the text is off register and blurry. Someone's made a table and chairs out of fluffy cotton balls.

"Oh my God! Look at those!" Fiona pushes us over to a wall near the windows. The Ben Franklin Bridge twinkles in the distance. The train, the one I ride home, is lit up and chugging its way back to Cherry Grove. But the art on this particular wall is what really grabs my attention.

There are a series of four enormous photographs, nearly floor to ceiling. Photographs of Philadelphia, I guess. Raw city decay. Metal that rusts, train trestles in steely black, railroad tracks, and cement drainage tubes. It's very urban. Gritty.

But that's not all.

On top of each photograph is a painting, a layer blocking out part of the image. These are the most beautiful nature scenes ever. Fields and rivers and beautiful trees at the height of autumn. The colors are way more intense than in real life. Like the beauty of it all has been amped up to the loudest possible degree.

"It's like a time warp," Fiona says, quiet. It's maybe the first time I've ever heard her quiet before.

"These are incredible," Robyn says.

"They make me wish I could paint," Adrian says.

July

I just nod.

We all lean in together and read the name scribbled on a piece of masking tape across the wall.

YATES

"I hope you guys aren't drinking, because that's going to put me in a very awkward situation as your teaching assistant."

We turn around and it's him, looking so cute in a slim-fitting white button-down shirt, tuxedo shorts that hit at his bony knees, and a pair of checkerboard Vans. Like dressed up, but not.

"You did these?" Fiona asks, absolutely, totally shocked. "What the hell are you doing teaching summer school to us?"

"Come on," Yates says, laughing and looking off across the party. "They're just okay."

Fiona steps past Adrian and lays both her hands on Yates's shoulders. "I'm not kidding! I am, like, so in love with you right now."

Adrian shrinks, and I shrink, too. I put my hand on his back, like a friend. It's sweaty, just like mine.

"Are you part of this place?" Robyn asks Yates.

"Well, technically yes, but I get studio space for free at school since I'm a TA. I'm friends with one of the founders. He's the guy who fills the studios. There's no real openings now, but he's the keeper of the list."

"Oh! You mean Slegel!" Fiona says, with a flirty smile. "I love his posters. I saw his show last fall at Skate Nerd Minnow. I was sort of stalking him. He does such amazing prints."

"I was there, too," Yates admits with a grin.

Fiona raises her hand for a high five. Yates obliges.

I try to suck up some of Fiona's overflowing confidence. After all, I've consistently made a fool of myself in front of Yates, looking like the inexperienced kid who doesn't know anything. "Well, I think your paintings are great," I say. "I mean, not great." My mind spins to find the right word. "Incredible." Ugh. Even when I'm inspired, I can't seem to express it.

"Thanks, Emily." Yates looks at me. "You look so dressed up, I hardly recognized you."

"I gave her a makeover," Fiona offers. "I'm plotting to steal Emily from the suburbs. She's too good for her hometown." And then she cackles deviously, like a witch.

What Fiona says makes me anxious, but mostly I just feel thankful. She's making me look better than I can make myself look.

A young guy in camouflage pants and a nose ring grabs Yates on the shoulder. "Hey. Some guy wants to talk to you about the whole set."

Yates smiles at us apologetically. "I gotta go. But you guys should stick around and hang out. Just don't let me actually see you holding any beers. Then I won't have to feel guilty not reporting you to Dr. Tobin, okay?"

We watch him disappear into the crowd. A few seconds later, a punk-looking boy in a mohawk comes over and puts little red stickers next to all of Yates's paintings.

Fiona bites her finger. "God, he is so hot, it's not even funny. How did I not notice this before?"

Adrian walks away from us. "I'm going to get a beer."

My phone buzzes in my pocket. Another text from Meg.

hello?!?!? i need you!

My excitement instantly evaporates. I wish I never told Meg I'd come back. I whisper into Fiona's ear, "I think I have to get going. Is the train station around here or should I take a cab?"

"No! Don't go! Tell your mom you're sleeping at my house. Things are just getting awesome!"

"But —" Robyn looks pissed. "I thought you were going to sleep over at my dorm and then meet my parents tomorrow for brunch!"

Fiona shakes her head at Robyn, embarrassed. These plans were a secret I wasn't supposed to know. But I do know, and now I can't help but feel left out.

"Oh right." Fiona contemplates. "Robyn, I'll just meet you in the morning for brunch. Emily will have to go home by then. Back to her real life, poor thing."

Robyn stares at me, and the niceness drains out of her. "Yeah, whatever."

"Excellent! Sleepover party!" Fiona hugs me before walking over to the open window with a cigarette and a lighter.

Fiona does seem to want me to stick around, enough to piss Robyn off, anyhow. I don't want to start trouble between Fiona and Robyn. And it seems like I already have, in a way. But, honestly, I don't feel like leaving yet. At all. So after I call my mom and convince her it would be much safer for me to spend the night with a friend than ride the train home alone, I send Meg a text. It takes me a few minutes before I have the courage to hit SEND.

don't think i will make it. soooo sorry!

I hold my breath and grip the cell tight, waiting for it to vibrate. An excruciating ten minutes later it does. The buzz rattles my bones.

My stomach sinks.

don't call me when you get home

"You okay?" Fiona asks me and hands me a beer. She puts her hand on my shoulder. She's not sarcastic or jokey at all. She's genuinely concerned.

"Oh yeah," I say, wiping the sad away. It's better not to think about it and let it ruin my time here. I can always explain things to Meg later, when I'm home and my life has settled back down. Meg never stays mad for long, especially not at me.

Sixteen

The sidewalk is already warm from a few hours of morning sun, and the dew on the grass sparkles as it waits for eventual evaporation. The train station is eerily peaceful on Saturday morning. Apparently, I was the only one coming to Cherry Grove, and no one else is interested in leaving.

While I wait for my ride, I rub the end of a thin, spindly stick in circles against the concrete. The bark leaves behind faint brown lines until it wears completely away, exposing a hot point of white pulp. I hold it just under my nose and feel the warmth radiating against my lip. The heat gives a smoky smell.

I don't know why, but I touch the point to my callus like a magic wand. A quick tap, just in case it burns. Then I hold it there longer, pressing down, because it doesn't hurt at all.

Mom's convertible speeds into the lot and pulls to a stop in the no-parking zone. The stereo blasts a chorus of bongos and maracas. Mom listens to this stuff exclusively since she asked our cleaning lady to make her a copy of whatever it was she was vacuuming to. Mom thinks she's some kind of expert now, because she picks out her own CDs from the World Music section at Barnes & Noble. It's so embarrassing. "Welcome home," she calls to me. "Did you have a nice time?"

I nod as I struggle to my feet. My legs ache like I've just run the mile in gym class. All evidence of last night's adventure is like this — hidden inside where no one else can see: I'm wearing my own clothes; Fiona's hand-me-downs are tucked inside a plastic Superfresh bag. I tried to sleep in my bobby pins so that my hair would still look twisty-cool, but it was too uncomfortable, so now it's all back up in my trademark ponytail. I washed my face clean of glitter eye shadow, but a few rogue flecks twinkle on my arms.

"You don't look like you got much sleep."

"Yeah, you could say that." I laugh as I click my seat belt. Then I realize I should be more discreet, if I ever want to stay over at Fiona's house again. "But it's always hard the first time you sleep at someone else's house. When it's not your own bed."

Mom sniffs the air. "Have you been smoking?"

"No."

"Well, was someone around you smoking?" She asks this equally accusatory, like she is everyone's parent.

"Yes, Mom. Geez."

She stares at me for a second, concerned, and then turns her eyes back to the road. "I'm glad you're making friends in Philadelphia, Emily, but it's strange for me to not know who you're spending time with. Why don't you invite your new friend to sleep over here one night, so we can all get acquainted?"

I can't help but laugh. "Fiona's not going to want to come here," I say.

July

Mom looks wounded. "Why not?"

"Because she lives in Philadelphia."

"So?"

I can't believe I have to spell it out for her. "There's nothing fun to do in Cherry Grove."

Mom makes the turn into Blossom Manor. The tires roll over the brick and make a buzzing sound that hurts my head. "I bet Meg would be surprised to hear you say that."

I sink low in my seat when we pull into the driveway. Meg's window is dark. She's probably still in bed; we always sleep in late after parties. I don't like the feeling that comes over me — how making a new friend feels a little like cheating. I guess I did lie to her, saying last night was a school obligation, even though I just didn't feel like coming home. But that's just not the sort of thing you can tell your best friend. Especially someone sensitive like Meg. She wouldn't get it. She'd take it too personally.

Mom offers to make me something to eat, but I'd rather just crawl into bed and take a nap. I walk straight to my room and toss my bag of clothes from Fiona on my floor. And then I peel back the covers.

I think if I had taken a deeper breath, I might have screamed. But all I do is suck in air, as much as I can take in as fast as possible.

Meg is asleep in my bed.

She sits up, startled and fearful. She's got on a cropped white sweatshirt, a jean miniskirt, and dangly white beaded earrings. "Where have you been?" she mumbles.

"I slept at a friend's house." It feels like I've been caught doing something bad.

Concern washes over her, and she pushes her hair off her face. "You didn't call my house, did you?"

"No," I say, remembering her text message from last night. She looks relieved and lies back down, inching toward the edge of the mattress to make room for me.

Meg doesn't seem mad, which is a relief. I kick off my flip-flops and get in next to her. The bed is warm.

"What are you doing here?" I ask.

She bites her lip. "I decided to sleep over at Rick's house, since his parents were at the shore. I told my mom I was staying at your house. That's why you couldn't call. Rick had to leave early for work, and my mom knows if I came home earlier than noon, I'd be lying. So when Rick dropped me off at five, I climbed in your window, expecting to find you here."

"Oh." I'm relieved. I guess last night worked out perfectly for both of us. But it's also crazy to think of Meg using me as an alibi. That's never happened before, because we're always together.

I wonder if she did anything with Rick. Like, anything serious. I don't want to ask her straight out, though. It could sound like I'm accusing her of something.

"So," I say, "did you have fun?"

"Yeah, I guess," Meg says. She closes her eyes. "Things just got kind of rowdy toward the end of the night, people being drunk and stupid. Joe Bukowski tried to do a keg stand to impress all the girls. He's so big, you know, and the guys and Rick had trouble holding him and he slipped and cracked his front tooth on the edge of the keg. I felt bad for him, but he thought it was funny and he was running around the rest of the night trying to bite all the girls with his snaggletooth." Meg taps around until she touches my hand. "Oh! And Chad and Jenessa were totally fighting the whole night. I doubt they're even together anymore." She gives it a squeeze. "Looks like you have a shot after all."

Nothing comes out of my throat, even though I open my mouth to let it. So I smile at her instead. I know it feels fake. I don't have to see it to know it.

Meg doesn't notice a thing. To her, everything's fine. I'm still the Emily she's always known. It sucks that she can't tell that something happened to me last night.

I feel even worse because she also hasn't bothered asking.

She rolls over, her back to me. "I am so freaking tired. Rick has a twin bed and he's so huge. I was on the very edge of the mattress the whole night, wide awake. He snores. Loud." She sighs. "It's weird to sleep next to someone for the first time. It's not like what you'd think, all cozy and romantic. You're aware of absolutely everything."

I pull the covers up to my chin. It only takes a minute before Meg's breathing slows down and she's back asleep. I give it a few minutes more before I reach out for the bag of clothes Fiona gave to me and push them far underneath my bed. Then I close my eyes.

Two hours later, we are at Starbucks, back at our favorite table. But nothing about this peppermint mocha trip feels like our normal routine.

Meg barely looks at me. She's just gazing out at the highway, like she's counting cars. And she still hasn't asked one thing about my night. It's like she's trying to punish me for not showing up at the party.

"My friend Fiona is so crazy," I say suddenly.

"Oh," she says, surprised, like she just remembered I was here.

"In this one gallery, Fiona started talking all loud about how the artist was a crackhead. Some old people nearby were obviously eavesdropping and, like, getting excited, as if being totally messed up somehow made his art more valuable."

Meg takes a slow sip. "It's sad when talented people have drug problems."

I shake my head. "He didn't. She made it up to be funny."

Her face pinches. Meg's not getting it. But instead of making me want to be quiet, I want to keep going, telling her more. Because this is how I always felt when she would go on and on about Rick. I sat there for months while she'd reenact their private phone conversations. I had to listen to her read the funny notes he'd write to her inside Hallmark cards sent for no particular reason.

"So, then we went to this other gallery, which was soooo stuffy, and everyone was giving us dirty looks like we didn't belong there. I went to use the bathroom and Fiona came in and drew my shadow on the wall with this big fat marker!"

Meg sets her drink down. "Like graffiti?"

I shrug. "I guess you could call it that."

"And this was on a school field trip?"

Whoops. "I mean, it's really lax. It's kind of like anything goes in art school. People are as wild and crazy as they want to be. It's actually encouraged."

"That doesn't sound like you." She says it like I am trying to trick her, like she doesn't believe I could be a part of something like that.

July

"Well, it wasn't me, exactly," I concede. "It was Fiona."

"Right." Her eyes drop to the table as she looks for a napkin. "Fiona."

We both get kind of quiet then. I take a sip of my peppermint mocha and stare out the window. Across the highway, workers are transforming the old Pizza Hut into a Taco Bell. A new sign is going up, and they've got a guy hanging colorful decals of burritos in the windows. But the actual building is the same tan rectangle, same sloped red roof, same flat top. Fast food architecture.

The view is achingly depressing in so many ways.

If only I had my sketchbook.

Seventeen

On Tuesday morning, Mr. Frank arranges the stools so we're all sitting in a straight line, facing the front of the room like the firing squad I feared on my first day. He tells us we'll go one by one, presenting what we think is the best drawing from our sketchbooks so far.

Most of the kids show traditional still lifes, where they've drawn a bottle of Snapple or a pair of sneakers. As boring as those kinds of drawings sound, a few are really good, like staring at black-and-white photographs. Robyn's sketch of Adrian's glasses is particularly amazing. The lenses truly look like glass. I have no idea how she did that.

"This is a good start," Mr. Frank tells a girl named Jane, who's drawn a basket filled with fruit. "But I can tell you shorthanded this drawing. Don't just make lines at random. Count the woven strips. Be as exact and authentic as possible. You are not drawing any basket, you are drawing a *particular* basket." He clears his throat. "Emily?"

July

I stand up and walk to the front of the room. Yates folds his arms and nods his head at me. Fiona makes a funny, presumably supportive face. Robyn stares out the window, completely uninterested. I open my sketchbook and flip to the last drawing.

Last night, after taking a late swim with Meg, I left to go home. And I did initially, but just to change out of my wet bathing suit and grab my sketchbook. Then I snuck out to the top of the sandy hill just outside Blossom Manor.

My hands split the pages and crack the stiff spine of my sketchbook. I hold it up in front of my face, so I won't have to see anyone's reactions.

"And what is this?" Mr. Frank asks.

"Well, I drew the same building twice. Once as a Pizza Hut and once as a Taco Bell, to show that they're actually the same thing." I cough away a tickle in my throat. "The same shape, anyway."

The room is silent.

I peer out at Mr. Frank from behind my sketchbook. "Can I sit down?"

"No," he says. Then he clears his throat. "Would anyone like to comment?"

I want to throw up. He hasn't asked anyone to comment before.

Yates steps forward, like he wants a closer look. "I think it's neat." He's just trying to be nice. Someone as talented as Yates couldn't possibly be impressed by my dumb sketch. "It's like an examination of suburbia and mass consumption. It's original thought presented through its antithesis."

Umm . . . *what?*

A few seconds pass and one of the two skateboarding boys raises his hand. "To me, it says corporations are soulless."

A few other kids add their thoughts — including Robyn, who says, "There's a self-hatred here, because Emily is clearly attacking the McMansion culture of her hometown."

"Yeah," I say. "Sort of."

Finally, Fiona says, "People just shove this processed food in our faces and tell us to chew, even though it's killing us. The proof is right there, right in front of us, but we don't do anything about it. It's absolutely disgusting, and I mean that in the very best way." She smiles at me.

"I would agree with all that," Mr. Frank says. "Emily, this is exactly what I hoped would come from these journaling assignments. Fantastic job."

I smile back, even though I'm not sure I had any of this in my mind when I was drawing. I thought it was just kind of funny, in a depressive way. But I'm thrilled that everyone likes it. It's my first piece that has gotten any kind of response in class.

When I sit down, Fiona grabs my arm. "See? Once you start seeing things the way they really are, it's like you can't stop looking. And think, if we never became friends, you probably wouldn't have ever noticed something like that."

I nod and whisper thanks. I don't mind Fiona taking some of the credit. She deserves it.

Fiona goes next and shows a page covered by black spots. They look like puzzle pieces, totally amorphous. There's a tiny newspaper clipping taped to the corner of her drawing, but I can't make out what it says from where I'm sitting.

July

"I'm very into shadows these days. Like, showing something in an undefined way, capturing something at its essence, stripping away the audience's pretension. Basically, I focus on the shell of something"— she winks at me — "and let you project whatever meaning you want to on the object. So these are a series of shadows that I saw in the water off Penn's Landing, drawn over one afternoon. I've also included a copy of the weather report for that day." Fiona is so sure of herself, so confident.

Everyone stares. I think the shapes look cool. But no one says anything. I think it's because Fiona kind of said it all herself.

"Interesting," Mr. Frank says.

Fiona curtseys, pleased as punch.

Mr. Frank goes through a few more sketchbooks until it's time for lunch. Then Fiona, Robyn, and I walk out and meet Adrian on the steps. He takes a graphic novel illustration class on Tuesdays, which is in the other building across the street. A bunch of papers falls out of his back pocket when he stands up to greet us.

"What's that?" I ask him.

"A mock-up of the first chapter of my graphic novel," he says, grinning as wide as the wingspan on his Batman shirt. He gathers them up. "I have to present it to my professor this afternoon. He's already making us fight for his nomination for a final gallery spot. So much for creating in a non-competitive environment."

"You should have seen our class today," Fiona says. "I left everyone totally speechless with my new shadow piece. Mr. Frank is in the palm of my hand."

We walk to the Vietnamese lunch shop and get sandwiches to go, so we can eat in the courtyard. I never thought I'd like Vietnamese food, but these sandwiches, with their spicy mayo and warm crusty bread and ham and pickled carrot shreds are better than anything I've ever had at Subway. And the almond bubble tea is really yummy, too. I think Meg would like it as much as she likes frozen peppermint mochas. She'd love that you get to pick your straw color. I chose purple, same as Fiona.

We're about to enter the courtyard when Fiona stops dead in her tracks and cries out, "Ouch!" I check to see if she hurt herself. She's clutching at her chest, but with a dopey smile on her face. "My heart hurts."

Yates is sitting on a bench in the courtyard, drawing. He stretches and reveals two tattoos . . . one on the inside of each bicep. They're of lucky horseshoes, like an old-timey sailor might have.

Ouch indeed.

Fiona runs her fingers through her blue stripe.

"Let's go talk to him."

I'd never have the courage to do that, but Fiona . . . she's fearless.

"He probably doesn't want to be bothered," Adrian says.

But Fiona walks over to Yates anyway and we follow her like she's the kite and we're the little ribbons dangling on her string.

"Hi, Yates," she says, and sits right down next to him on the bench.

"Hey, guys. Are you enjoying today's lesson?" he asks in a corny voice, like he's playing the part of our teacher on a television show.

"We sure are!" Fiona says, equally hokey, and they both laugh. "Listen. I'm seriously considering applying to this college next year. Do you think you could give us a tour?"

July

He gets shy. "The admissions office runs tours. I wouldn't know what to say."

"We don't want to go through those boring, stiff tours where they just read facts out of the catalog. We want to know about the school from your perspective. Like, how it *really* is to go here."

Fiona elbows me.

"Yeah," I add.

Yates debates. "Well, I mean, I guess I could show you guys around a little tomorrow, after the field trip."

"Awesome!"

We walk away. Robyn massages Fiona's shoulders and moves the lock of blue hair away from her ear. "Oh my God, you guys are totally going to be the cute, artsy couple," she says. "And then you will both move to Paris and show your work in my gallery and we'll all get rich!"

It stings a little bit to hear this, but I know it's true. Fiona deserves someone like Yates. She's confident enough to go and get him, even though he's our TA and it's totally taboo. That challenge probably makes Fiona even more excited about the whole thing.

I see Adrian looking glum.

"You're going to come with us on the tour, right?" I ask.

"Yeah, come on . . ." Fiona says, draping herself all over Adrian. "Are you just going to let Yates win my heart without making a stand?" It's weird that she's flirting with Adrian if she doesn't honestly like him in that way, but I can tell it makes him happy, so what's the harm?

After all, there's something about Fiona that makes everything seem worth the risk.

151

Eighteen

After Wednesday's field trip to the Painted Bride Art Center, the four of us meet Yates near the elevator bays in the main building. Fiona is nervous, I can tell by the way she keeps scratching the scabs on her arms. She looks pretty, though, dressed in a white tank and a frilly, pink skirt made out of a vintage apron with all these pretty drawings of cakes and cookies on it. It sets off the blue of her hair, and she's painted her nails blue, too. Her hair is flat and shiny, her bangs trimmed perfectly even.

"Hey, guys," Yates says as he comes around the corner.

Instantly we all shut up. Except for Robyn. She laughs.

I think Yates knows what we might be up to, but he just smiles sweetly and says, "Okay. Follow me."

Yates takes us through the school. The main art building is divided by majors — each one has its own floor. The fibers floor is full of old looms and big vats to dye fabric. The ceramics floor smells earthy like clay. The temperature of the metals floor is extra hot from all the torches.

Yates walks with Fiona, explaining class options and stuff

while the rest of us hang back. I try to stay near Adrian, because he looks bummed, like this is painful for him to watch.

I can sympathize.

"Have you ever told her how you feel?" I whisper in his ear.

"No," he says. "She knows. It's obvious."

"That's the thing. Fiona doesn't necessarily go for obvious. She wants . . . more of a production." I'm definitely rooting for Adrian. He's a really nice guy. But maybe also because I still like Yates. I can't help it, but I do.

"Yeah," he says, and flicks his hair out of his eyes. "I guess."

As we go from studio to studio, Yates introduces us to a lot of interesting-looking students. Everyone seems to know him.

"You're, like, the king of the campus, huh, Yates?" Fiona laughs, and loops her arm through his.

Yates shakes her off, not meanly or anything. But if anyone was to see that, I bet he'd get in trouble. "Oh no. I mean, the college isn't that big, so you end up meeting pretty much everyone in the first few weeks."

Fiona looks frustrated, but she quickly replaces her grimace with a smile. "Cool."

I try to imagine myself going to a college like this. I always assumed I would go to Trenton State with Meg. Meg's going to do premed, because she wants to be a doctor who delivers babies. I'm not sure what I want to study yet. But there's a lot I like about what I see here.

"So, you guys are really thinking about applying?"

"Absolutely," Fiona says. "Art is the only class in my high school that I haven't failed. In fact, none of my teachers know what to do with me anymore. They just send me to the art room. For me, it's either art school or majoring in Fries at McDonald's University."

"Well, this place seems to be very forgiving when it comes to that kind of problem. My transcripts from high school were all random, too, since I went to an art high school and never took much math or science."

"Ah, so we're both art geeks." Fiona bumps him playfully. "But seriously, that's good to hear. I mean, I wear the fact that I can barely survive in a 'normal' school like a badge of honor, you know? This is definitely the kind of place I belong."

I find myself next to Yates in the elevator. I want to ask him something, too, so he knows I am actually interested. So I blurt the first thing that comes to my mind, a question Meg had asked on our tour of Trenton State. "Does this college have any sororities?"

Yates looks over his shoulder at me and smiles. "Oh no. I mean, people definitely get cliquey within their majors. Like the painting kids hang out with the painting kids, and the sculpture kids hang out with the other sculpture kids, but nothing like a sorority."

"Oh my God, Emily!" Fiona cackles. "Like I'd ever apply to a school that had sororities!"

I let my hair hang over my face to mask my blushing. Meg and I had always talked about pledging together, though I was never that excited about the idea. I'm sort of a picky friend. I don't like being shoved into a place and then told I have to be friends with a bunch of people. It can be overwhelming. I'd rather have one good friend over a hundred acquaintances. Those are the kinds of friends you can count on.

July

"Where are you from, Yates?" Fiona asks.

"Rhode Island," Yates says. "I was so afraid that I'd have to spend the summer in my hometown, but then I got the TA position with Mr. Frank."

"I don't know how you manage to look so interested in that old man's rambles," Fiona says. "Mr. Frank is such a stiff, he's practically dead."

"What? Are you serious? Mr. Frank is one of the most amazing painters ever. His TA position is the most coveted one in the whole school. I was competing with almost a hundred other painters. He's totally inspiring."

It's cute to watch Yates gush. His cheeks get red and he stares up at the ceiling, as if he were actually looking up to an invisible Mr. Frank towering over him.

"Well, it's obvious you got the position because you're so talented," Fiona says. "I completely get it. That's how it is with me and my mom. Her work is so inspiring to me. I just hope I can be one little bit as good as she is."

Robyn says, "Yeah. I mean, your pieces at Space Invaded were seriously amazing."

Yates smiles. "Well, thanks. That never gets old."

"Where is your space?" Fiona asks.

"It's on the painting floor."

"Well . . ." Fiona laughs. "Can we see it?"

Yates looks around, cautious. "Do you guys really want to?"

We all say, "Of course!" Yates walks us to the painting floor, and down a long hallway. He fishes a key from inside his shorts pocket and unlocks a blue door. Fiona looks at me and smiles all goofy. She's excited. I am, too.

Yates's studio is a large rectangle. Huge canvases sit on the floor. All of the laughter and the chitchat quiet down, like we just walked into a real gallery.

The canvases display more of his huge landscape painting/ photographs, like the ones at his Space Invaded show.

"These are all amazing," I say. I look over to Adrian and see that even he's impressed.

Yates scratches his head. "I'm kind of bored with them, actually. But I've been really struggling with what I'm going to do next."

"Painter's block?" I ask.

"I guess so. Though I'm quickly discovering there's a very fine line between painter's block and procrastination. I'm just hoping some inspiration strikes me soon."

Fiona sees a digital camera on a table. She grabs hold of it. "Take a picture of us!"

Yates looks shy. "For what?"

"For the debut issue of the Yates Fan Club Newsletter!" Fiona giggles. "I call president!"

That's about all Adrian can take. He walks out into the hallway. Robyn moves forward to pose next to Fiona, but Fiona loops her arm around me instead.

Yates points the camera at us. I try to channel my inner Fiona and stick out my tongue playfully. I want to be seen by him, the way Fiona is seen by everyone.

"Nice," Yates says. "Well, I should be taking off."

"Take us with you," Fiona whines.

"Sorry. It's a work night for me. I'm going to my friend's band rehearsal. They've got a huge show tomorrow, opening up for a much bigger band, and it will give them a ton of exposure. The only thing is, their show is kind of . . . complicated. So they need my help."

I am definitely intrigued. I can tell Fiona is, too.

"What band is it? Where are they playing?" She gets close to him.

Yates takes a deep breath and starts adjusting some of the jars of paint up on his shelf. "I wish I could tell you guys, but I could get in serious trouble fraternizing with students outside of school. I mean, seeing you at Space Invaded was totally random, but I can't be inviting you all out with me."

I'm instantly embarrassed for coming here and doing all this in the first place. But Fiona shakes her head. She's not going to accept that answer. "Listen, Yates! We are all practically the same age. In fact, a little over a year ago, we were all in high school together. And Emily and I don't even live in the dorms. We're from around here. So it would be like ten thousand percent probable that we'd end up at the same show anyhow!"

All I can manage to do is nod. I can see Yates cracking, as his determined mouth, lips pursed tight together, blooms into a grin.

He whispers the band name to us. *Romero*. To me it sounds like a boy band or something, which would be really weird and unexpected. And then he tells us the show is at the Electric Factory.

I totally feel the sparks.

Nineteen

iona does my makeup for the concert. I've got my back turned to her mirror, so I can't see how it looks, but I'm freaked out by the tiny pot of black eye shadow she's got cupped in her hand, and the fact that she's dabbing her finger underneath my lids instead of on top, like normal.

"So, in my Performance Art class today, my teacher taught us how to make moss graffiti using yogurt. It was so awesome." Fiona steps back to admire her work and smiles. I guess that's a good sign. "How was Mixed Media? I didn't see you at lunch."

"I kind of lost track of time." Hanna and Charlotte want everyone in class to build a library of interesting images that we can draw from when we make collages. I stayed in the studio all afternoon, looking through a stack of musty, cloth-covered books and old Sears catalogs for interesting pictures. I found some cool stuff, like a diagram of a heart from an old medical textbook. When I saw the picture, my stomach tingled. A heart waits to be pasted on a sleeve. "What did you guys do last night?"

July

"Ugh, it was a total bust. I let Robyn pick some foreign movie playing at the Ritz Five, and of course we were all bored out of our minds. Adrian and I played hangman by cell phone light, using chalk on the back of the seats. We switched seats for every new game, and covered practically the whole theater. He's extremely good at hangman. I don't think he died once."

"Adrian loves you," I say.

Fiona looks down at the floor. "He's sweet. But he's not my type at all."

I'm surprised. Fiona definitely likes attention, and Adrian would give her lots of it. "What's your type?"

"Yates," she says, and laughs. "I mean, he's talented, he's hot. We get what each other is trying to do, you know? And anyhow, Adrian and I could never work. He's too . . . safe. And what good is a summer romance with a guy who lives across the country? At least if Yates and I hooked up, it'd be like a real relationship that could last all through the school year. Then I could spend my senior year hanging out with him at Space Invaded instead of at my sucky high school." Fiona's so matter-of-fact here, it takes me by surprise. She's looking for an escape, too. "But anyway, I'm really going to go for it tonight. Mark my words, Yates and I are totally smooching."

Poor Adrian.

"Anyhow . . ." Fiona digs in a shoe box for some red lipstick. "Can I just say that I'm kind of over Robyn. I mean, she thinks she's, like, the expert on everything just because her parents run a gallery. Honestly, I can barely stand her bragging."

It's funny. I see it more from Robyn's side. I mean, she only says the stuff she does to impress Fiona. And it's not like she's making things up to look cool. It's her real life. But the more she does it, the more Fiona pulls away from her. Not that I mind.

I say, "When I first saw you and Robyn together, I thought you guys looked like you were meant to be friends. I never thought that we'd be friends."

"Yeah. I didn't, either. But it's way more fun to hang around with someone like you, someone who doesn't really know anything. It's like this place gets to be new to me because I'm showing it to you. Seriously, before this summer, I was kind of over Philadelphia and I was burnt-out on art, too. But now I'm all inspired again, partly thanks to you. You've given me fresh eyes." She perches herself on top of a pile of clothes on the bed and struggles to do the tiny buckle on a pair of black heels. "I was thinking . . . maybe I could come to your house this weekend for a sleepover. I want to see what this weird little town of Cherry Grove is like. I loved your last sketchbook piece. It got me thinking I needed to experience your life for myself."

"Are you sure?" I'm surprised. I didn't think someone like Fiona would willingly step foot in the suburbs. After all, she's always making jokes about how I need to be decontaminated. Cherry Grove is this thing about me that Fiona forgives, because it's not my fault. But it's also not something she likes about me.

But Fiona's lighting up like it's the best idea ever. "Seriously, it'll be so much fun. We could run around and do dumb stuff like go to the mall and the Applebee's and make fun of everything."

I shake my head. "You don't really want to do that."

"I do! I want to see where you come from." She sounds hurt, as she lies on the bed and stares at the ceiling. "I mean, you've been to my house like a million times already."

160

July

I've only been here twice, but I don't say that. Fiona's been awesome about keeping me included and showing me things from her life. It's just that nothing at home seems worth sharing with her. And what am I going to do about Meg? Maybe I could introduce them, but I don't think so. Meg would probably be sweet and friendly, if not overly so, to cover the fact that she didn't understand why I'd be friends with someone like Fiona. And Fiona would think Meg is super corny.

But it might be cool to have Fiona come and shake up Cherry Grove in a way that I can't. Hearing her take on things could give me more confidence to go my own way, some validation to save up for September.

"I'm warning you, I doubt you'll have a good time."

Fiona laughs off my concern as she jumps up and wriggles her way into a white tank dress. "I'll have a good time. I always have a good time."

I spin around to check my makeup. Hollow black circles are painted under my eyes, and face powder dulls what little summer tan I've managed to accrue. I look like I'm dead. Dead, but with red lipstick, put on like an old lady who can't see herself in the mirror anymore.

I'm about to say something, but Fiona nudges me out of the way of the mirror and wipes some black eye shadow under her own eyes. I guess she sees the confusion on my face because she says, "Don't worry, Emily. I checked out the Romero band website and this is exactly how we should look."

"Okay," I say, and watch as she cuts some holes in her dress, and then approaches me with the scissors. "If you say so."

Twenty

We take a cab to the Electric Factory — a humongous old building converted into a concert space, just underneath the Ben Franklin Bridge. The parking lot is packed with kids and showgoers, singing lyrics along with car stereos to songs I don't know. Fiona loops her arm through mine and takes off toward the entrance. No one else has makeup done like ours. More than a few people turn and stare at us. Fiona throws her shoulders back. She really does relish the attention. But I don't know if I'll ever get used to it. In some ways, it's nice to be invisible.

"Are we meeting Robyn and Adrian inside?" I ask. I have no idea how that'll happen. Considering the size of the crowd outside, the place must be packed. I had thought that we would pick up Adrian and Robyn in the taxi, but Fiona gave the directions to the driver, and we sped right past Broad Street, where the dorms are.

Fiona threads her fingers into mine and squeezes. "Come on. Let's see if we can find Yates."

July

We go inside and it's not nearly as crowded as I thought it would be. "Where is everyone?"

"Romero is the opening band, and most people don't give a shit about the opening band. In a couple of months, when they make it big, all these people will be crowding to the stage. It's ridiculous, how people judge talent. Or, rather, don't judge. They just default to what everyone else thinks."

The room is a huge raw rectangle, with a small balcony hanging over the right side. Speakers and lights dangle from the ceiling. An old crackly jazz song plays quietly through the space, dulling the voices of the people mingling and moving around for a good spot near the stage. There's a bar in the back, and a folding table where a guy in tight jeans and a beanie sells T-shirts and CDs. Fiona walks toward the stage door.

Every time someone walks out, Fiona cranes her neck and rises on her tiptoes to see inside. But there's no sign of Yates. Just a lot of burly-looking roadies and scantily clad girls in little camis and skirts. They look delicate and feminine, the exact opposite of us.

After a few minutes, the lights dim. The place is still barely half full. It all feels pretty anticlimactic.

Still, when I went to that summer radio concert last year with Meg on the Jersey Shore, we didn't even bother going until the headliners would start . . . about three hours after the official concert start time. But the bad thing was we were stuck way out on the lawn. You couldn't even see the bands play unless you looked at the JumboTron. They looked like tiny specks.

This place is much smaller, and it definitely changes the energy. About forty kids have gathered at the foot of the stage, anxiously staring up at a black velvet curtain, waiting for the show to begin. People with weird makeup and torn clothes, just like us. They don't care at all that the place isn't packed.

"Let's see how close we can get!" Fiona says.

I'm about to suggest we stay where we are and wait for Robyn and Adrian, but Fiona takes my hand and pulls me through. It looks like a wall of people standing shoulder to shoulder, but somehow Fiona manages to sneak and snake her way until we are right at the stage's edge. It's about as high as where my ribs start. A few people give us the stink eye, but everyone makes room for us. The lights go completely dark. Feet stir around just under the edge of where the curtain skims the stage.

"Oh my God, we are so close!" I shout.

"This is going to be awesome!" Fiona shouts back.

A bass guitar strums out a low, fast beat. The people behind me start to growl at the curtain. Growl? I look at Fiona, embarrassed and caught off guard. She laughs and growls right in my face.

I turn and look over the five rows of people standing behind me. The rest of the place is empty, uninterested people waiting for the headliner, mingling toward the back of the venue. At least if Robyn and Adrian come in late, they'll figure out where we are pretty easily.

And then, I turn back around, take a deep breath, and growl. I growl, and I don't even know what for, but I growl. Though I think it might sound more like a purr. Fiona takes my hand and starts jumping up and down to the strumming beat, growling super loud. I let her bounce me along with her, and soon my growl grows so loud and low that I can feel my throat start to hurt in the best way.

The curtain lifts and the stage is empty, except for the drum set.

July

The strumming continues from some unseen place, thumping like a fast heartbeat. I look left and right for the source, for the hiding guitar player, but all I see are three muscular shirtless boys struggling with a pulley offstage. And then a large plywood helicopter is lowered from the stage. It's like a prop from a low-budget movie — hokey, but that's the point, I think. The crowd goes absolutely crazy for it.

Inside the helicopter are the band members — five adorable punk-looking boys with guitars, a keyboard, and a set of drumsticks attached to them like weapons. When the helicopter crashes to the stage floor, they climb out and survey the crowd.

The crowd's growling intensifies. People throw their arms up and shuffle forward, pressing into my back, pushing me closer and closer into the stage until I worry that I might actually be crushed to death.

"What's going on?" I shout at Fiona. I spread my legs and try to anchor myself against the surge.

"It's punk theater!" she screams back.

The lead singer commandeers the microphone — a tall skinny boy with white-blond hair, dressed in head-to-toe camouflage. "Get back, zombies!" he screams. And then the band puts on their "weapons" and, after a speedy countdown of "*three two one*" tapped out on drumsticks, they rock intensely. And by that, I mean Romero makes the most insane, fast-paced, hardcore music that I've ever heard in my life.

Everyone around us begins to dance and thrash like wild. I'm nervous at first, but then I let the whole thing take control of me and shake along with it (the music) and them (the crowd zombies), until I'm spinning and jumping and generally just freaking out. Fiona grabs me and we smile and scream in each other's faces, and even though I'm supposed to be dead, I'm more alive than ever.

Four songs into the set, I am dripping with sweat. In the quiet space between one song ending and another beginning, I long for more. The lead singer announces that this is the last song and everyone *awws*. A hand taps my shoulder and I turn around. Robyn is standing behind me, totally pissed off. Adrian lurks in the background behind her, trying his best not to get pulled into a pit of pogo-ing zombies.

"Why didn't you pick us up?" Robyn says to me. Her hands are shaking.

"Umm . . ." I tap Fiona for her, because she's just out of Robyn's reach.

"Hey," Fiona says, and turns back toward the stage.

Robyn leans in past me and grabs at Fiona's shoulder. "What the hell? Why didn't you come pick us up?"

"I thought we were meeting here," Fiona says.

I think Fiona's lying about that, but I don't say anything.

"Don't you check your phone?" Robyn says.

The finale gets started. Everyone is dancing. Everyone but the four of us. I understand why Robyn is upset, but I hate her for stealing this last song from me. I don't even have her cell phone number, so what do I have to do with these messed-up plans? Fiona holds her cell up to her ear in the noise and shrugs, like, *How am I supposed to hear that?*

Robyn shakes her head and storms off with Adrian.

I feel bad, because I know exactly what's going on. The unwanted feeling. So I chase after them. Fiona follows me, grudgingly. Robyn stands over by the wall, arms folded. Adrian is right next to her.

Fiona cozies up to him. "Do you hate me as much as Robyn does?"

"I don't care," Adrian says, in a long, slow drawl that shows he obviously cares. He stuffs his hands into the pockets of his shorts. He doesn't want to melt. And in a way, I kind of don't want him to melt, either. I know Fiona has no intention of making out with him tonight. She's after Yates. I feel a bit bad that she's essentially leading Adrian on, flirting with him so that he won't be mad at her anymore.

"Listen, I'm sorry that plans got messed up. We can still have a good time." Fiona throws her hand up for a high five. When neither Adrian or Robyn slaps her back, she slaps her own hand. Hard and annoyed. "Fine, whatever. Let's just go."

I can't believe Fiona's going to leave without seeing Yates first. I know she doesn't want to, but I'm glad she offers.

The last song ends, the crowd cheers. When the lights go up, and the zombie people go back to being normal again, Yates appears at the stage door. "Hey, guys!" he calls out. He waves four yellow plastic wristbands in his hand. "Do you want to come backstage?"

Any sympathy that Fiona might have had for Robyn and Adrian vanishes from her face. "Hells yeah, we do!" Fiona says. She strips her arm from around Adrian and skips toward the door.

The opportunity seems to rid Robyn of most her gloom, though Adrian seems more skeptical. We all follow Fiona anyhow.

The backstage area is much less glamorous than I imagined it would be. It's just a windowless room no bigger than our classroom. The boys from the band are there, stripping down to their underwear and changing into dry clothes. A battered leather couch is shoved against a wall, next to a cooler filled with beer. I decide not to take one even though my throat is raw from growling. I feel uncomfortable drinking in front of Yates, since he's still our teacher and all. But Fiona helps herself without asking.

"So, you made that helicopter?" she asks Yates, cracking a beer open. "It was so rad!"

I'm impressed, too. Yates, the same guy who makes those incredible photo-paintings, can also make a helicopter prop for a punk band.

Yates's face tightens for a second, but then he turns his back to Fiona and looks more relaxed. "Yeah. I guess I'm Romero's resident special effects guy." He looks at me, sitting on the couch. "Did you guys like the show?"

"What I saw of it was cool," Adrian says, and shoots Fiona a glare.

"Does Romero ever have shows in New York?" Robyn asks the band. "It's too bad CBGB closed, because I could see you guys playing there. My friend's dad owns a couple of bars on the Lower East Side. Maybe he could book you some shows." The lead singer breaks off and starts talking to Robyn, near the door. I watch Fiona watching them, her lip curling a little.

"What did you like best about the show?" Yates asks me.

I feel put on the spot, like I'm in class or something. "I don't know . . . everything?" I say, and then fall onto the couch.

"Come on," Yates says, smiling at me. "When I first saw these guys, I didn't know whether to rock out or run screaming. So, tell me. I want to know what you think."

July

"She loved it," Fiona says. Then she drops into my lap like a kid and kisses me on the cheek. "But you should have seen how freaked out she was when I was doing her makeup. She had absolutely no idea what Romero meant."

Fiona's laughter rings in my ears. My face gets hot. She's right. I don't know what it means, and I'm definitely not going to ask now, now that I've been called out in front of everyone. I know Fiona thinks it's cute how much I don't know, but in front of everyone else, it's incredibly embarrassing.

Yates sits down next to me. "I had no idea, either, Emily, so don't feel bad. But the band is named after George Romero, director of those creepy *Night of the Living Dead* zombie movies. I could get you a CD if you wanted. All of you," he says, even though he's only looking at me.

I manage a thin smile. "Thanks."

We all hang out for a while longer, talking while some music execs drop by to chat with Romero, and then everyone goes to the wing of the stage to watch the headliner band perform. They're good, but no Romero. None of the fans are dancing or anything. They just stand there, rocking ever so gently to the beat. The music is quiet and pretty, but too measured.

Even though I keep my eyes on the band, I can still tell that Yates is looking at me. And Fiona's on my other side, watching him. It makes me insanely uncomfortable. I wish I could just disappear. I don't understand why Yates isn't paying more attention to Fiona. She can get nasty when someone takes her spotlight. I've seen it firsthand with Robyn. I don't want her anger to move over to me.

After a while, Robyn, Fiona, and I leave to use the bathroom. Even though the room is lit with red lightbulbs and the mirror is

169

dirty and cracked, I can still see that my makeup has run all over my face from the sweat. I rip a length of rough brown paper towel from out of the dispenser and wet it under the faucet.

"I think Yates likes you," Robyn teases as she perches herself up on the sink next to me.

Fiona goes inside an empty stall and shuts the door fast.

I give Robyn as hard a look as I can. "He does not."

"I'm serious! I keep catching him staring at you. You can't tell me you don't feel it." Her head dips back and she smacks her forehead. "I mean, he's been flirting with you ever since that first day of class. Remember?"

I close my eyes and splash water over my face. "No," I say. And then, "You're wrong." I make my voice as defiant and stern as possible, so Robyn shuts up and Fiona knows that I am not asking for any of this.

The stall door swings open without the sound of a flush. Fiona walks to the sink and washes marker ink from her hand. In the mirror I see the outline of the toilet drawn on the side of the stall door. "Robyn's right," she says. "He likes you." Her voice sounds surprisingly even.

I feel like I've unintentionally betrayed her.

"Don't look so sad," Fiona says, in that Big Sister voice.

"But —"

"Yates isn't my type. He's too . . . introverted. I mean, can he speak in a normal voice, or does he always have to mumble like that? And sure his work is cool, but he's also a huge suck-up. He's so afraid to break the rules, he barely wants to be seen with us. Come on, dude. It's not that big a deal. No one's going to tattle on you. Live a little."

July

"I . . . I feel weird. I mean, he's still my teacher." And also, as of a few hours ago, Yates and Fiona were inevitable. Is she really over him that quickly?

"You were telling me to hook up with him before!"

"I know . . . but that's someone like you," I say.

Fiona shakes her head knowingly, and leans into the mirror to apply some more lipstick. "Don't worry. I'll help you make it happen. Just follow my lead." She stares at Robyn as she presses her lips together to spread the shiny red around.

We return to the backstage area. My mind is swimming. Fiona liked Yates so much, but she basically gave me her blessing to pursue him. Not only her blessing, but her help, too. Honestly, this makes me feel so amazing. If a guy can't come between us, I guess we really *are* friends. Friends for real. It's almost a stronger bond than I have with Meg. It's crazy to think how far we've come in so short a time. How far I have come.

Yates stands up and makes room for me on the couch. As I sit down, I feel like everyone's watching. Fiona makes a beeline for Adrian in the corner, where he's chatting with some of the boys in the band. My heart skips a beat for him, thinking maybe now he has a chance with Fiona. But instead, she pushes past him and touches the arm of Romero's lead singer, the same boy that Robyn was talking to before. Robyn stops dead in the middle of the room and watches, her mouth ever so slightly open.

Fiona inches closer, tickling his cheek with her long lock of blue hair. "You should let me do some backup growling on your next record. I'm really, really good at growling."

It's too much for Adrian to bear. He grabs Robyn's arm and whispers in her ear. The two walk over to me.

"We're leaving," Robyn says.

"No. Guys, stay. Come on."

Adrian shoots daggers across the room. "I'd rather poke my eyes out with a dull pencil."

"Listen," I say, and lead them away from Yates. "Please stay. You know how she gets sometimes." I don't want to sound like I'm talking bad about Fiona, but it is the truth. "She likes attention."

"You can tell Fiona I said 'screw you,'" Robyn says to me, but so loud it carries across the room.

If Fiona hears, she certainly doesn't show it. Her face is locked against the lead singer's. She guides his hands onto her hips. She growls for him.

Twenty-One

I don't kiss Yates.

There are a few times when I think it might happen, when we're talking but not actually having a conversation. At least not one that's registering. It's more like we're both spitting out words to pass the time until one of us has the courage to lean in.

But neither of us does.

He says to me, "This TA thing isn't all it's cracked up to be," and he sighs and raises his arms up for a stretch, lacing and cracking his fingers and giving me a glimpse of those horseshoe tattoos on his inner biceps. I feel lucky.

But I don't want Yates to risk getting in trouble. The attraction — the urge — is there. But it's held back by the caution. There isn't even a place for us to be alone backstage. There are no secrets here, and this would need to be a secret.

So I try to enjoy the flirtation of it all, the fact that I have his attention, until finally the show ends and the after party breaks up and Fiona and I go back to her apartment. For once, I understand completely why Fiona's obsessed with having all eyes on her.

It does feel like a drug, or like helium, making you lighter.

We're both pretty tired. Fiona kicks some random stuff on her floor into a pile near the wall, and then unfolds a foam chair into a thin twin mattress for me. She lends me a pair of pajama pants and wraps a spare pillow in a T-shirt, because she can't find any clean pillowcases in the linen closet. It's too hot for a blanket, so I use a sheet.

"It sucks that you guys didn't kiss," Fiona says as we climb into our beds. "If you want this, you're gonna have to grow some balls, because Yates is never going to make the first move." Fiona falls asleep pretty quickly. From the floor, I see the tops of the Philadelphia skyline out of her window. Staring at it, I realize that the night sky isn't really black, which is the way I've always thought of it. It's actually a dark shade of blue, the darkest possible.

When I get back home, I find myself wanting to talk to Meg. It feels weird to be on the brink of something and her not know anything about it. She doesn't even know Yates's name. I want to tell her, as soon as we get some time alone. But I can't exactly get the subject to come up, not when all I can get Meg to commit to is a quickie Starbucks run between a lunch date with Rick and a trip to the car dealership with her mom to pick out her birthday-mobile. It's like Meg only wants to hang out with me in spare moments, instead of making real time for us. Lately I've been guilty of that, too, but she did it first.

When we meet up later that night, Meg casually mentions that she has a craving for funnel cake, and since there's nothing else to do, we pile into Rick's truck and decide to drive to the boardwalk. It'll be a long trip, about forty minutes, but I don't mind. I haven't been to the shore once yet this summer.

We're about to get on the highway when Rick fumbles for his phone. "Oh," he says awkwardly, the way the one senior jock cast in the school play delivers his lines. "Chad just texted me and asked what we were doing." His head spins toward us, smooth and measured. "Should we ask him to come?"

Meg taps a finger against her lips, contemplating. "That's a great idea. You don't mind, do you, Emily?"

I scrunch up my face. "No," I say, suspicious.

We swing by Chad's house. He's waiting outside on the curb, his hair gel reflecting in the moonlight. We decide to take his car, since it has more room than Rick's truck. I'm automatically given shotgun.

Meg reaches around my headrest and tucks some hair behind my ears. I pinned up most of the pieces in those twisty buns that Fiona always wears, but I left a few strands in the very front loose. "Your hair looks so cute down, Emily. I mean, people would kill for hair like yours." She leans forward between our seats and winks at Chad.

"I like my hair this way," I tell her, gently guiding her hand away.

"Oh yeah," Meg chirps. "Me too. I was just saying . . ."

Everyone talks and laughs on the drive to the boardwalk. I participate every now and then, but really, I just take note of the things in Chad's car. It's a typical messy boy car, with so much sports equipment and dirty T-shirts piled up on the backseat floor that Meg has to sit sideways and drape her legs over Rick's lap. Dirt from the ball field dulls the black floor mat where my feet are, and empty foil wrappers from protein bars catch the highway lights and flash inside the car like stars in a garbage constellation.

It was warm and nice in Cherry Grove, but the closer we get to the beach, the air thickens with moisture into a dense, wet fog. Chad puts on the windshield wipers, even though it's not actually raining. Not many people are out. We get a parking space, no problem.

As soon as I get out of the car, I'm shivering. I'm dressed completely wrong — in a jumper Fiona gave me. It's apple green and has tiny blue stars printed on it, and two oversized blue buttons hold up the straps. My white lace-trimmed cami peeks out the front. Fiona said I could wear it with nothing underneath — but I think she greatly overestimates the size of my boobs.

"Here," Chad says, and pops open the back hatch. He gives me his green nylon baseball windbreaker. It has the softest lining inside, a heather gray T-shirt material that feels like it's been washed a thousand times. His name is stitched on it in a bulge of little lines of gold thread. I trace the script letters with my finger. I remember Meg telling me how thrilling it was to get Rick's windbreaker, like it was a prize she'd won. I slip it over my head, and when I poke my head out of the hole, Meg's right on top of me, giving this high-pitched *squee* that makes my stomach drop.

The boardwalk is mostly deserted and the fog makes it hard to see. But I can hear the waves crashing against the sand. As much as I like swimming in pools back at Cherry Grove, nothing comes close to the ocean. Swimming in the ocean has an element of danger, when the tide wants to pull you back in.

The boys walk just slightly ahead of us. I take advantage of the privacy.

July

"Is this a setup?" I whisper to Meg. Even if I can't tell her about Yates right now, she might as well know that it's not going to happen with me and Chad. I don't want things to get anymore awkward.

"Noooo," she says, but I can tell she's lying. Meg is the worst liar. Ever.

"Meg, I —"

She turns her head toward the ocean breeze, so her hair doesn't fly in her mouth. "Remember all the summer days we'd spend here with my family? I wish they never sold my grandma's house. They tore it down, you know. To build some crappy hotel."

"Really?"

"Yeah."

I sigh. It's so weird, when something like that, something as real and tangible as a house that you've been in, is suddenly gone. "Remember how we'd boogie-board the waves until our stomachs were cut raw from the sand?"

Meg laughs. "Remember that time we were lying out and a seagull pooped right on your stomach?"

"Ewww," I say, and slap her arm. "Remember the first time you got your period and you were so afraid of tampons that you wore a pad in your suit and it swelled up all huge from the water?"

"Emily!" Meg shrieks and covers my mouth with her hand. The boys don't even notice us. They've faded into the mist. "Those were the best summers," she says quietly.

"Yup," I say. But these memories don't make me happy. Even though I can see them in such sharp detail, I feel fuzzy and confused. Like déja vu. Like maybe none of it was real.

SAME DIFFERENCE

The funnel cake shop looks warm and inviting. Popping white lightbulbs chase each other around the glowing sign. I smell sugar. And butter.

Meg races to catch up with Rick. "Will you get me my own plate?"

I guess we're not sharing, like always.

"You're not going to eat a whole plate of funnel cake," he says.

"Yes, I am," she insists. "I haven't had funnel cake once this summer. I've got to make up for lost time."

Rick leans against the counter. "Come on, Meg." He laughs. "I've only got twenty bucks on me."

I watch as she slides herself against him, her legs clenching against his thigh. She wraps her arms around his waist. A smile creeps across Rick's face. "Okay, okay," he concedes.

I've never seen Meg do something like that before. Something so . . . Jenessa.

Suddenly, the light in the place is too bright and harsh. I sit down in a plastic booth and shield my eyes with the windbreaker, giving the place a wash of emerald green. Chad buys me a funnel cake and a lemonade.

"Say thank you, Emily," Meg jokes as he plops them in front of me.

"Thanks," I say quickly, even though I didn't ask for it.

Everyone sits down. And then something weird happens. Chad slips his hand into mine underneath the table. It feels warm and cold at the same time, or maybe I'm getting our hands confused because his fingers squeeze mine tight and there is no room, not even a little, between our palms.

July

There's a moment where I think I should just go with it. Let this happen so everything in Cherry Grove can go back to normal. Meg wants me to hook up with Chad because it will tie us together again, like the beach house and the Starbucks. She wants that closeness back, and there's a part of me, a little one, that does, too.

Then Chad's finger rubs against my drawing callus. It's rough and hard and completely ungirly. His grip loosens with surprise. I pull my hand free.

"I have to go to the bathroom," I announce and bolt from the table, speed-walking through the empty store, leaving their chatter behind.

There's a full-length mirror mounted to the bathroom wall. I stand there and stare at myself. My hair is all frizzy from the fog. And the windbreaker looks ridiculous, bagging out over my jumper. I look like two halves of two different people mashed together. I wonder what Fiona would say about me, about tonight. Is it possible to be a poseur in both worlds?

When I come back out, my purse has moved from the seat to the tabletop. It's open, and my sketchbook peeks out. My walking slows but my heart rate increases.

"Were you guys looking through my sketchbook?" I ask.

They all say no with super straight faces.

I don't sit down. "Just tell me if you did." I don't want them to protect my feelings, but I am scared of what they think.

Rick says no again, but Meg cracks. "Okay, we peeked! But only because you never share anything with us. Seriously, Emily, you are so talented!"

"Yeah," Chad says. "You should draw something for us right now."

"Come on," I say, falling into my seat. My body temperature drops back to normal. "Give me a break."

"Seriously. Draw something!" Meg's eyes search the place and land back on our table. "Draw this funnel cake."

A tingle comes over me. The funnel cake does have an interesting shape. It's like a long, skinny rope twirled around itself. And there's a lot of texture, too, with the way the bread glistens with oil in some places and looks dull where the powdered sugar was sprinkled on. Also, I do want to show Meg what I'm capable of. I want to impress them with who I really am.

I press my pencil to the first blank page, and everyone's quiet, watching me. I get the curves of the long, spiral tube. I do it like Mr. Frank says, paying attention to the real thing, and not just shorthanding a version of it. My eyes trace the funnel cake, my pencil follows. I don't even look down. Then I draw the rim of the paper plate, and start the shading.

Suddenly, my pencil skips out from under me, like a needle jumping the groove of a record. A thick white interruption in my gray line.

When I look up, the boys start to laugh. Then I notice, deep in the crevice of the spine, the rough jagged edges of paper and a loose string pulled from the binding. A page has been ripped out. Sloppy. Careless.

They've done something to my sketchbook.

I lay my pencil flat on its side and abandon my drawing. I scribble all over the sheet, hard and fast, blacking out everything in sight. But my pencil keeps skipping over the groove.

A form starts to take shape as the laughter grows into hysterics. The white lines curving and then long and then curving again. It's a big shape. It takes up almost a whole page.

They've drawn a big cartoon penis.

I flip to the next blank sheet and rub my pencil over it. They must have pressed pretty hard, because it goes through two, three, four, oh my God, five sheets. Five sheets wasted. My sketchbook, my diary, compromised.

I look up, heat burning behind my eyes. Rick and Chad slap hands over the table. And Meg looks like a kid who's been told a dirty joke for the first time — euphoric. It takes all my self-control not to throw my lemonade in their faces.

"Who did this?" I say.

Meg's face falls hard and fast like the first drop of the rickety old coaster roaring outside. "Emily — "

"Did you do this?" I shout in Rick's face. It feels good to stand up for myself.

Rick looks stunned. "Hey, Emily." He puts his hands up. Surrender. "We were just joking."

"It's not like you don't have cocks drawn all over that thing," Chad snorts.

"Those were nude models, you idiot." It's one thing to be critiqued by people better than me. But this is worse, because it's people who don't get it at all. I stand up and bump the table, spilling a bunch of lemonade. "I want to go home. Now."

Meg tries to pull me back down. "Emily, no. Come on. We just got our food."

"I'm serious," I say. I grab my purse and start walking.

Meg runs after me. "Emily, listen—"

"I honestly can't believe you."

She throws her hands up, like I am being way too intense, way too mad. "What? I thought your drawings were great. We were having some fun with you. It was just a joke."

"You think that was funny? You honestly think that was funny?" Meg is the one who's a poseur. She pretends to like baseball for Rick's sake, and she pretends this is funny. The old Meg would never, ever think that. She would have gotten how important this sketchbook is to me.

Now, at least, she realizes the night is over.

A heavy silence blankets the car ride back to Cherry Grove, even though the radio pumps a happy summer song, the kind that is supposed to make nights like these feel infinite. Chad takes corners too fast. He can't drop me off quickly enough.

"You're going home, too?" Rick whines when Chad pulls into our cul-de-sac and Meg starts to scoot out.

"I'll call you later," she says, kissing him fast on the cheek before climbing over his lap.

I cringe as I'm getting out of the car. I want to tell Meg not to bother. I want to tell her to go and be with Rick. I pass Chad's windbreaker through the open window. He just stares straight ahead, so I drop it on his seat.

They peel out. The sound of screeching tires is ultraloud.

"Emily, come on." Meg's trying to stay patient. "I worked so hard to plan something fun for us tonight!"

My heart sits in my throat, cutting me off from taking deep breaths. "Why? Why did you do that, Meg?" I'm yelling. And we

July

both look around for a moment. Our fight echoes through Blossom Manor. My mom's bedroom light flicks on. Sure, we've had little tiffs before, but nothing like this. Nothing so absolute, where I didn't see a way out.

Meg backs away from me slowly. "Why are you acting like this?" She shakes her head. "You think I forced Chad to come tonight? I didn't, Emily. He was totally down to hook up with you. Rick and I barely had to say anything about it. He knew you liked him and he was interested."

"I was never interested!" I say. "I was just tired of being the third wheel with you and Rick, okay?"

"So now you're mad at me because I'm dating Rick? I'm sorry if you're jealous that I have a boyfriend but . . ."

"Jealous? Of Rick? Are you kidding?" But my throat tightens up when I hear the twinge of hesitation in my voice, and the fact that Meg doesn't look at me means she hears it, too.

But it's not just about Rick. Maybe it used to be, but it's become so much more.

Meg pulls off her tortoiseshell headband. "Whatever. I'll deal with it. I'll smooth things over with the guys." It's not that she's comforting me — she's just tired. "I just hope things won't be totally awkward the next time we all hang out." Her last sentence hangs in the air like a warning, like this isn't going to happen again. She's standing up for them, not me. And then she does something she's never done before. She walks away without saying good-bye.

183

Twenty-Two

"Soooooo," Mom says. "Is everything okay with you and Meg?"

"Everything's fine, Mom."

"Good." She taps her steering wheel. "Because I thought I heard you girls fighting last night."

"We weren't fighting," I lie.

Mom and I sit in silence as her blinker ticks away the uncomfortable seconds. The 12:30 p.m. train from Philly glides into the station as we turn into the parking lot. Mom sighs and opens her mouth like she wants to get into it with me. I glance over at her and try to stare her down into a concession. Does she really want to get into this now?

"Fine, Emily," she says. "Whatever you say."

The train doors ding open and Fiona climbs down the steps of the first car. She's got on a red slip dress with a purple cardigan, black fishnets, and black round-toe heels. Her hair matches the cardigan, dyed purple. You wouldn't think purple could be summery, but the shade is exactly the color of grape ice pops that come in long plastic sleeves. And the long lock is stripped to a flat blond.

Fiona sees the convertible and races over. My mom's eyes get wide, and then she quickly slides on her sunglasses.

"Hello, Mrs. Thompson," Fiona says as she approaches the car. She doesn't climb right in, even though I get out of the convertible and hold the door open for her. Instead she walks around to the driver's side and gives my mom a very firm handshake.

"Hello, Fiona," Mom says, smiling. "I'm so glad you decided to visit us."

"Are you kidding?" Fiona says, climbing into the back. "I had to beg your daughter to invite me."

Mom eyes me over the tops of her sunglasses, like I am a terrible hostess. "I think Emily was afraid you might be bored coming to Cherry Grove."

"Hardly," Fiona says with a snort. "I can't wait to see this place with my own eyes."

I get in the backseat next to Fiona and play Cherry Grove tour guide, pointing out the huge cement mass of the mall, the red-and-black movie theater, my Starbucks, the Putt Putt Palace.

"Oh my God, your town has its own miniature golf course? Cherry Grove is like freaking Disneyland!"

"Not exactly." I take it in for myself. Putt Putt Palace is way cheesier than I remember from when Meg and I would come here in middle school. The place is filled with bad knockoffs of Disney characters, like a Mickey Mouse with drunk eyes that look in two different directions and a Little Mermaid statue whose hair is the wrong shade of red. A fountain spits foggy water.

I can almost smell the mildew from the AstroTurf carpet.

"We should totally go there tonight!" Fiona says.

"Maybe," I say. As much as Fiona is excited to traipse around Cherry Grove, I kind of want to lie low, especially after what happened last night. Hopefully Fiona brought a bathing suit like I asked so we can hide out in my pool. Suddenly, the whole making-fun thing doesn't seem like such a good idea. Maybe because July is already half over, and there's barely three weeks of the summer program left. Then I'm back here, full-time.

"Emily thought you might want T.G.I. Friday's for lunch, Fiona," Mom says.

"Not that it's good or anything," I clarify. "I just thought it would be funny."

"Oooh!" Fiona says. "I've never had T.G.I. Friday's before. My mom is going to flip when she hears. She's very anti the whole chain fast food thing."

Even though we're obviously not nine years old, we force the hostess at the podium to give us red balloons and goody bags. Inside are crayons and a coloring book. Fiona and I draw madly on it, ignoring the cartoon burgers and dancing sodas by blackening the pages with tracings of our hands. Then we draw each other's faces without looking down. They look squiggly and weird and wonderful.

Mom peers over the top of her menu, trying not to obviously look at what we're doing. But she is looking.

When we're done eating, the waitress brings my mom the bill. Suddenly, Fiona's face gets tight. She kicks me under the table.

July

"I don't have any money to give your mom for lunch," she whispers.

"Don't worry about it," I say. "She wouldn't take your money anyhow. It's our treat. Welcome to Cherry Grove."

Fiona looks relieved and then her face suddenly lights up. "So guess what? My mom sold a whole bunch of her new paintings to a gallery owner she knows."

"Wow! That's great!" I say.

"I know. She really wants to meet you, by the way. She feels bad that she's been working so hard on her paintings this summer. But now that everything's sold, she should be around more often."

When we drive into Blossom Manor, Fiona says, "This is where you live."

"Yeah."

"You're loaded. You know that, right?"

I shrug my shoulders.

Mom turns onto our cul-de-sac and my stomach drops. Rick's truck pulls away from Meg's house and Meg is on her way up the front steps. When she sees my mom's convertible, she starts walking over toward my house. Her pace slows and she stops halfway across the street, right on the manhole cover, when she sees Fiona in the back of the car.

"Oh God," I say under my breath.

"What?" Fiona says. She looks over my shoulder at the girl in the middle of the road. "Who's that?"

"Nobody." I don't want this to happen right now. I unbuckle my seat belt the second Mom puts the car in park and leap out. "Just keep walking."

"You're not going to say hello to Meg?" Mom interjects, with this look on her face like I am the worst friend, the worst person in history. She doesn't know anything, though. She has no idea what's been going on.

"You never tell me about Meg!," Fiona says. "Let's go say hi." I'm afraid of the smile she's got on her face, like this is going to be fun.

"Hey, Meg," I say when we get to where she's standing.

"Hey," she says back. "You must be Fiona. It's nice to finally meet you." She's 100 percent happy, sweet Meg. There's not a trace of the turmoil from yesterday.

It makes me mad that Meg refuses to see what's going on. But Fiona is a piece of undeniable proof. And I know with my new friend, I am daring her to say something. I am issuing a charge to her to try and overlook this one.

Try to pretend that this isn't happening, Meg.

Fiona's quiet for a second. I see her eyes jump from my E necklace to Meg's M necklace and back again. A wry smile spreads across her mouth, and she says, "Charmed."

Meg's smile doesn't waiver. "Is Emily giving you the grand tour?"

"Oh yeah," Fiona snickers. "I've gotten all the highlights."

"Well, despite what Emily might say, it's a really nice town," Meg says, as if she needs to do damage control or something, to protect her beloved Cherry Grove from me tarnishing its image.

"I didn't say anything that bad," I snap.

Fiona slings an arm around my shoulder. "You can't blame Emily for being disillusioned. I mean, she's been practically living in a city now for the whole summer. She's made new friends, she's one of the best artists in class, *and* she's got a new boyfriend.

July

You should see Yates! Did she tell you that he's in college?"

Meg looks at me like she can't even process what's going on. She shakes her head, defiant. "I don't think you know Emily at all. As much as you might want her to be like you, she's just a regular girl." Even though Meg's still talking to Fiona, she moves her eyes over to me. "School is going to start in September and everything will be back to normal."

My mouth drops open. How could Meg say something like that? Something so humiliating in front of my new friend?

I want to step forward. I want to fight back, take her on, show her that she doesn't know me at all anymore. But the fire, the passion, and the confidence, isn't in me. It's in Fiona. And even though Fiona is right next to me, I'm aware that there will be a point when she won't be.

I run as fast as I can away from Meg. Knowing I can't go far, that there's really no escape, doesn't slow me down at all.

"Emily, wait!" Fiona calls after me.

I sprint across the lawn, up the stairs, and straight to my room. Fiona's footsteps pound behind me.

The whole place feels like a cage.

I want to get rid of everything in here, all the things that tie me to being a person I hate.

I tear through my closet, ripping my clothes off the hangers. I jam them down inside my white wicker trash can. Of course they don't all fit but I like the feeling of stuffing them inside, hearing the delicate wicker snap and pop from the force. I punch them down down down.

Fiona stands in my doorway, watching. She doesn't try to stop me.

But it is completely unsatisfying, too. I know deep inside that this isn't trash, and tomorrow the maid will come and do my laundry and all my clothes will be hanging back up where they once were. And the summer will eventually end and I'll be back in Cherry Grove and everything will be like it used to be except much, much worse. I start to cry. I fall on my bed and smother my face with my stupid rosebud comforter.

"She's wrong about you, Emily."

"Is she?" I sound desperate and scared. I hate it. "Look at this place. This is who I really am. It's pathetic." Tears stream down my face.

Fiona glances around. "I remember this. From your sketchbook," she says. "But this isn't you, Emily. Maybe it used to be, but not anymore. And you don't have to pretend like it is." Her hand runs over the wall and stops on a seam, where the rosebud wallpaper doesn't exactly line up. "You've got to start fresh." She slides her nail underneath and slowly rips a piece away from the wall. A long, lean strip.

I walk over to my bookshelf, and though it takes a few jumps, I manage to grab hold of one of those ballerinas. It slips free from my hands — and I let it. It shatters on my floor.

I finally feel a release.

Three hours later, my room is unrecognizable, transformed to the sounds of Romero-on-repeat. Fiona's done a bunch of shadow tracings on every available surface — doors, my dresser, the hardwood floor. I've reconstructed my ripped rosebud wallpaper into larger flower shapes and glued them to the rough walls. Now Fiona's pulling stuff out of my closet. I'm holding a garbage bag open.

The old Emily is officially gone.

July

My parents keep walking by my closed door, mustering the courage to see what's going on. When they finally knock, Fiona shouts, "Come in!"

It swings open, and there's Mom and Dad and Claire. Claire runs in and says, "Wow!" My parents, both absolutely stunned, stand in the doorway.

"I, uh—" I stutter.

"We did some redecorating," Fiona explains.

Dad starts nodding. Slow at first, and then faster and faster. "Okay, okay," he says.

"Emily," Mom says, like she needs to make sure it's still me. She looks around the room, frightened.

I know that I have to say something. I have to start speaking up for myself. "Mom, it just . . . didn't feel like me in here."

"I want to redo my room!" Claire shouts.

Mom moves past her, over to the trash can and sees the smashed ballerinas. She picks up one long, graceful, disembodied arm. And then she spins around and walks right back out.

Dad leans against the doorframe. "We'll talk."

He drags Claire out with him and closes the door.

My heart finally starts beating again.

"Holy shit, your parents just freaked out!"

"Dad will be okay, but my mom." I sigh. "I wish I had a mom like yours," I say. "Someone who'd understand."

"Who cares if they understand? Artists can't worry about what other people are going to say."

I nod, but the aftermath suddenly closes in on me. I know now that there's no turning back.

Not with my family, not with Meg.

Twenty-Three

Fiona stands at the front of our class on Tuesday, holding a huge black poster board just to the side of her face. On it is mounted a piece of paper, her abstract shadow drawings, smudges creeping across the page. They look random, but I know they are painstakingly deliberate.

"More of your shadows," Mr. Frank says.

"Yup," Fiona says.

"And what are these of?"

"I'd rather not say. If you knew, my piece would be compromised."

The class thinks in silence. Or at least the polite ones do. The rest avert their eyes, or occupy themselves with something else. Fiona's losing her grip on them, and it makes the whole room feel off center.

"I'm concerned," Mr. Frank says.

"Concerned?" Fiona asks, genuinely confused.

"I think you need to try a new approach. The problem with doing the shadows in such an abstract fashion is that they lose their power to inform. They don't become shadows anymore. They become nothing."

Fiona drops her chin to her chest and gives Mr. Frank the look of death.

"I agree," Robyn says haughtily. "I think the artist needs to innovate more."

I shoot Robyn the same death stare. I know she's pissed at Fiona, but it's totally not cool to go after her like that.

Fiona's arms go limp, and her piece falls sloppily to the side.

"Don't get defensive," Mr. Frank says.

"How could I not get defensive?" Fiona walks back toward her stool. "You're attacking me."

"I'm not attacking you, Fiona. I'm giving constructive criticism about your work."

"Same difference," she says.

I look at Yates, wishing there were some way to stop this from happening. "What does everyone else think?" he asks.

"I really like these pieces," I offer meekly. "And I think the abstract stuff works. It plays with audience expectations. You might not know what you're looking at, and you might want to dismiss it, but you're definitely looking at *something*, something that really does exist."

"I agree with your vision, Emily," Mr. Frank says. "But I don't think Fiona's expressing that clearly enough." He turns to her. "Fiona, I'm not saying there isn't something to your shadows. I've enjoyed all of the pieces you've shared with the class. I'm just encouraging you to push yourself. I want you to solve the problem you've created here. Give us more than what's on the surface."

Fiona walks back to her stool, shaking her head.

"And as you all know, our closing gallery reception is on the horizon, and the selections for the juried portion of the show will take place in the next two weeks. You should be producing your best work now. Believe me, I am waiting for it."

Fiona won't even look at me for the rest of class. I think she might be mad. Maybe I said the wrong thing about her piece. I wasn't trying to side with Mr. Frank. I was trying to defend her. I love her work. It inspires me.

At one point, Robyn corners me near the pencil sharpener. "You know Fiona only likes hanging out with you because she gets to be the star."

"Fiona and I are friends," I tell her, unable to hide the bragging in my voice. "That's why we hang out."

"Why do you think she tossed me to the side? Because I was too much competition. I'm just saying, be careful."

"Whatever, Robyn. Why do you care what happens to me? You never liked me in the first place."

"You're right," she admits. "I was wrong about you. And you know who else I was wrong about? Fiona. I bought into her whole schtick. But now I think her shadows are totally lame, and the whole thing is a cover for the fact that Fiona doesn't have any real artistic talent. Sooner or later, everyone's going to figure it out."

"You don't know what you're talking about." I turn my back on her. But a part of me wonders why Fiona has done the same sort of piece again and again. It's definitely her trademark, and I still think the pieces are great, but perhaps Mr. Frank is right that she needs to take it to the next level.

July

When we break for lunch, I try to get Fiona to talk to me, but she's doing what I used to do when I felt insecure — painstakingly cleaning up her supplies while the rest of the students file out. "Don't worry," I say. "Mr. Frank likes your stuff."

Fiona rolls her eyes. "Shadows are my thing. I mean, how does he not know that by now?"

"I don't think he meant to upset you, Fiona. He wanted to inspire you. You've only scratched the surface of what you're capable of."

"I honestly couldn't give a shit what that old idiot thinks. He's a nobody. He's nothing famous. He's just a lame teacher at this lame school."

Unfortunately, Yates is still hanging around in the room, cleaning up the supplies. He must have heard Fiona trashing his idol. He walks over to us.

"Seriously, Fiona," he says, "don't let it get to you. You know what you have in mind for your pieces. It's a lesson every artist has to learn. You can't please everyone."

I love that Yates is saying this. Any other person would take Mr. Frank's side and give some condescending speech about how you need to bend to other people's expectations.

"Thanks," Fiona tells him. I can't tell if it resonates at all, but I hope it does. "Emily, do you want to go get a cheese steak with me for lunch? I seriously need greasy comfort food like a-sap."

"Sure," I say. But a part of me wants to hang back with Yates. It's like we have this conversation that's been paused for days now, ever since the concert. A conversation where neither of us knows what to say. But Yates isn't the one who needs me right now — Fiona is. Even if she'd never admit it.

We don't talk for a few blocks. I just follow Fiona and enjoy the view. Philadelphia is a beautiful city. One second we're walking down a main street with stores and high-rise apartment buildings, and then we duck down an alley and find ourselves in a maze of tiny cobblestone side streets with tiny houses and hitching posts for horses from the old days. After a few of those, I've completely lost my sense of direction. But Fiona leads the way and before I know it, we hit South Street.

On South Street, there are a bunch of shops you'd never see in the mall — like an incense store that blasts Bob Marley or a place that sells only condoms. There's also a big comic book shop, lots of bars, and a record store that Fiona tells me is the spot where all the local DJs go to buy music.

A few apartment buildings and alleyways we pass are covered in mosaics of glass and mirror and broken pottery that glitter like diamonds in the afternoon sun. Fiona explains they are done by a local artist named Isaiah Zagar.

"He always puts the words 'Art Is the Center of the Real World' somewhere in his mosaics. Isn't that badass?"

I nod, unable to defocus from the jagged shards, until I am forced to completely spin around or fall flat on my face.

We stop at Jim's Steaks, a greasy-looking diner on a corner. The lunch line is reeeally long. Like out-the-door-and-down-the-street long, full of all types of people, from traffic cops and construction workers to old ladies. I'm starving and the smell of steak and onions and gooey Cheez Whiz wafting down the street is brutal torture.

July

"Should we wait? I think we should wait," Fiona says.

"Yeah," I say. "Let's definitely wait."

We walk to the back of the line. I turn to Fiona but she's suddenly not there. She's staring inside the window of a shop a few stores down from where the line actually ends.

"Oh my God, Emily! C'mere!"

I run over to her side and find her standing in front of a tattoo shop called Philadelphia Eddie's. Inside, there are three tattoo stations and a huge wall of drawings you can choose from, like dragons and Chinese symbols and delicate fairies. I hear the buzzing through the glass window, a combination of the needles and the neon.

Fiona fishes in her bag and pulls out her sketchbook. "Come on."

I'm nervous as I follow Fiona inside, like someone's going to kick us out or call the cops because we're not eighteen. I hang back by the boards while she steps up to the counter and talks with a guy who has literally every inch of his body covered in tattoos. Even his knuckles. Even his earlobes. And when he opens his mouth, even on the insides of his lips.

"Do you have ID?"

"Umm." Fiona pats herself down, despite the fact that her tank and shorts don't have pockets. "I must have forgotton it in the dorms. I have this, though," she says, and pulls out the college ID from her owl tote bag.

He glances at it dubiously. She curtseys. He breaks into a smile. "I'm not supposed to do this," he says. "But my boss is away at a tattoo convention and that's my alma mater. So today's your lucky day."

The man opens the gate and ushers us in.

I can't believe it.

"This is what I want." Fiona shows him a drawing in her sketchbook. It's of a tree, branches bare and spindly. You see the detail of the trunk, the knots of the branches. And then, stuck off to the side, its dark shadow.

"Do you think this is a good idea?" I whisper as she hands me her tote bag. "I mean, tattoos are permanent."

"It's not like I'm picking something random off the wall, Emily. I made this. This is me. This is who I am. I believe in my art, and I don't care if anyone else gets it or not."

I understand what she's saying, especially after Mr. Frank's crit, but I'm still nervous for the pain she's going to feel. The man takes the sketchbook back to a photocopier and returns with a spray bottle and a plastic Bic razor. "So, where did you want this?"

Fiona takes off her shirt and hops up onto a long black medical table, the kind you'd see in a nurse's office at school. She lies there on her side, in her bra and a long beaded necklace and a pair of ripped denim shorts, and cranes her arm up over her head.

"Wait, you're getting it on your *ribs*?" I cry out.

Both Fiona and the tattoo guy laugh at me.

He sprays her side with the solution and gently shaves away any small hairs on a six-inch section of her creamy white skin, from the top of her rib cage to the bottom. Then he uses the photocopy to transfer the drawing right onto her skin.

It's not as big as I thought, just maybe five inches tall. It looks cool . . . I think.

"Aren't you nervous?" I ask.

"Yes!" she says. "Come hold my hand!"

July

I step forward and position myself next to her. The man gets the tattoo gun ready, pressing his big black boot on a petal to make it buzz. I can't watch him actually touch the needle to her side, but I feel her body tense up.

"Are you okay?" I ask, squeezing her hand. "Does it hurt?"

She talks out of the corner of her mouth, trying not to move. "Kinda. But not as bad as you'd think. More like my entire chest is vibrating."

After a few minutes, I muster the courage to look. Fiona's skin is red and tender and inky. The tattoo guy runs the needle for a few seconds at a time, then wipes the skin with a paper towel. I can see the shape forming.

"Do you think your mom is going to get mad?" I ask her.

"What? No. Of course not. If anything, she'll be pissed that she wasn't here for my first one."

"Hold still," the man says, refueling with more black ink.

She takes a couple quick breaths like women who are in labor do. Her whole face scrunches together. "What's it like to draw with a tattoo gun?" Fiona asks him.

"It's definitely different than a pencil. I was a Fine Art major, but I wanted my art to have more of a life than just hanging on someone's wall. So I got an apprenticeship here a few years ago and did a bunch of tattoos on honeydew melons to practice."

"Cool," we both say at the very same time.

Since the tattoo isn't that big, it doesn't take long for him to do the outline, which he says hurts the most. Then, he fills in the shadow portion all black. Finally, it's time to do the shading and detail of the actual tree. He mixes up a bunch of different paints inside these tiny plastic thimbles, combinations of gray and one of pure white. Fiona is able to relax. In fact, she says she doesn't even feel the needle anymore. Her side is totally numb.

"So, Emily, what are you going to get tattooed?" Fiona asks me.

I freeze. My mom would absolutely kill me if I ever did anything like that.

"Come on. Pick something in your sketchbook! I'll pay."

I'm too chicken.

Fiona looks over at her side and smiles. "Breathe, Emily. I'm just kidding!" Then she takes a deep breath. "But I wanted to thank you for what you did in Mr. Frank's class today. I know I don't handle criticism well. And I really appreciated that you had my back."

"Of course, Fiona. I love your stuff. And I do think —"

"We don't need to get into it again. It's just great to have a friend who understands how important this is to me. I mean, I can't see doing anything else in my life but this, you know? It's just art for me, I know it. And for someone to get that, to believe in me. It's just . . . awesome. It sounds corny, but I'm so glad we became friends."

I give her hand a squeeze. "Me too."

It takes about thirty-five more minutes before the whole thing is done. And when he's finished, it looks really pretty. It looks so great I almost wish I have the courage to get one myself. I look at my watch and know we're going to miss the afternoon session of Mr. Frank's class. I kind of feel bad about that, but I know Fiona needs this right now.

"I absolutely LOVE it!" Fiona screams and hugs the tattoo guy.

July

Fiona sends me to the ATM with her card to get the $200 the tattoo costs while the tattoo man takes a picture of her for his portfolio and bandages up her side with some ointment and a fresh paper towel. I enter in her pin and try for $200, but get rejected. I check her balance, and she only has $40 in her account.

I put in my own card and withdraw the difference. After all, that's what friends are for.

Twenty-Four

On Wednesday's field trip, we visit the Institute of Contemporary Art up near the UPenn campus. They have a big exhibit of Nara — a Japanese artist who makes cartoon-looking sculptures and drawings, but instead of being happy like the ones on cartoons usually are, his characters are all a little sad and weird. There's one enormous sculpture of a white puppy with sleepy eyes. And lots of drawings of a small girl with the creepiest, most mischievous look on her face — like the dark side of a little kid world.

When we return from the field trip, Fiona and I walk off together. Yates lurks by the headlights and when I step out to the street, he taps me on the shoulder.

"Hey," he says. "Do you have a second? I want to show you something."

I freeze and glance back at Fiona. "Um, we were going to walk to the train station. I usually catch the five o'clock back to Cherry Grove."

Fiona interrupts and hip-checks me. "Trains run like every fifteen minutes during rush hour. Don't worry, Emily. I'll see you

July

two later," she says, and walks toward the train station, away from me.

I hear Fiona's voice in my head: *If you want this, you've got to make it happen.* I wish I could be that sure of myself. And I only ever see Yates during school hours. When he's off-limits.

But then again, classes are technically over for the day. This could be an extracurricular field trip.

Yates and I race across the street and head into the art building.

"You never came back to class yesterday," he says, holding the door open for me.

"Did Mr. Frank notice?" I ask, twirling past him.

"Of course he noticed. But it wasn't a big deal. I told him that Fiona wasn't feeling well, and that you took care of her."

"Thanks. That's not far from the truth, actually. She was really hurt by the stuff Mr. Frank said."

"What did you think of her piece?"

"I love Fiona's stuff. She just gets really sensitive when anyone challenges her. It's because she's so passionate."

"Yeah, I totally understand that, but it's also a dangerous state of mind. People are going to tell you over and over that you're not good enough. Not everyone can love your work, you know? But you have to have the strength to overcome that and to keep going if this is what you want to do."

I raise my eyebrow. "She's got the strength. Believe me."

We take the elevator up. A few other kids are in it, and I notice that Yates edges over a few steps away from me. I understand him being careful, but we're not even doing anything. We're riding the elevator. So I do something bold. I slide next to him, close so that

our arms touch. His muscles tighten. He's definitely nervous, looking around out of the corner of his eyes, checking if anyone sees.
But he doesn't pull away, either. He lets me do it.

The elevator doors open, and Yates and I walk down the empty
hall together. We stand so close, our arms touching, but not holding hands or anything like that.

"I've been working on a new painting and I wanted to
hear what you think," Yates says as he opens the door to his
studio.

We step inside. The door closes behind us, before Yates can
get his hands on the bulb cord overhead. The room is suddenly
super dark, and the only light is a strip that seeps from the hallway
through the gap between the door and the floor.

Yates fumbles and swats the air. When he finally clicks the
light on, we're practically standing on top of each other. He's
behind me, and so tall he could put his chin on the top of my head.
The heat of his body tingles against my back.

Then he steps past me and grabs a corner of a paint-splattered
sheet. It's covering a huge canvas, nearly as tall as the ceiling.
When it drops, I almost drop with it.

It's a painting. Of me.

Sort of.

The canvas is a huge photograph. It takes me a second to
recognize that the picture is the one Fiona and I took the last time
I was in his studio. Maybe because Fiona, who was standing right
next to me, has been all but cropped out. She is background.
Blurry. I am the focus.

Yates has painted over my picture, just like he did in the Space
Invaded show. But he's taken it a step further. Instead of painting

beautiful landscapes over urban shots, he's painted over my face, a thin layer that still allows the photograph to be visible underneath.

I stuck out my tongue for that picture. The sight embarrasses me now, and I feel myself blushing. I was doing that to impress Yates, to make him think I was more like Fiona. But he's painted over my contorted, funny face and made me look classically beautiful, like the old Victorian portraits we saw in the Philadelphia Museum of Art.

"Do you like it?"

"I . . ." Somehow, the collision of those two images, those two versions of myself, presents the most accurate split that my personality has gone through this summer. "I feel like you get me better than I get myself."

He stares at the floor. He wants to tell me something.

"What?" I say.

"Emily," he says, "I've liked you ever since that first day I met you out on the sidewalk."

I shake my head. "But why? I was just this idiot girl from the suburbs."

"You were never an idiot," he insists, and finally looks me in the eyes. "You're so pure and genuine and humble."

"Humble?"

"I'm telling you, Emily. You have so much talent — only without the confidence to match it. Mr. Frank knows it. I know it. Fiona knows it. Everyone knows but you."

"You can't be serious."

"Why? Just because you don't look like the rest of these kids here, you think that makes you less than they are? Your potential is . . . limitless." He steps closer to me. "I just wish that circum-stances were different." He rustles his hands through his hair, frustrated. "As a TA, I had to go to this crazy day-long seminar about how it's completely unacceptable to fraternize with the stu-dents. I went through the same thing when I got the RA position for next semester. I need these jobs. The paintings I'm able to sell cover my tuition, but that's about it. I can't risk getting in trouble with you, even though I really, really want to kiss you right now."

"Me too."

Only instead of kissing me, Yates turns away and puts the sheet back over the painting. I feel the moment slipping away.

But the Fiona part of me takes over, and suddenly I feel a charge of confidence. I walk over and squeeze in the small space between him and the painting. I reach up and grab his face and pull it down to mine. I kiss him first, soft on his bottom lip.

And a second later, he kisses me back.

Twenty-Five

I lean across the car door and stare at myself in the side-view mirror. After you kiss someone, you're so much more conscious of your lips.

I can't wait to run up to my room and call Fiona. I would have called her from the train, but I just sat quietly and let it all wash over me.

As Mom pulls into our driveway, her car screeches to a stop. I look up. She can't park because Rick's truck is already there. He's standing on our front lawn with a shovel and a wheelbarrow, scooping dark wet dirt on top of a brown patch of dead grass.

"What are you doing?" I ask. Rick is probably the last person I want to see right now.

"I noticed this a few weeks ago and I thought I could help. It might be a soil issue, but I figured I'd try some of this heavy-duty fertilizer first."

"Well, stop." I fold my arms across my chest. "I like it the way it is." It's true. I love the imperfection. There's about a million shades of brown in that patch of dead grass. A million shades, right in my very own front lawn.

Rick opens his mouth to argue with me, but he thinks better of it, and jams the shovel into the pile. "Listen, Emily," he says, wiping his brow. "You have to talk to Meg."

"Why? I don't have anything to say to her."

"Look, I'm sorry about your sketchbook, okay? It was a stupid joke. But don't use that as an excuse to be mean to Meg."

I don't need an excuse. "Rick, you don't know anything about our friendship, so stay out of it."

"Maybe not. But I know Meg's needed you this summer and you've been nowhere to be found."

Please. The only thing Meg's needed me for is to pass the time in between her hangouts with Rick. "What could she need?" I ask. "She's got you, Rick. I honestly have no idea what you're complaining about. Isn't this your ideal situation? You've finally gotten rid of me! Congratulations!"

"Get over yourself, Emily. All I've tried to do is pick up your slack. But I'm not Meg's best friend. You are. So start acting like it."

"No, seriously. I'm sure Meg's had tons of big, emotional problems to deal with, like which bikini to wear when you came over swimming and what lie *about hanging out with me* to tell her mom so she can sleep over at *your* house. She's got it rough."

Rick steps up. All the kindness and dopiness washes off his face. He's pissed. "I know you think I'm some jerk who isn't good enough for your best friend. Well, I love her, okay? There's nothing I wouldn't do for that girl. I only want to see her happy. Which is more than I can say for you." He lifts the wheelbarrow and dumps

208

July

his whole pile of fertilizer on our lawn. Some falls over my feet.

Rick doesn't say another word. He just gets in his truck and roars out of my driveway. I stare across at Meg's house, wondering if she's watching from one of the windows. They all look dark, but in case she is, I smile like I don't care in the slightest and strut back up to my house, wet dirt squishing between my toes with every step.

Twenty-Six

hen I was a kid, I measured growth in lines on the pantry doorframe. Every couple of months, I'd press my back to the wall and let Mom rub a pencil across the top of my head. Then I'd step back and look at the white space.

The gap between two lines represented so much — old sneakers now too tight, the realization that I suddenly needed a bra, skinned red knees that healed to pink and then back to creamy white so fast I didn't even remember getting hurt. I used to think that if there was so much about me that could change in a millimeter's time, I might just grow straight up to the sky.

That's the first thing that comes to mind when my Mixed Media teachers explain our final project.

Hanna steps forward. "Your self-portrait should use the techniques we've been discussing — collage, painting, graphic design."

"Hopefully you've been amassing a nice image library to draw from." Charlotte holds up two fists full of paper snippings. "This piece can be as abstract or realistic as you want. Basically, anything goes."

July

"Just have fun with it," Hanna says. "And make it as *you* as possible."

It occurs to me that maybe my self-portrait shouldn't be about who I am now, but how I've figured out who it is I *don't* want to be anymore. Mr. Frank's lessons roll around my head. This must really be that personal perspective stuff he talked about when he first assigned us the sketchbooks. This project shouldn't be about staring at my face in the mirror, like some of the other kids in class are doing around me. It's about what I've lived.

Only it seems impossible to catalog how much you've changed or grown with a single picture. How do you track the history of transformation? How do you make sense of where you used to be?

Yates did it one way, covering things up with layers. But that's not how I want things to be. I can't avoid who I used to be. My past is fresh, just seconds behind me.

I've been collecting images in a large manila folder. I dump them all out on my worktable. There's the ticket stub and the backstage bracelet from the Romero show. The textbook heart I found.

I take a look at the salvaged scraps from my old room, stuff that I was sure was garbage but kept anyhow, because something inside told me to rescue it from the trash. Strips of rosebud wallpaper, a cut of fabric from my drapes, a slice of the red halter, shards of broken porcelain, an old Starbucks receipt. It's a complicated, colorful snakeskin of my path to this moment.

I weave all these things together in a silhouette. I cut out delicate images and sew them together with a needle and thread. I make a patchwork shape of myself. Then I draw my street on the middle of a fresh sheet of paper. It's funny, how a cul-de-sac doesn't actually lead anywhere. You walk straight down, like you're going somewhere, like you're on your way, but you could get lost forever in the loop at the end, rolling round and round.

When I lay the silhouette shape down on the paper, it's as flat as a paper doll. Dimensionless . . . but still interesting. I move the shape to its side. It looks like a shadow.

The shell no longer represents the mystery I'm supposed to be. It's the shell I'm leaving behind.

I work straight through lunch. I lose track of time, of blinking, of breathing. I lose track of myself in finding myself.

I make a reverse shadow, where the me is the thing that is empty, full of possibility. My shadow, the stuff I'm leaving behind, is a catalog of the old me. Only the shadow isn't stuck to me anymore. I draw my black shape lifting my foot just off the page, off the shadow, off the cul-de-sac. Really, finally stepping away.

My professors perch over my shoulders.

"This is so evocative, Emily."

"I love the texture."

"I feel the energy."

The rest of the class gathers around. Everyone compliments, congratulates. But it doesn't matter. I only care about one opinion.

My first instinct is to find Fiona and show her. She'd be so proud, to see how inspired I've been by her. To see the mark she's left on me. But Fiona's more into the big moment. So I decide I'll just let her see it, hanging with the student work, at the final show. It will solidify our friendship after this program is done. She's left her indelible mark on me.

It's for her. I'll call it *Thank You.*

Twenty-Seven

I spend most of Friday staring out my window at Meg's house. I plan on walking over to talk to her as soon as her parents leave. I want to get this over with now that I'm absolutely sure about things. It's not going to be a fun conversation, but Meg needs to hear what I have to say. It makes no sense for us to pretend that everything's fine, that we're still best friends. I'm tired of pretending. I feel like I've been doing it my whole life.

But as soon as her dad leaves for work and her mom leaves to run errands, before I barely have my foot out of my room, Rick's truck appears.

There's no way I want him to be around for our talk. He'll just make things more difficult. No. This is between me and Meg. So I wait for him to leave.

I kneel on the floor, fold my arms across my windowsill, and stare at Meg's house. After about an hour, I hear the vibration of the diving board echo through the air as Rick cannonballs into the water with a huge splash. I don't need to actually see the backyard to know it isn't Meg on that diving board. Meg hates the diving board, because on the first day it was installed, she slipped and fell.

"Okay, Maria." Mom pushes open the door of my room with her foot. "Just be careful in here. There might still be some broken ceramic on the floor. I don't want you to get cut."

Maria has the vacuum hose slung over her shoulders. Her mouth drops. "Emily!" she cries. "What happened to your beautiful room?"

"She's going through a phase," Mom reasons.

"It's not a phase," I snap back. Mom and I have avoided talking ever since Fiona slept over for this very reason.

Mom doesn't even acknowledge what I say. She just keeps talking to Maria as they disappear down the hall. "And all of Emily's clothes in the garbage bags downstairs are actually clean, so please be careful not to throw them out by mistake."

Another thirty minutes pass before Rick emerges from the stone path. As soon as he's gone, I sneak out the front door and walk over.

Meg lies on a lounge chair, reading a magazine.

"Hey," I say. "We need to talk."

"We've needed to talk for a whole week, Emily." She looks at my Meowie tank and then back to her magazine. "Thanks for finally fitting me in."

I'm a little startled at Meg's lack of fake cheeriness — I guess we're beyond that kind of pretending now. Still, I'm not going to let Meg intimidate me from saying what needs to be said.

"I needed time to cool down," I tell her. "You really upset me. It was like you were purposefully trying to embarrass me in front of Fiona."

July

"*You* were embarrassed?" Meg flaps her magazine closed. "How about you trying to avoid even saying hi to me? And the fact that Fiona obviously had no clue who I was?"

A car pulls into the driveway. It's Meg's mom, carrying a bunch of grocery bags.

"Emily!" she chirps out. "So nice to see you!"

"Hey, Mrs. Mundy."

"You girls having fun today?"

"Oh yeah," Meg says in a flat voice. She stands up and grabs her towel. "Loads."

"Listen," Meg whispers in my ear, "I can't talk to you here. My mom has been driving me crazy, acting all nosy about why you never come over anymore. I think she knows we've been fighting."

"She's probably been talking to my mom. Every day, she's on my case to call you or whatever. She thinks this is just a phase, but it's not."

Meg shrugs. "So, should we go to Starbucks? It feels weird to go there, knowing we're going to be fighting, but I can't think of anywhere else."

Starbucks would be a bad idea. I'm tired of going to Starbucks. "Actually . . . I was planning to go to Goodwill at some point today," I say. "You could come with me."

She makes a scrunched-up face. "For what?"

I ignore her face and readjust one of my bobby pins. "I need to get some new clothes and some furniture for my room." I'm tired of borrowing all of Fiona's clothes. I want my own. I'm going to need my own.

"Furniture? Why do you need new furniture?"

"I did some redecorating." My white Pottery Barn furniture isn't cutting it anymore. I want more color, more patterns. I want a mix-match of things, things that no one else will have. Actually, I'd love to show Meg my room. I think, more than anything else, it would get across the point that I'm trying to make. But Meg doesn't ask to come over and see it, and my mom's home anyhow, so I let it go.

Meg flips open her cell and pounds out a quick text. "Okay. Let's go." Then she snaps her cell closed and heads for the gate.

We walk through the natural fence and up over the hill. We pass right by the Starbucks. About a quarter mile down Route 38 is the Goodwill. It's a little tricky to get to by walking, because there's no sidewalk on the highway. Meg and I just sort of scurry along the side of the road from parking lot to parking lot, being careful to watch for passing cars whizzing by and the broken glass on the pavement. We can't talk. We walk in a straight line.

I've never been inside a Goodwill before, and it takes me by surprise. It's hot inside. Hot like no-air-conditioning-at-the-end-of-July hot. There aren't many other people shopping, and no one looks . . . cool.

I thought Goodwill would be like a hip department store, where I'd have my pick of interesting, retro stuff. But it isn't like that at all. It's sort of junky. There's no amazing find, like a leopard-skin armchair or a fuzzy green rug. It's just . . . trash. But I don't let on to Meg. I just grab myself a shopping cart and head toward the big overhead sign that says HOME FURNISHINGS.

"What are you looking for, exactly?" Meg asks, wrinkling her nose up at a set of ugly brown dishes.

"I'll know when I find it."

June

It ends up that Home Furnishings is a misleading categorization. It's not just furniture there. There's a bunch of random kids' toys and lawn ornaments and weird old televisions that couldn't possibly still work. And things aren't even separated into aisles. Everything's in big mounds you have to dig through. It's kind of gross.

Meg picks up a hunk of white plastic and walks it over to me. "Look! A Snoopy Sno-Cone maker! Do you remember when we decided to open up our own ice cream parlor next to the security guard booth? But it took an hour to grind up all the ice and everything melted before we could even sell one?"

This should inspire me into a happy memory. But I'm tired of reminiscing, now that my real life has begun.

Maybe it's the heat in here, or the stale smell, or the bright lights, but I just can't take it. "Do you remember when we used to have conversations that weren't trips down memory lane? When we had an *actual* friendship?"

Meg takes one last look at the Snoopy Sno-Cone maker before putting it down. "Are we not actually friends anymore? Is that what you're saying?"

"I just think we've grown apart," I say, and hold an ugly gold metal lamp up to my face because I don't have the courage to look at her.

"We haven't grown apart, Emily. You're forcing us apart."

That's absolutely not true. Meg just doesn't want to see the truth. "You can't deny that things have changed, Meg. I mean, I'm guilty of not talking about it, but you have to understand that I'm not even close to the person I was when summer started."

She sighs. "Emily, I really hate when you do that."

217

"Do what?"

"Act like you're so grown-up, just because you spend a few days a week in Philadelphia. It's ridiculous."

I shake my head. "You don't get it."

"Get how much you suddenly hate it here? You're right — I don't. This is our home, Emily. This is the place where we became friends. We grew up here, we've had so many good times here. Why are you trying to forget them?"

"That's not it, Meg. I'm just seeing this place different than you." I glance outside. There's more fast food architecture. "See that? See how that Wendy's looks just like a Taco Bell? Doesn't that make you sick?"

"That's not a Wendy's. The Wendy's is near the mall. That's a Burger King."

"Same difference. Whatever."

"No." Meg shakes her head. "It's not the same difference. And I would have thought an *artist* would pay attention to details like that."

I'm not going to be made fun of, especially by someone like Meg. "Listen, you've got Rick, so go ahead and do your thing at the Dairy Queen and watch those boring Babe Ruth baseball games and whatever. Because I've got a new boyfriend and a new best friend and she's cooler than you, anyway."

"Right. Because going out and doing graffiti is so cool and mature."

"Oh! You mean mature like you and your boyfriend drawing freaking cartoon penises in my sketchbook? Grow up, Meg."

"Are you kidding me? You think you're so grown-up because you draw penises? Well, I've actually touched a penis before,

July

Emily. I've had sex, actually. So I guess that makes me more mature than you."

"Congratulations," I say. And then the reality of what Meg just said hits me. I think of the hour she and Rick spent alone in the house today, and the way she was so flirty with him at the funnel cake shop. And the night she slept over at his house and used me as her cover.

She's lost her virginity to Rick.

She did it, and I didn't even know.

"You're not the only one who's growing up," Meg says. But unlike me, she doesn't sound proud or happy. She looks like she's going to cry.

An employee pushing a huge cart piled with old wedding dresses passes us in the aisle. "I can't believe you didn't tell me," I whisper. Maybe I should have expected it, but I didn't. A part of me wants to comfort her, but I feel so small. It's true — I'm not the only one who's changed. Meg has changed, maybe in a bigger way than I have. She's left me behind, too.

"I tried to tell you! In fact, that night that I wanted you to come to Rick's party, I was hoping you'd keep me from doing it. But you blew me off. Every single time I've said that I've needed you, you've blown me off."

I say "What?" even though I know exactly what Meg's talking about.

"And then, when I finally did try to talk to you, you'd start to brag about how much fun you were having in Philly. And you'd complain about how you don't think Rick's good enough for me." She's so angry, I can see her start to sweat in the corners of her forehead. "And stupid me didn't want to make you feel bad. You've been so weird since Rick and I started dating. Like I was breaking up with you or something. Well, I wasn't. I was just acting like the rest of the kids in Cherry Grove. But you couldn't catch up. You couldn't catch up even if — "

"Hello! I don't want to catch up to you." This is impossible. We're moving in two different directions. "I don't want anything close to your life, Meg. In fact, I wish I could fast-forward through senior year and just get the hell out of Cherry Grove."

Meg shakes her head. "You know what? You're right. We've both outgrown each other. So let's make a clean break of it."

"That's fine with me." And I realize: It *is* fine with me. It's over.

"Why wait until next year when we graduate? Why prolong the inevitable? Let's just say it's over and then we won't have to feel bad about ignoring each other anymore."

"Meg!" I say. "FINE! That's why I came over to your house in the first place!"

Meg nods once, like a genie who's just cast a spell. Then she turns and walks right out of Goodwill, leaving me in a sea of memories that have all been given up, given away.

Twenty-Eight

Yates sends me a text on Saturday.

meet up today?

It's a welcome invitation. I feel like Blossom Manor's become my prison, especially after my fight with Meg. I write back and say yes. Yates wants to know if I can get into the city by 2:00 p.m., but seeing as it's already 1:00 and I'm still in my pajamas, I don't think so. But if I hurry, I can be there by 2:45. He says that's fine. He'll meet me at my train platform.

I toss my phone onto my bed and run to the shower. My phone buzzes once more.

bring your sketchbook

I make the 2:15 p.m. train just on time. As it chugs past the parking lot, and then the back side of the mall, I feel myself relax, unwind. Everything with Yates has felt like a first — first flirtation, first hesitation, first realization, first kiss. Now it's another first — although I'm not entirely sure how far this first is going to go. It makes me equal parts nervous and giddy.

As promised, Yates is waiting for me on the platform. He looks adorable, in a red T-shirt and his ratty jeans and his old fluorescent Nike sneakers. He's brought a cup of coffee for me. Iced. Milk and sugar.

Instead of leading me to the street, he takes me down a flight of stairs to the subway.

"Where are we going?" I ask, high on this surprise.

He hands me a token. "You have your sketchbook, right?"

"Right."

"Okay," he says, and takes my hand in his. "Let's go."

The only hint Yates gives me is that the place we are going is one of his favorite places to draw, and that no one in the summer program will see us there.

I wonder if that means we'll kiss again.

Finally, it's our stop. Pattison.

We climb up to the street. City Hall is waaaay off in the distance. William Penn looks like a speck. When I turn around, I'm face-to-face with a big stadium.

"We're going to a baseball game?" I know I sound disappointed, but I can't help it.

"What? You don't like baseball?"

"You do?" I ask. I mean, how can the artsy boy who loves Romero be the same boy who wants to take me here? Unless he means it ironically?

"All boys like baseball." The earnestness in his voice conveys that there's no irony here.

July

"Not all boys," I say. "I bet Mr. Frank won't be here." Yates looks disappointed. I try to explain. "I'm not saying I don't like baseball. It's just that my best friend," and I pause for a second, because Meg and I aren't best friends anymore, but I'm not going to stop and correct myself now and look like a weirdo, "has a boyfriend who plays and she always drags me to his games."

Yates brightens. "So you've never been to a professional baseball game then?"

"No," I say. Is there a difference?

Apparently, there is. Yates takes off at a slow run toward the ticket window. "Come on! We've already missed the first three innings. And I'm dying for a hot dog!"

I shrug my shoulders and laugh. "Okay." And then I chase him as fast as my flip-flops will allow.

Yates buys us two seats up in the upper deck. I have to say, it's beautiful there. You can see everything — the green grass, the blue sky, all the people walking around the concourse. He gets me Cracker Jacks.

First thing I do is dig for the prize. I reach way down inside, and the caramel corn sticks to my hand. But I can't feel the little paper envelope anywhere. "Oh my God, this box has no prize!"

"Are you for real?" He takes it from me and shakes the popcorn around. "I've never heard of this happening before."

"Just my luck," I say.

"Here," he says, and gets out his sketchbook. "I'm going to draw you a prize."

I take out my sketchbook, too. Drawing is a great way to pass the time at a baseball game, which is full of slow and boring parts. We draw the people we see, the crushed peanut shells on our laps, the pennants waving in the breeze.

"Your sketches are so great," I say. They are all simple and sure. He doesn't put in too many details, but you get a perfect sense of what he's looking at from just a few lines. He makes it look effortless.

"So are yours," Yates says.

I still have the urge to cover my sketchbook whenever someone says something like that. "You've got to be kidding. All my drawings are so random. There's no consistency except for the suckiness." I flip through a few pages and cringe. "I'm having so much trouble with perspective," I tell him. "Do you have any more genius tricks you could teach me?"

"As a matter of fact, I do! You can actually use your thumb and forefinger like a protractor to measure angles and length. Here, let me see your hand." He grabs my hand and as he moves my fingers into an L shape, he accidentally touches my callus.

I pull my hand free. "I'm sorry. It's so gross."

"Are you kidding?" He holds his hand up and shows me an identical callus.

"Wow."

"And check this out." He twists his hands over. His fingerprints are all inky, black deep in the grooves of his already dark skin. "I seriously can't get them clean, no matter how hard I scrub. I think I'm permanently stained."

"Whoa."

July

He leans back in his seat, pleased. "This is just about the best date I've ever had."

We both pause at that. He's said it. Out loud.

"Really?"

He folds my hand in his and nods. "I just feel so comfortable with you, Emily. It's been hard for me to feel that way at college this year. I've barely made any friends."

"Are you kidding? You seemed to know everyone."

"But I can't be myself around those people. Art school is like a bubble, you know? There's only so much air inside a bubble until you can't breathe."

"I don't understand."

"There's this whole game going on, where everyone tries to be cooler or more artistic than everyone else. It isn't even about the work anymore. It's more about convincing people that you're a real artist."

I laugh and shake my head. "Come on."

"Seriously. I have to play the part to get the attention, to be able to make things that are important to me and have people notice them. I don't like it, but I do what I have to do."

"Like what?"

"Well, for instance . . . would you be surprised to know that Yates isn't even my real name?"

I nearly choke on a peanut. "Huh?"

"Swear to God." He pulls his license out of his wallet and hands it to me. "Would you want to buy art signed by this guy?"

I look down at the Rhode Island license. It's Yates's face, adorable as ever, but not his name. "Leonard Jones?"

He drops his head into his hands. "See what I mean? It's all about the image. Do you think anyone wants to buy a Leonard Jones original for their wall? Not at all."

"Yates is definitely a more interesting name," I say, patting his leg. "But your paintings are amazing. Isn't that what people ultimately see?"

"Yes and no."

"I don't know . . ."

"I mean, aren't you doing it, too? You've changed the way you dress, the way you carry yourself. And Fiona, too. She's all about the game, the persona. She lives for it."

"I guess."

"I have to say, Emily — the thing I like best is that I feel like I can be Leonard in front of you."

I raise my eyebrows. "Do you want me to call you Leonard?"

"No!" He laughs hard. "God no! Call me Yates. But remember who I really am underneath it all."

The crack of the bat echoes through the murmurs of the crowd and the whole stadium suddenly springs to life. Yates leaps to his feet to cheer and high-fives the two old men sitting next to us. I quickly draw him on a fresh page in my sketchbook.

I will remember. Always.

Twenty-Nine

O f course, the only time I'm late for Mr. Frank's class is the one that he starts right on time. I had burst through the door, expecting to see students hanging out and talking while Mr. Frank and Yates prepped the room. But the lights are dimmed and everyone is really quiet, focused on a nude male model seated on a platform of boxes. All eyes turn to me, even the model's.

"Sorry," I say, and rush to find a seat. Luckily, Fiona has her owl tote bag perched on the stool next to the one she's sitting on. An easel is set up nearby. It's reserved for me.

"Did you miss your train or something?" she whispers, and moves her stuff to the floor.

Fiona's got on a baggy black tank top that's way too big. Even though she's twisted and pinned the shoulder straps together into an X across her back to keep them from falling off, the armholes still scoop so low that her bare stomach, the waistband of her black leggings, and her tattoo show through the gaps in the fabric. Underneath the tank, she's wearing a magenta bandeau to cover her boobs and keep the outfit from being X-rated. I guess that's the problem with getting a tattoo on your ribs. It's sort of hard to show off, unless you're in a bikini.

"I was over at City Hall, finishing up my perspective assignment," I tell her, climbing onto my stool.

"Aww, you're such a good little student," Fiona teases. "I give you a triple A plus." She actually does, too. She leans forward, grabs my foot, and pulls it into her lap. Then, with black marker, she scribbles inside the white squares of my brand-new pair of checkerboard Vans, the pair I had insisted Mom buy me at the mall.

My mom will probably get mad at something like that, but whatever. When I was a kid, she'd get really insane about keeping my Keds as white as possible. She'll never understand that you're practically required to write on your Vans. It's, like, mandatory.

Yates circles the room and hands out some papers to the class. When he gets close to where I'm sitting, a smile breaks across his face. He hands a paper to me, and casually asks, "Hey, Emily. Did you have a nice weekend?"

"Yeah, it was pretty good," I answer, trying to camouflage the excitement in my voice. I tilt my head forward so that my blushing cheeks sink below the popped collar of my gray polo shirt. It used to be plain, but I customized it with some pink, white, and red embroidery floss from the craft store. Now there's a whole pattern of intersecting broken hearts stitched, exploding around the word ROMERO.

"Emily, your shirt rules!" Fiona says. "Make me one!"

I turn back to Yates, feeling a high from Fiona's compliment. "How about your weekend?"

July

"It was very nice. Thank you for asking." He rests his hand on my shoulder for the quickest second before walking away, but it still feels weighty and warm, exactly like the subway ride back from the baseball game, when Yates held on to me instead of the subway pole and everything in the world rushed past us at a billion miles an hour.

I catch Robyn watching from her stool on the other side of the room. She smiles at me, but I pretend not to see. I know she was around when all this stuff between Yates and me started, and maybe if it wasn't for her opening her mouth at the Romero show, none of this would have ever happened. But I still don't want word of it getting around. I can't trust her.

Fiona punches me in the arm. "I seriously want to stuff you and Yates inside a heart-shaped balloon and let you fly away together."

"Shhhh!" I lean over to cover Fiona's mouth with my hand. My stool tips over and crashes onto the ground, and I barely manage not to fall with it. We try really hard not to laugh.

Fiona and I had talked on the phone for a full hour after my date with Yates. It was so much better than talking to someone like Meg. Fiona didn't want just a plain old recap. Instead, she asked the best questions, the kind that let me relive the whole day over and over in the most beautiful detail. She wanted to know stuff that no one else would even think to pay attention to, like what Yates's hair smelled like (oranges), how tightly he held my hand (medium, fingers interlocked), if he chewed with his mouth open (eww, no!), or if his laugh was the kind that made me laugh, too, or made me be quiet because I wanted to concentrate on the sound (it depended).

229

But as excited as Fiona got over those kinds of details, she did think the larger picture was boring. According to Fiona, going to a baseball game was a lame date. I tried to explain that it was actually pretty fun and how we'd done a bunch of drawings of each other in our sketchbooks, but she wasn't convinced. In fact, she said that she expected better of Yates. So I decided not to tell her anything about Yates's *real* name or the stuff he said about the bad side of art school. Those felt like secrets only he and I should share.

Mr. Frank circles the room and says, "Yates is handing out anatomy charts so that you may continue your study of the human body. It would serve you well to memorize all the proper names of the bones, especially if you are planning on applying to this college. You need to know exactly what it is you are drawing."

Fiona crumples up the paper and throws it carelessly into her bag. "I'm going to art school, not *med* school. He's got to be kidding."

"What does it matter, so long as we can draw?" I whisper back, rolling my eyes. But I slide the paper into my bag carefully. Just in case.

"Emily! Fiona!" Mr. Frank calls out. "I would appreciate you not ruining our last class for the rest of the students."

I double-take from Fiona's equally shocked face back to Mr. Frank. "Wait. Don't we still have another week?" It's only the end of July, and the program goes one week into August.

"Yes, but your final class will be spent primarily cleaning up the classroom, emptying out your studio space, and prepping the gallery for the final show. This will be your last day of actual drawing."

All the happiness drains straight out of me. I can't believe this is my last drawing class. I rush to get my sketch pad and pencils out of my bag. The egg timer *tick, tick, tick*s the time away.

I draw as fast as I can for the rest of the model's pose, five dif-ferent sketches on my paper. I feel like I have to stock them up, since when this class is over, I don't know when I'll have the chance to draw a nude model again. And I'm a little nervous that I won't keep up with my drawing, knowing that Mr. Frank won't be check-ing it every week. I have a tendency to get lazy, and I really, really don't want that to happen. At least Fiona and Yates will keep me accountable and inspired. There's no way Fiona will let me slack off.

An hour later, the model gets dressed and leaves. Mr. Frank disassembles the platform and says, "So, let's share the perspective drawings you've been working on. Who would like to go first?"

Fiona's hand shoots up. I'm really excited to see her piece. I know she worked all weekend on it. She really wants to impress Mr. Frank, especially after her last crit.

Fiona walks up to the front of the class and flips her big note-book around. She's drawn a portrait of a sleeping woman curled up on a couch. The paintings on the wall, the weird old lamp with the fringe shade, the stack of art books — it's her apartment. And the woman must be her mother. She looks younger than I imagined.

"This is something I didn't expect to see from you," Mr. Frank says.

I agree. I've never seen Fiona draw something like this before.

"You said you didn't want shadows, so . . ." Fiona shifts her weight from side to side. I can tell she's nervous, but I hope no one else sees. I don't want her to crack in front of these people. Especially not Robyn.

"I definitely appreciate you trying something new. But I do think there's something about the perspective that looks off here. What does everyone else think?"

"The lamp looks a little too big and it throws the piece off balance," offers a girl named Gabriella from the front row.

Fiona looks at me and sighs, deep and painful. I smile back as best as I can. But the truth is, I think Gabriella's right. Fiona's drawn the lamp way too big in the foreground.

"Yes, and I'm not getting the sense of a room with any real angles. Do you see how the horizon rises as it heads to the left of the page?" Mr. Frank gets up and walks over to Fiona's drawing and points to the line that carves the wall from the floor. "I feel like we're undulating here. We're at sea. For this to be a successful portfolio piece, it would need some reworking."

I see what he means, though I really wish he wasn't using Fiona's piece to illustrate this lesson. Fiona's lines don't look as smooth and fluid as they do when she's sketching shadows. Instead, they are jagged and impatient. Like she was trying too hard.

Fiona shakes her head. "I told you so," she says, smug and under her breath.

"I'm sorry?" Mr. Frank cocks his head to the side.

"I told you shadows are my thing and whatever. So no wonder this sucks. This is exactly why I didn't want to do this kind of drawing in the first place." Her voice is loud. Her hands flop down at her sides.

I make fists and dig my fingernails into my palms. Fiona's not good at taking criticism, and Mr. Frank isn't exactly sensitive at dishing his out. It's a volatile combination.

July

"Fiona, perspective is something that all artists must master." He's trying to stay patient. "It takes lots of trial and error."

But Fiona's only getting madder. Her jaw locks up tight and makes her face red. "I . . . I shouldn't have compromised my artistic vision for you. I should have just done what I know I do well."

"There's no need to be so defensive, Fiona. And I didn't want you to give up shadows," Mr. Frank says. Disappointment hangs on his every word, and it makes his voice lower and more quiet than usual. "In fact, I was hoping that this perspective assignment would have sparked a way to solve the issues we were talking about last class. I assigned it just for you."

"Oh right. That's why every time I show one of my pieces, you make this big show of ripping it to shreds." Her voice is loud, self-righteous. She jabs her finger into the air, like she's throwing darts right at Mr. Frank's head. "You hate that I don't care about your stupid drawing exercises and assignments. I'm sorry, but I don't need to know which bone a femur is to be a good artist. I just need to make art and not listen to hacks like you."

"Fiona, I . . ." Mr. Frank is in shock. So is the rest of the room. No one is speaking. I don't even think anyone is breathing.

"Next! Go ahead! Next person!" Fiona says, walking back to her seat.

I make eye contact with Yates. He might be the most shocked of all. And sad. I can't bear to look at him. I feel terrible for Fiona. I want to apologize for her. She takes her work so seriously. She wants Mr. Frank's praise so badly. But I also feel embarrassed.

Mr. Frank shakes his head. He's still trying to compose himself. "Emily? Do you want to go next?"

SAME DIFFERENCE

I walk up to the front of the class, turn my paper around, and show my perspective drawing. And in a way, I'm glad it's unfinished, after what just went down.

"Why is this incomplete?"

"I didn't get it done in time."

"You've never turned in an incomplete project before. Were you working things out and ran out of time?"

Yates looks at me, and cocks his head to the side. I have pages and pages inside my sketchbook of false starts and attempts to get things right. It wasn't until Yates gave me that tip on perspective that things started to come together. But I don't want to show progress when Fiona's literally standing still. It's not worth it. "I just didn't get to it. Sorry."

Mr. Frank sighs. Everyone is letting him down. "For the love of God, someone *please* say something insightful."

"Nice line weight," one of the boys, Jim, offers.

The rest of the room stays quiet.

I return to my seat, so glad not to be singled out by Mr. Frank with a compliment. I try to say something to Fiona, but she won't look at me. She's too busy sketching. Mr. Frank and his shadow. It has devil horns and a long, long tail.

Mr. Frank gives us a break after the crit is over. Fiona storms out of the room and I chase after her into the bathroom. She leans against the sink and stares at the mirror.

"You were so badass in there," I say, trying to cheer her up. "You really told Mr. Frank off. I swear, I thought he was going to crap his pants."

July

Instead of smiling, Fiona drops her chin to her chest. "Don't talk, okay? Just stand here with me for a minute."

I nod, though I don't know if she sees. Then I rub my hand on her back gently for as long as she'll let me.

On our way back into the classroom, Jane and Gabriella stop me at the door.

Jane chews on her fingers while she talks. It's hard to make out what she's saying. "Hey, Emily. Do you want to come with us to go see the William Penn statue at lunch? There's this big observation deck under the statue and you can see the whole city from there."

Gabriella twirls her hair up and secures it with a pencil. "And it's free."

"Ummm . . ." I say, conscious of how quickly Fiona is stuffing her supplies inside her bag across the room. "I don't think I can make it today. But thanks for inviting me." I mean, it sounds like a cool thing to do, and I've been weirdly in love with that building since the first day I saw it. But it's not like I have to see it today or anything. Fiona needs me today.

The girls shrug and walk back to their seats.

"Don't be upset," I tell her.

"I'm not upset," Fiona spits out as she climbs back up on her stool. "I'm just glad this summer thing is almost over."

I reach for a new, sharp pencil in my art box, but all the points are dull. "Yeah," I say, even though I don't actually agree.

Thirty

I am standing in front of the Gates of Hell. Literally.

Our last field trip of the summer is to the Rodin Museum. Rodin did sculptures in bronze, and one of his most famous is called *The Gates of Hell*. It's a humongous piece, a set of doors that don't open, covered in hundreds of tiny people, gnarled and ensnared and desperate for escape. Agony. It's really an unsettling thing to look at.

And it just so happens that Fiona's mood fits in perfectly. She leans with her butt up against the marble pedestal of *The Thinker*, Rodin's other famous statue, and says, "You know this is a reproduction, right? It's not even the real thing. The real cast that Rodin made is in Paris. He pimped his students out to make hundreds of these knockoffs." Two German tourists want to take a picture of *The Thinker*, but Fiona is both impossible to crop out and oblivious to them.

I take her by the hand and drag her away.

"Seriously," she continues, raising her other hand up to point back at the statue, and then letting it fall back down like deadweight. "We might as well take a field trip to the poster shop on South Street to see Monet's *Water Lilies.*" She pulls out of my grip and walks away.

I let her, because I don't think I'm helping.

A hand taps my shoulder. I turn around and see it's Adrian. "Hey, Emily. Long time, no hang."

"Hey," I say back. I feel myself blushing. I've seen Adrian a few times around school and stuff, but never felt like it was okay for me to say hi. Sides were taken, and I wasn't on his.

Luckily, Adrian is really smiley and sweet. He quickly puts me at ease. "Can you believe the summer is almost over?" he says.

"I know." I sit on a bench and pat it. "How have things been going?"

"Busy. I started this new graphic novel." He pushes up his glasses and flips his hair out of his eyes. "It's pretty much done. The first chapter, anyhow. My class gets to make a bunch of photocopied versions of them to hand out at the big closing reception, which is cool." His face scrunches up like he has indigestion, and he checks who's standing around us. "Listen . . . is Fiona dating that guy from Romero?"

"Who?" It takes me a second to remember Fiona making out with the lead singer. I haven't heard her mention him since. "Oh no. I think that was just a one-night thing." I don't know if this answer makes things better or worse.

"Ah. Okay."

"Why?"

He flicks his hair out of his eyes. "No reason. I was just thinking about what you said, about having to make a big statement to get someone like Fiona's attention. So I made something for her.

237

But I'm going to wait and give it to her at the show. You know, for maximum dramatic effect."

"I know exactly what you mean," I say with a laugh. But then I wipe the smile off my face. "I . . . I'm sorry about everything that went down that night at the show. I was definitely hoping Fiona and you would, you know." And the truth is, even with Adrian planning some big play for Fiona's feelings, I still don't know if she'd reciprocate.

"Yeah. Me too."

Yates walks by, coughing to get my attention. I turn, surprised. We really don't talk much in public, but he flashes me a toothy smile and a big thumbs-up.

"What?" I whisper, because I have no idea what he's trying to say.

But there's no time to tell me, because Dr. Tobin claps her hands in the center of the courtyard. "Gather round, students."

We do. Yates drifts away from me and stands next to Mr. Frank.

"As you all know, this is the last week of regular classes for the summer program. Next week, you will help prepare the gallery for our closing reception, finish up your projects, and clean out your studio spaces. On that note, the faculty met this morning and discussed the outstanding work you have all completed. Each teacher was asked to present the best piece from his or her class, and then all teachers voted on the best five pieces from that selection of work. Again, please let it be known that this juried decision was a very difficult one."

Fiona appears by my side. She doesn't say hello to Adrian. "What's going on?"

July

"They're announcing the selections for the jury show."

"Oh." She bites her finger. I think she knows it's not going to happen with Mr. Frank. But Fiona thinks she really has a shot with her Performance Art class. I hope she gets picked. Especially when I see Yates wink at me.

Right then, my stomach drops.

"Emily Thompson, Mixed Media, for her collage entitled *Thank You*."

The first name. I am the first name called. And I am so scared, so nervous about what Fiona will say, that I can't even look at her. Everyone claps politely. I close my eyes.

Four more names are called. A boy from the Sculpture program. A girl from Jewelry. A boy from Adrian's Graphic Novel class who I remember him saying was amazing. Each one is followed by applause. I don't even pay attention to the final name, because it's not *Fiona Crawford*.

I muster the courage to look at her and immediately I wish I hadn't. She's got this confused look on her face. And then a second later it's gone.

Robyn finds me in the crowd. "Congratulations, Emily. It's very deserving."

Like she's even seen my piece.

I take Fiona by the hand and walk away. I don't even stop to say anything to Yates, who has a proud smile on his face.

We all board the buses. I know I have to say something to Fiona, but I have no idea what.

"Listen, I—"

Fiona shakes her head. "Emily, I am so over this place. Don't even worry. This whole jury show is ridiculous. I mean, what do they think they are? A real gallery? It's going to be a bunch of parents there. And all these teachers. On a real First Friday? It's pathetic."

I half believe her. But I figure out a way to make it better. So when the buses park in front of school, I force Fiona to come up to my studio space. "I want to show you my piece."

"I'll see it at the show."

"Come on, please?" I want to show her that what I made, what I've become, is all thanks to her.

"Emily, it's no big deal."

"Please?"

Fiona rolls her eyes, but manages a smile. "Okay, okay."

We step into my studio space. But my piece isn't here. "Oh. It might be in the Mixed Media room," I say.

Fiona lingers a bit at the door, looking at some of the other projects I've been working on.

I pull her hand.

The Mixed Media room door is closed and the lights are off. I step in and turn them on. There's my piece, hanging up on the pushpin wall. I put Fiona dead center.

She doesn't say anything.

"I call it *Thank You*," I tell her.

She snorts. Then she turns and looks at me. "Are you serious?"

I nod. "I made it for you."

Fiona starts laughing, like it's some kind of joke. And then she runs out of air. She turns red.

I feel an ache spread through my chest. "Don't you like it?"

"*J'adore!*" she says, her French accent unhindered by her sarcasm. "I particularly like your use of shadow." And then she turns around and walks out. The last word rings through my ears.

Oh shit.

"Fiona! Wait!"

I chase after her, but she's already gone.

Panic sets over me. She thinks I've copied her. I wander out of the school, not sure exactly where to go or what to say.

Yates sees me in the hallway. "What's wrong?"

"Fiona. She thinks I stole her shadow idea for my collage."

"Emily, don't worry about it. She'll come around."

I shake my head. "No, she won't."

"Yes, she will. She knows you're her friend, not to mention her biggest supporter."

I feel a little better. Fiona has to know that I'd never do something like that to her. Never, ever.

"I don't know why she's so possessive over this whole shadow thing anyhow." Yates goes on. "Artists are inspired by each other's work all the time. Everyone innovates off everyone else. And it's not like . . ."

Part of me wants to let his voice trail off, but I also want to defend Fiona, even if only to make myself feel better for what's happened. "Not like what?"

Yates puts up his hands. "Emily, I mean, you have to realize that Fiona isn't really that talented. I mean, I know she's your friend and all, but she's more attitude than execution."

"I don't understand." I really don't. Art is Fiona's entire persona. It's in her genes.

She's nothing without it.

Thirty-One

I don't see Fiona all of Thursday. It's on purpose. I'm hoping to let her cool off.

Yates and I have made plans to meet at his studio after class, so that's where I go. I knock on the closed door. Quietly at first, and then louder when no one answers. I press my ear to it and don't hear a sound on the other side.

I hear footsteps coming down the hall and whirl around. But it's not Yates. It's Dr. Tobin.

"Emily. Just the person I was looking for. Would you come back to my office, please?"

"Um, sure."

I walk with Dr. Tobin out of the art building and back toward the atrium. I'm afraid that I'm in trouble for something at first, but every time I look at Dr. Tobin, she's smiling at me, so maybe not. "Your collage was extraordinary," she says to me. "And Mr. Frank mentioned that you've amassed quite a few portfolio pieces. Have you given any thought about applying to our college this fall?"

July

"A little," I say.

"Well, if you do, I hope you'll let me know. I am very close to the Dean of Admissions, and he loves when I hand-deliver talent to his desk. We also offer a special scholarship to former summer program students. You would, of course, be a top candidate." She holds open her office door for me.

"Thank you," I say, and step inside.

The office is very, very modern. I sit down on a couch made of large fabric circles in primary colors, bolstered by thick metal rods. It looks uncomfortable, but it's actually quite nice. Each metal rod has its own spring, and the whole thing forms to my body.

"So, Emily, you must be wondering why I brought you here."

I don't have to wonder for long. As soon as Dr. Tobin closes the door to her office, I see Yates's portrait of me against the wall.

"I've gotten wind of a breach in the code of our Teaching Assistants. I'm just going to ask you straight out — have you been romantically involved with Yates?"

"What?" I bite the inside of my cheek. "No. Of course not."

Dr. Tobin stares me down. I shift uncomfortably in my seat.

"You obviously fraternized outside of class for something like this to be produced."

"Well," I say, choosing my words carefully. "I mean, Yates was my TA. And I did ask him a lot of questions about the classes and the college, and once he showed me his studio. My friend Fiona was there, too. You can see her at the edge of the photo."

"I need to know if anything inappropriate happened, because that would obviously jeopardize other students' experience here."

"No," I whisper, but I can tell Dr. Tobin doesn't believe me, with the way she stares at me over the tops of her square black frames, her fingertips laced together, all but the pointers, which rise straight up like a church steeple and *tap tap tap* like a metronome. "Who would say such a thing?"

It's a stupid question that I don't need the answer to, because I already know.

Thirty-Two

I run straight from Dr. Tobin's office to Fiona's Performance Art class, but she's not there. I check her studio, and she's not there, either. So I run to the train station and buy a ticket to Fish Town.

I feel so betrayed. I supported Fiona through everything. I was her biggest cheerleader. She should have believed that I didn't steal from her. I was inspired by her. And anyhow, her problem should have been with me. I don't understand why she had to bring Yates into it.

When I get to the platform, I see Fiona sitting on a bench, waiting. She's surrounded by all her shadow pieces and supplies. She's obviously cleaned out her studio already.

I storm up to her. Words fill my mouth, but before I can push them out, Fiona sneers. "Don't even start with me, Emily." There it is, that Big Sister voice. "I've got nothing to say to you."

Only I'm not the little sister anymore. I've grown up.

"Are you kidding me? I've got a lot to say to you! If you're still mad at me, fine. But why did you tell on Yates? He had nothing to do with it!"

"Didn't he, though? Don't you think it's strange that you, the girl who was obviously the worst in our class, gets picked for the final show? You honestly don't think Yates had anything to do with that?"

She's trying to rattle me. And it works. But I know I'm not the worst in class. I know that the compliments that my Mixed Media professors and Yates and Dr. Tobin gave me were all real. "It was a consensus by *all* the teachers. And who cares about the stupid final show?"

"I care!" she screams. "You knew that shadows were my thing — and you stole them! You can just go back to the suburbs and your perfect life, but this is all I have, okay? This is it!"

"What are you talking about, *perfect life*? You saw what my parents are like. You saw my best friend. I don't have anything in Cherry Grove."

Fiona's not moved at all. "That's right! First you were a carbon copy of your old buddy, Meg, and then you latch on to me and try to become me. I didn't know any better. I thought you were just some nobody loser from the suburbs who I felt bad for. I took you under my wing, gave you clothes, and turned you cool. And this is how you thank me? By taking over my life?"

"Stop trying to make me sound like a bad friend! I'm the only one who's been there for you! I've defended you so many times!"

"Oh yeah? To who? Robyn? You think I care what Robyn thinks of me?"

I second-guess myself fifty times in the matter of one single second. But I say it anyway, because I want to hurt Fiona. I want to hurt her the way she's hurt me. "Yeah, I do think you care.

246

July

I think you care that Robyn thinks you're a poseur. And she's not the only one. All you can do is draw shadows. And you do it because you don't have any real talent." As soon as I say the words, I want to contradict them. Because I do think Fiona has talent. I think she's afraid, afraid to go deep, afraid to fail for whatever reason, but I do believe in her.

Only I don't get a chance to say any of that. Because it's too late.

Fiona gasps for air. She starts to laugh, even though a few tears fall down her face. "You know what? Maybe I should thank you, Emily. In a way, you saved me. Now I know that this college fucking sucks and that I don't want anything to do with you or this place anymore. Maybe I'm the idiot for caring so much. If people like you, people who don't give a shit about art and about what it means to do this . . . if people like you are the ones that succeed, it's better that I just give up now."

A whistle sounds, and the roar of the train pulling into the station drowns my ears with noise. I know our conversation is over. She's going to get on that train and leave. I doubt I'll ever see her again.

But then Fiona does something unbelievable. As the train chugs forward, she scoops up all her shadow work, all her drawings, and even her sketchbook, into her arms. She walks over and throws everything down onto the tracks.

By now, she is full-on crying. Hysterical.

I stand there, my mouth wide open as the train clicks over the pile. Fiona climbs onto the train. A second later, the doors *ding* closed and it pulls forward. Every single car that passes by crunches the paper.

247

SAME DIFFERENCE

When the train pulls clear out of the station, I take the smallest steps up to the edge. I peer down and see a mangled pile of dirty confetti, of colored chalk ground into dust, of a sketchbook sawed to pieces.

It's no longer art. It's no longer anything.

Thirty-Three

I run up to the street and send Yates a text message.

where are you?

I wait as long as I can possibly stand for him to write back. It could be five minutes, it could be fifteen. It feels like forever. Then I send him another text.

please. i have to talk to you.

I stare at my phone, not even blinking, until it finally vibrates.

space invaded.

I step off the curb, throw up my arm, and hail a taxi. "Can you take me to ten twenty-six Arch Street? It's by the Convention Center."

The cab driver makes a funny face. "I can, but it's only three blocks away."

I guess I still don't know the layout of the city as well as I thought I did. I take off in the direction he points, and wish I was in shape like Claire. There's a sharp pain in my chest. It might not be from running, though. It might be guilt.

When I get to the gallery, I climb the stairs fast, stretching my legs to take them two and three at a time. I push open the door and the gallery looks so much different in the daylight. Smaller. Dirtier.

A boy sits at a junky wooden table, lit by the glow of his MacBook laptop.

"Is Yates here?"

"He's in the back."

I walk down a long hallway, leading away from the gallery and into the divisions of studio spaces. It looks like a weird hotel, where the doors are all personalized with paint and fabric and pictures. The last door is open. Yates is inside with another boy. They're unwrapping his canvases.

"Hi," I say, my bottom lip trembling. They both turn to look at me. I manage to bite down on it and keep from crying until the other boy exits. But once we're alone, I lose it. "Yates, I'm so sorry!" I blurt out. "I didn't tell them anything. They tried to make me admit it, but I wouldn't."

"It's okay, Emily," he says. His voice is tired and soft and somewhat comforting. But he doesn't come and hug me or anything.

I choke back my tears just enough to talk. "Are you kicked out of school?"

"I don't think so," he says. He touches my arm lightly. His fingertips are icy. "But I lost my internship with Mr. Frank. And my studio space. And my free housing next year, because they stripped me of my RA position."

July

I tip my head back and focus on the old paint chipping off the ceiling. I've messed everything up. "It's not your fault. I told them that."

"It doesn't matter. I shouldn't have kissed you. I knew that deep down, but I did it anyway."

Then I really start crying. Because Yates wouldn't have kissed me if I hadn't kissed him first.

He reaches out like he's going to pull me into a hug, but he stops short. "I don't mean to be paranoid or anything, Emily." He steps around me and walks over to the window. The dirt on the glass makes the sunlight look stale. "I don't think we can see each other anymore."

"Why? What does it matter now?"

"Things are complicated. I don't even have a place to stay and classes start in three weeks! I've got to try and find an apartment I can afford, which is pretty much impossible." He closes his eyes. It's all too much. "Everything's really messed up, Emily. Don't you understand?"

Helplessly, I say, "But we both have feelings for each other. I know we were breaking the rules, but it's not like we don't have something real between us. And I'm not even a student anymore."

Yates shakes his head. "I was known as the painter. Yates. I worked really hard to play the game and work my way up through the other students. Only now, the faculty is going to think of me as this . . . lecherous TA who hooked up with his student."

"But that's not how it is. You know it's not."

He looks at me over his shoulder, face tight. "It doesn't matter. People see what they want to see." He motions toward a canvas,

251

wrapped up in plastic and leaning against a big trash bin and some collapsed cardboard boxes. It's far away from the rest of the carefully arranged pieces. I can see my painted face blurry through the clear plastic layers, like I'm being suffocated right before my very own eyes. "I probably should have left this in Dr. Tobin's office." His arm drops to his side. "I can't show this to Mr. Frank. It's tainted. It's worthless now."

"Who cares what anyone thinks?" I ask quietly. "You said yourself that it's all a game, everyone playing pretend."

"You don't get it. The painting, and what everyone thinks of it, *is* the important thing. It's bigger than who I am. I want to be an artist. I want people to take me seriously. That's what I care about."

I can tell Yates is getting annoyed with me because I'm not just agreeing with him. I do feel terrible about everything that's happened to him, so terrible it makes it hard to stand up straight, but I don't feel like this is even Yates talking. At least, not the Yates who was with me at the baseball game, the guy who was so many layers all wrapped into one.

"I guess I don't get it," I say, shuffling backward toward the door. "I thought you wanted to show me your true self, but here you are, going back to the role. That's not you."

He doesn't say anything, though. He turns back to the window, leaving me no other choice but to walk down the hall. He's sorry — I sense how sorry he is. But he's not going to say it.

I move slowly at first, giving him a chance to come after me, to prove me wrong.

He doesn't.

Then, I run.

Thirty-Four

I sit on the floor of my room. The crickets hiding in the lawn sound more like nails on a chalkboard than a summertime lullaby. I stare at my new and improved room. I appreciate the way it looks . . . but I'm not feeling it.

All I feel is absence. You can decorate absence however you want — but you're still going to feel what's missing.

I want to believe in art. But art isn't a boyfriend who can hold you and make you feel better. Art isn't a best friend who'll always be there for you.

I turn off the lights. I sit in the dark. The art disappears.

This is what I'm left with:

My thoughts.

My doubts.

My absences.

What have I done?

I tell myself that Meg and I were destined to outgrow each other. It's just what happens to friendships where the common denominator is the cul-de-sac you both live on. I try to believe this. I try to believe we were meant to grow apart.

I felt suffocated.

We both felt suffocated.

Now it's over and I'm still finding it hard to breathe.

I wish things could have ended better. I wish I'd let myself stretch and bloom in my own light. I wish I hadn't gotten scared. I wish I hadn't stepped into someone else's shadow.

If only I had let myself be more open. If only I'd made a big group of friends. If only I'd looked for chances instead of changes.

Maybe I could have really become myself.

Now I have nothing. Nothing but the drawings on my walls and a portrait of a me, a me who only has a shadow.

They're not enough.

They'll never be enough.

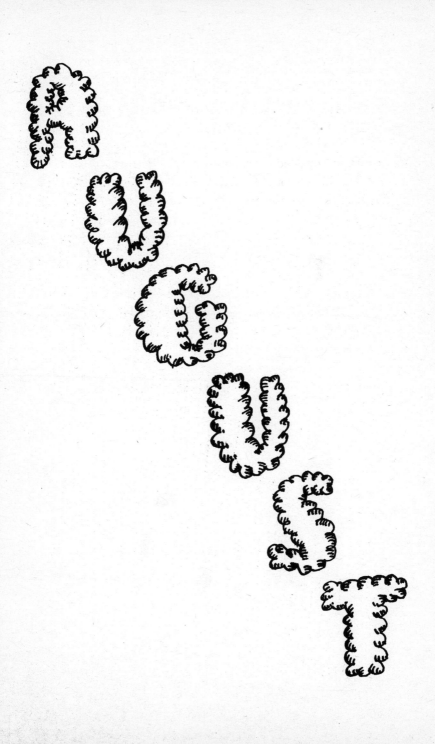

Thirty-Five

Instead of normal class on Tuesday, all of the summer students meet down in the gallery to prepare it for Friday's art show.

Fiona doesn't appear.

I'm not surprised.

We're all given jobs and tasks, like spackling the holes in the wall from the last show, touching up the white paint where it's dirty or scuffed, sweeping the floor, adjusting the spotlights. Robyn and I go down the lists of students and put strips of masking tape up on the walls where their pieces will hang.

"I honestly can't believe Fiona ratted out you and Yates," Robyn says.

I tap my pencil against the clipboard, afraid to look up at the eyes that might be trained on me. "Does everyone know?" For some reason, I didn't think gossip would work in the same way here that it does in Cherry Grove.

Robyn looks around the room. "Umm, yeah. Pretty much. I mean, Yates isn't here. And Mr. Frank has been snippy with you all day."

She's right. I asked him a simple question about where our class would be showing our pieces, and he almost bit my head off. I wish I could tell him that it's not my fault, but I know that's not true. It's Yates's fault, and definitely Fiona's, but I'm not innocent, either. I knew what I was risking when Yates and I kissed. All I was thinking about was what I was going to get. I didn't think once about what I might lose.

I reach FIONA CRAWFORD on the list. Robyn must figure it out from the look on my face, because she writes the name down on a big strip of masking tape, even though I don't say it out loud.

"Do you think she'll show?" she asks me as she presses the tape against the wall. "She might. Like, storm in all dramatic and turn this place on its head? I can see her doing that."

I don't say anything. Maybe because a part of me hopes that she *will* show up. It still kills me to think that Fiona might give up her art forever. Even though I'm mad at her, furious even, I don't want that to happen.

Adrian comes over. "Hey," he says. "Sorry about what happened."

"Geez," I say, annoyed. Everyone *does* know. And then I notice the huge box in his arms. "Hey! Is that your graphic novel?"

"Yep." Adrian grins. He opens up the box and hands me a full-color copy. It's got a funny cartoon boy on the cover, with two thick black swirls across his upper lip. It reads MR. MUSTACHE FALLS IN LOVE.

"Oh my God!"

"I know. I thought about what you said. About making a big statement. I know she's done some bad stuff to you, and she's definitely hurt me, but you have to admit . . . hanging out with her was pretty amazing."

"Yeah, it was," I concede. "But Fiona only kept me around because I made her feel good about herself. I was her ego boost."

Adrian considers this. "She was yours, too, though . . . right?"

"I guess." I mean, I did have loads of fun being with Fiona. She made me feel bigger. "But that doesn't erase what she did. It's obvious that Fiona wasn't as strong as we all thought she was."

"There are definitely some deep insecurities there. I mean, everyone has insecurities. But we have to work to get over them." He sighs. "I guess this is mine. To really admit to her how I feel. And not to care what anyone says about it."

"That is brave," I say. "Really." We both wear sad smiles, because we know that, with Adrian going back to Kansas, there's really no chance for this love story to have a happy ending. But for Adrian, that's not what it's about. It's about him making something with the feelings he has.

"Only thing is, I'm afraid she won't come on Friday night. You've been to her house, right? Could you get this to her somehow?"

I really don't see myself being in touch with Fiona ever again. But I want to do this for Adrian. To give him closure. "Yeah," I say. In my sketchbook, I have the directions to Fiona's apartment. I could put Adrian's graphic novel in the mail. "Sure."

Something over my shoulder grabs his attention. "Umm," he says quickly. "I'll talk to you later."

I turn and see Mr. Frank walking straight for me.

I look for an escape, but I'm surrounded by a crowd, by other students who are quickly becoming aware of this impending show-down. I try to look brave.

I don't come anywhere close.

"Emily, can I speak to you for a minute?"

"Sure."

He walks past me and I follow, out into the hallway.

"I want to talk to you about something that happened in class the other day."

"Okay."

"When you showed your perspective drawing in class that day, I knew you had been lying about your progress. I know you did that drawing fifteen times. I saw you getting better with each assignment."

"Oh."

"Emily, you must never stifle your own potential to make concessions for those who don't have your gifts. Hiding will never give you the perspective you need. You can't help the fact that you are who you are, just like Fiona can't help who she is."

Lesson already learned. But what good will it do me?

He continues. "If there's one thing I've discovered, it's that stifling yourself will only lead to more misery. For a time, I tried not to make art. I felt undeserving. But my life was miserable. I polluted all other happiness because I was afraid to let myself create and change. You have to have courage. Real courage to explore, to fail, and to pick yourself back up again."

He stares at me, trying to gauge how much of his wisdom is penetrating. I wish it was more than it is.

I still feel undeserving. Maybe I always will.

Maybe I just have to learn to accept that.

Thirty-Six

I'm sad when it's time for lunch. Sad, but not lonely, because I don't really want to be around other people. So I don't go eat lunch with Adrian and Robyn when they ask.

But unlike when I used to take lunches by myself, now I'm not afraid to walk or wander. So that's just what I do, opting for the narrowest cobblestone side streets and alleyways, where houses sit but cars don't drive. I find peace and quiet in these secret little avenues. I like the way the uneven stones feel under my flip-flops, crooked and unsure, but also like a massage. I've worn my Havaianas so much now, they are molded to my feet. They know their place on me. They're sure of where they sit.

I walk east until I hit the river. Then I follow the bike path along the water, watching ducks swim by and cars drive by, where the city mashes into the country. It's like neither side wanted to give up, so they just called a truce.

I'm ready to call a truce.

And then I come upon the Philadelphia Museum of Art. It's not the grand, dramatic staircase at the front of the building.

Instead, I've stumbled upon the much less majestic parking lot. It's half full. There are Dumpsters there. And trash on the ground. It's much more . . . approachable. So I approach. With caution, but also something else.

I think it might be excitement.

My pace changes, from meandering to purposeful. Even though my steps are quick and rushed, I still take the time to see what's on the walls, what colors jump at my eyes, the curves of carved stone, the undulations of a gilded frame that rivals the artwork it showcases.

I go back to Duchamp. To *The Waterfall*.

There are a few people inside the gallery. I stand next to the opening, not quite inside, as two old ladies rush through, lean forward, and gasp.

Their reaction momentarily breaks my courage, but it is only a hiccup because then they walk past me, shaking their heads and smiling.

Something good to be seen.

When I am in the room, the fear comes over me again, but this time it feels more euphoric than scary. Because with the worry of what is there, I realize I need to be brave enough to go and look for myself, to face the fears and not to run.

Six weeks ago, I was so scared. I'm still a bit that way, but now I'm more excited to see what's underneath when I strip everything else away. When it's just me.

I take slow, measured steps toward the dark wooden door. I press my face against the holes. This is one of the only pieces in the museum you can touch. I am touching art.

August

Fiona's voice rings in my ears. Duchamp didn't tell anyone about this work. He built it in secret, while everyone else thought he was retired. He didn't care what people thought of him, what they were going to say about his work.

I used to think that was why Fiona liked Duchamp so much. He was her badass equal.

Only, when I peek through the door, I see Duchamp *did* care. He cared so much that he took great pains to preserve this experience, to give it to people like me.

I stand there and stare through the door for what feels like forever. And then I leave, changed.

Fiona definitely got me to this moment. She opened my world up, for the better. And maybe the things that I thought were in her, the things I so desperately admired, are really in me.

But they can be in her, too. They must be, because she got me here. Instead of following her lead, I see now that we were on a journey together. Fiona helped me get to this point. I can't abandon her now, when she needs me the most and doesn't know how to ask for help.

Just as in your sketchbook, you never throw out a drawing. You have to learn from mistakes. I ruined things with Meg, deserted her when she needed me most. I have no idea how to fix things, or if they are even fixable at all. It's probably too late for that. But one thing I do know: I am not about to make the same mistake twice.

Thirty-SeveN

Instead of taking a cab from the museum, I follow her directions. Two buses and one train. It takes me almost an hour, but it isn't complicated. I enjoy the ride.

I get to her apartment and look up to her window, but I can't tell if anyone's inside. I go to the front door and check out the buzzers. Unfortunately, none of them are marked with names, and I don't remember Fiona's apartment number.

"Can I help you?" a woman says from behind me. She's struggling to carry three huge bags of pet food.

"Maybe," I say. "I don't remember my friend's apartment number. Her name is Fiona Crawford."

The woman gasps and drops a bag on the ground. It spills and a few tiny brown pellets fall on the sidewalk. "You must be Emily!" she says and sweeps me into a big hug.

When she pulls away, I recognize her from Fiona's perspective drawing. Fiona's mom has a few wrinkles around her eyes but she still looks kind of young. Maybe because her short, choppy hair is split into pigtails. It's sort of funky hair and jewelry for the outfit she's wearing — a bright blue polo shirt and khaki pants. On the pocket of her shirt, just above her chest, is a small cartoon of a googly-eyed pooch and bubble letters spelling PETSMART.

I guess I make a face, because Fiona's mom blushes. "I know. Isn't this the lamest thing ever? I hate these uniforms. But you have to pay the bills somehow."

"Yeah," I say and smile. But I'm totally confused.

Fiona's mom struggles to pick up the bag she's dropped. "I don't think Fiona's home, unfortunately. But would you mind helping me bring this upstairs? I can't manage on my own, not without a birdseed trail."

I take a bag into my arms.

"Did Fiona go to class today?" Ms. Crawford asks.

I don't know what to say. "I'm not sure. I didn't go."

"Oh." She shakes her head and fumbles for her keys. "She was pretty upset all weekend long, but of course she wouldn't tell me what was wrong. You know how defensive Fiona gets."

I carry the stuff into the living room. And because there's all this awkward silence, I say, "I love your paintings," gesturing to the ones on the wall.

"Oh, those? God, they are so embarrassing. Fiona found those under my bed and insisted we hang them down here. She's always trying to get me inspired to work again. It's sweet, but I haven't painted in so long."

"Really?"

"I know — it's terrible. I wish I was as passionate as Fiona. She has the drive to make something of herself. She always says I'm too good to be working at PetSmart. Maybe she's right, I don't know. At any rate, I should have had a better backup plan for us, to get our bills paid. Fiona always says she's going to be famous someday, and then I'll never have to struggle again."

I swallow, because I don't really know what to say. "Can I just leave her a note upstairs?"

"Sure."

I walk up to Fiona's room. It feels like trespassing. I stand in front of that Andy Warhol poster and think about the altered quote, and why Fiona wants so badly to be famous. Maybe it's to save her mom. Or maybe she thinks that if she's not good enough, she'll have nothing but PetSmart.

But she doesn't have to be afraid, to rely on her old tricks. Fiona has what it takes. I know she does. She just has to keep moving forward.

I leave Adrian's comic on her bed. And I write her a note on a scrap of my old wallpaper.

I write on it that I looked through the door.

I write that I get it.

I write that I get her, too.

Thirty-Eight

Mom comes in my room without knocking. It's early, so she opens the door slow and smooth, careful not to cause any dream-shattering squeaks from the hinges. She cranes her neck around the door and looks around my room, equally cautious, as if some booby trap might be sprung and her head sliced off by a DIY guillotine. Her eyes settle on me — sitting up in bed, arms folded, staring her down.

"Oh! Emily!" She puts a hand to her chest. "I thought you'd be sleeping."

"Nope." The truth is, I haven't slept all night. Nerves, fear, and anxiety kept me spinning. As tired as I was, I couldn't relax thinking about what might happen tonight. I'd try to shut my eyes, but they'd spring back open, like two like magnets pressed together.

"Well, good. I've got a surprise for you. I've made us all appointments at the salon, so we can get our hair and nails done. Why don't you go ahead and get dressed and we can stop at the Starbucks on our way over and grab some croissants."

I pull the covers up to my chin. "Why would you do that?"

"I thought you'd want to look extrafancy for your big gallery show. You know, have your hair curled or blown out. Maybe we could get it done half up." She reaches out to touch me.

I lean back as far as my feathered pillows will let me. "It's not prom, Mom. And I'm tired of letting you stand behind the chair and tell the stylist how my hair should look. It's my hair and I'll do what I want with it."

"I thought you liked my help! We always have fun looking through the magazines together." I shake my head and her wide, toothy smile falls. "Fine. Then get your split ends trimmed and choose clear nail polish. But you are coming with us." Mom takes a deep breath to calm herself down. "Do you know if we're driving Meg with us tonight, or if her boyfriend will be taking her to the gallery show?"

"Meg's not coming."

"What?"

"I never told her about the show. And anyhow, we're not even friends anymore." I say the last part like I don't care, because I want my mom to be upset.

Mom scratches along her hairline with a polished fingernail. "I don't understand. You and Meg have been inseparable for years. And you're just going to throw that away? Just because you made a new friend in Philadelphia?"

"It's not just me throwing it away, Mom. But thanks for assuming it's all my fault. You don't know anything about my life, so I wish you'd just stay out of it."

Mom lets loose a laugh. "How can I stay out of it when you won't let me in? You barely even talk to me anymore."

August

"Of course I don't. It's obvious that you don't like the way I've been changing, Mom. But just so you know, this isn't some phase. I'm not going to go back to the girl I was. I know you don't want to accept it, but I have. And I'm sorry Meg and I aren't so close anymore. But it happens, okay? It happens all the time. Friends stop being friends. It's no big deal."

"Okay. Okay. I'll admit, it has been hard for me to understand you, Emily. When I look at you, I see a stranger." Her voice is tight, and the words pop from her lips like jabs. "And not only because you've changed your room or your clothes, but because you're no longer acting like my daughter, or acting like Claire's big sister."

"What does Claire have to do with it?"

Mom looks at me like I'm crazy. "Do you really have zero idea how nervous she is about high school?"

"Please." I roll my eyes. I may have let down Meg, but what could be wrong with Claire? "Claire's going to be fine. She's got the perfect role model right next door."

"Claire doesn't want to be like Meg," Mom says. "She's begging me to take her out and buy her a pair of those chessboard sneakers. She wants to be like you, Emily. Have you seen her soccer ball?"

"What?"

Instead of answering my question, Mom stands up. "I know you think you're so different, Emily. But Claire is more like you than you realize." Her eyes water and it takes me by surprise. "Both my girls have been blessed with all the beauty, potential, and talent in the world, and yet both of you have some kind of gap in your brains that keeps you from ever truly realizing how special you

269

are. Anyhow, you should take a look sometime, when you're not so consumed with yourself."

I get up out of bed and walk across the hall and into Claire's room without knocking.

"Hey!" she says from her bed. She's watching Nickelodeon. In her pajamas and her big yellow comforter, with her hair all dented and matted, she looks like a little kid.

I step around the trophies and the piles of toys and clothes until I see her soccer ball. In every single panel, she's drawn something. Some are just basic stuff — like a star, or her name. But she's also drawn a really nice soccer player. I mean, it's a little cartoonish, but the proportions are all there.

"Claire!"

"What?"

"This is so good."

She sits up. "Really?"

"Really." I throw it at her. It goes way over her head, higher than I plan it to, but Claire has no problem catching it.

"Come on. Get dressed. Mom's taking us to the salon."

"Updos!" my mom calls from behind us.

"Noooo," Claire says. "I hate getting my hair done."

"I'm not getting an updo," I say, and duck my head down so I can see my reflection in her vanity. "But I do think it's time for a change."

Thirty-Nine

I don't stay long in the front gallery, where my piece hangs with blue ribbon distinction in its very own spotlight in the window. Instead I stand in the very back of the room and center myself where Fiona's piece should be hanging. People shuffle easily around me, like I'm a piece of sculpture. I fill the gap between a comic-book panel bursting with steroidal superheroes and a cracked water pitcher still life done in oils that still smells of turpentine.

"Hey, Emily." Robyn saunters over. Her parents stand right behind her — two sharp-looking older people, slightly androgynous, slightly bored.

"You leaving?" I ask. This night has been full of good-byes, of friends hugging and exchanging numbers and tears. Mostly I've watched from across the room.

"Yeah." She pauses, and an awkward, embarrassed look comes over her face.

I think Robyn and I both know that we are on different paths. I'm still not sure about art school next year, and Robyn isn't planning to go to college. Sure, I've had some okay memories that I'll keep of Robyn. She's played a small part in who I've become. But there's not really anything else to hold on to. So I let go.

We hug. Briefly.

"Look me up if you're ever in New York."

"Same for you, if you're in Cherry Grove," I say with a grin.

I spot my parents near the refreshment table. Mom looks gorgeous in a tangerine dress, and Dad looks dapper in his suit. They've taken about a million pictures of me tonight, which is sweet. They were really impressed, and there's been this look across both their faces like they are suddenly starting to get me. I guess tonight was a way for me to let them back in. Their weird kid suddenly makes sense. Aha.

Claire especially. I've been following her with my eyes, her and her new stripes of white-blond highlights, the tamer version of my new hair color. She's literally running around the room, taking everything in with a huge smile on her face. It makes me feel warm inside.

But I feel disappointment, too, heavy inside my stomach. I really hoped that Fiona would have shown up. Especially after my note and Adrian's comic. Maybe she didn't even see it, in her mess of a room. Or maybe she did, and she just doesn't care. Maybe there's no bringing her back. Still, I keep watching the entrance, and the people who lazily meander through the doors looking for air-conditioned escape from the steamy pavement outside the glass. I keep waiting for her big show to start.

Adrian does, too. He started tonight with a big, expectant smile. I've watched it wane like the moon into the smallest sliver as the night's gone on. His hope has been all but eclipsed by the reality that she's not coming.

There's a tap on my shoulder.

I spin around, expecting Fiona. But Meg is the person I actually see, standing in front of me in a pair of white linen trouser pants, silver sandals, and an emerald-green silk tank.

"Hi!" The word falls out of my mouth.

She takes me in with squinty, suspicious eyes. "I wouldn't have recognized you if Claire hadn't tipped me off," she says. She gently takes a lock of my newly white-blond hair into her fingers and rubs them together. "You look amazing."

"Thanks," I say. "You know, I always wished my hair was this color. I don't know what was stopping me." I push my bangs off my face, still surprised by their existence. Aside from the dye job and bangs, I also got about three inches cut off, so that the piecey ends barely graze my shoulders. Everyone at the salon was freaking out over me and Claire, side by side in the chairs. I think Mom was nervous at first, letting us call the shots, but as the stylists *ooh*ed and *aah*ed over us, she relaxed. There were practically fights between them as to who'd get to do our hair. And when I finally saw myself in the mirror, it really did look like the me I've always wanted to be.

"So . . . your mom called my mom and told her about the art show."

I look across the room. My mom waves and pops a cheese cube in her mouth. "I told her not to do that," I say. But I smile. Because I'm glad she did.

"It didn't have to be this big conspiracy." Meg shrugs her shoulders. "I was hurt you didn't invite me yourself, but I wanted to be here for you anyway."

I feel like such a jerk. I haven't even thought much about Meg since our fight. And here she is, to support me.

"Is Rick with you?"

"No. I left him at home."

"Are things . . . okay with you guys?"

"Things are fine. I told him not to come because tonight is about you. I think it'll be better for us that I do some things separate from him. But . . . I do love him, Emily. I know you don't think he's good enough, but he's a great guy. And yeah, I was scared and all that to" — she looks over her shoulders to make sure my parents aren't nearby — "*you know*, and it would have helped to talk to you about it. Honestly, I still don't know if I made the right decision. Even though you weren't there for me then, I need you to support me now."

I think about how brave it was for Rick to call me on what I was doing that day on my front lawn. How upset he was over the fact that Meg was hurting, and how I wasn't helping. "I was jealous of him, Meg. I'm sorry. He is a great guy. And he loves you like crazy."

Meg smiles.

"What about your new boyfriend? Is he here?"

I drop my head back and stare at the ceiling. "No."

"I'm sorry."

She touches my hair again. "You look so different."

"No, I don't. I still look like me."

She smiles. "I guess you're right."

"I feel like we've both been afraid to deal with how things have changed. And they *have* changed. But that's what happens in life, right? And we just have to roll with it."

August

I get it — friendships take work. They just do. And by Meg showing up for me tonight, she's proven to me that she's willing to give things a shot if I will. That she really does care about me, whoever I've become, like a true best friend.

"Exactly," Meg says with a decisive nod. She loops her arm through mine. "So, where is your piece?"

"It's up here." I walk her over to the front gallery. We both stare up at my self-portrait.

"It's beautiful," Meg says, her voice quivering. She gives me a tender squeeze.

I feel a surge of pride run through me, for the piece, for me, for Meg, for everything. "Thank you."

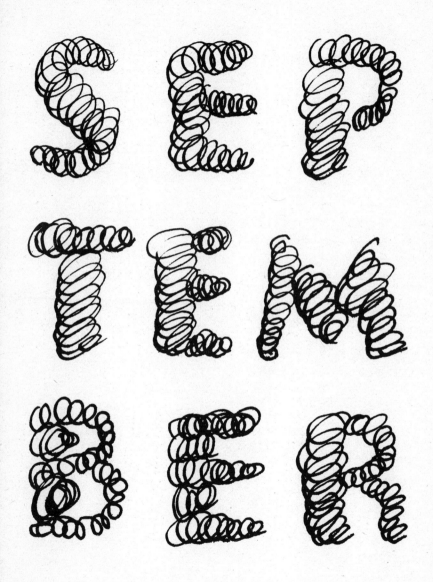

Forty

Meg beeps three times. Her new convertible's horn is cheery and tart and all too perfect.

"Let's go, Claire!" I call out as I shove my books inside my bag, gather a few bobby pins from my dresser, and tuck my makeup bag under my arm. Even though school started two weeks ago, I'm still not used to getting up early. I'm not even really awake until third period.

The front door opens and closes. I lean out my window. Claire sprints down the front walk toward Meg's car on her tiptoes, soccer bag slung over one arm, book bag over the other. She climbs in the back. Shotgun is left vacant for me.

Claire's so happy to ride to school with us, instead of having Mom drive her. It's sweet. She even offers to give Meg money for gas, which of course Meg refuses. But I sort of get how even a ride to school can feel like an anchor sometimes. Like, no matter how many people talk to you in a day, or don't talk to you, you still have a ride.

279

I step outside and the chilly air tightens the skin on my bare arms. Summer has ended all too quickly, and some of the leaves on the trees have already started to burn with the colors of fall. Fall colors are funny. They're so bright and intense and beautiful. It's like nature is trying to fill you up with color, to saturate you so you can stockpile it before winter turns everything muted and dreary.

"This stinks," Meg says. She drops her head back against the leather headrest and stares up at the black cloth roof. "I've had my convertible for two whole weeks now, and there hasn't been one day nice enough to have the top down!"

"At least you have your license," I remind her. "I've still got another three weeks to wait. Anyhow, I don't think I'm getting a car. So it's not like it even matters." I'm not complaining or anything. It's fine if I don't.

"What? You are so getting a car," Claire says. "I heard Mom and Dad talking about it."

I spin around in my seat. "Really?"

"Mmm-hmm. And, I probably shouldn't be telling you this, but they're talking to some guy who deals with classic cars. I think they're trying to get you something *cool.*"

I feel my insides light up. I'm totally surprised that my parents have thought about this, and that they'd be cool letting me drive something that wasn't brand-new and safe and with a million air-bags. It would be awesome to have a classic car, like an old VW Bug or some weird little import in a funny shape and color. Whenever you see cars like that on the road, you feel happy. People point and smile. They stick out in a good way.

September

I can't wait to tell —

I turn back around and sigh. This exciting development is diluted with the reminder that Fiona's not really in my life anymore. She'd probably flip, over a car like that. I wonder when this empty feeling will go away, if ever. The instant reflex kind of thing that happens whenever I see something cool. Something inspiring. And I think about her. I always think about her.

"Your mom really seems to have come around," Meg says.

"Pretty much," I say and smile. I flip down the visor. The white blond has softened over the last few weeks and my roots have started to grow back in, but I actually think the contrast makes it look better. Soon I'll have to make a decision to dye it platinum again, or try something new. I'm still not sure.

Meg pulls into an empty parking space next to Rick's truck — it's new, it's huge, and it's very shiny. Rick steps out in a navy fleece pullover and pulls Meg into a bear hug.

"Hey, Emily," he says over her shoulder.

I say hi back. A twinkle catches my attention — for her birthday, Rick bought Meg a thin gold ring that loops into a tiny heart. Even though it's on her right hand right now, sometimes I catch Meg wearing it on her left. It looks suspiciously to me like a promise ring, but Meg insists it's only a *ring* ring.

Meg's mentioned a few times how nervous Rick is for this year, and how he can be cheering her on about her SAT study prep one second and then act weird about her going away to Trenton State the next. Meg's not sure what's going to happen, and I haven't pressed her to talk about it. Even though we're back to being friends, Rick is still kind of a weird subject with us, even as much as we hoped it wouldn't be. But she knows I'm behind her no matter what.

"I'll see you later," I tell Meg.

"Salad bar lunch?" Meg says.

"Great." Since we're seniors now, Meg and I are allowed off campus for lunch. There's a new salad café that's opened up on Main Street. Meg and I have been going every day. Each time, we try a new dressing. They have, like, a million different kinds there. So far, my favorite is Vidalia onion, and Meg's is ranch. Both of us are afraid to try the blue cheese.

It's a new little routine. We hardly ever go to Starbucks anymore.

"Okay! Bye, Claire!"

Claire and I head toward the front doors of school. "So, you have a game tonight?"

"Yeah. Can you come?"

"Sure."

A bunch of freshman girls walk by Claire and pull her along with them. They all say hi to me. I'm the big, cool older sister. I kind of love it.

I walk into school alone, past the kids who sit underneath the tree. They look less weird to me now. I smile at them. Breaking the ice. It takes a while, but we're definitely getting our melt on.

The next twenty minutes are mundane and routine. Homeroom. Bell. Lockers. Bell. First Period. So it goes and goes.

School has only been in session for two weeks, and I am already totally lost in my first period Pre-Calc class. Maybe because I don't ever pay attention. Instead, I doodle in my sketchbook, camouflaged inside my notebook. Drawing has become like coffee for me — I feel like I'm not really awake or alive unless I do it.

This sketchbook isn't like the one I had for Mr. Frank's class. The paper is a little thicker, like cardstock, and the pages are all perforated. They are meant to be ripped out.

This morning, I draw Mrs. Dernelle's coffee cup, perched precariously close to the edge of her desk. The rim of white ceramic is covered in several half circles of coral lipstick, snaked with little tiny lines from the dryness of her lips. Like fingerprints. It takes most of the period. When I'm done, I rip the sheet out, flip to the backside, and address it like a postcard.

I've been sending drawings to Fiona in the mail since the night of the gallery show. Drawings of everything — sketches like this, people, places, funny bits of conversation, Claire's dirty soccer cleats. Sometimes I don't send any for a few days, sometimes it's a big stack all at once.

I want to encourage her, to show her that I haven't gone back to the old Emily, and she doesn't have to go back to the old Fiona. We can both move forward, so long as we keep drawing and not giving a crap what everyone else says. I keep waiting to hear something. But so far, silence.

When I get home from school, Mom says, "You got an interesting piece of mail today." She looks a little confused, flipping a glossy white square over and over in her hands.

My heart surges. Is it Fiona?

She hands me a postcard. My face, the painting Yates did of me, is on the front.

It's an invitation to his First Friday gallery show.

Forty-One

I don't feel steady on my feet, and it's not just because I'm in heels.

Yates's solo show is not at Space Invaded. It's at one of the more traditional galleries. There's wine, there are hors d'oeuvres on silver platters — little pieces of barbecued salmon, tempura asparagus rolls.

It's hard to squeeze through the door, there are so many people inside, from old patrons dripping in furs to the guys in Romero. The glass windows are fogged with body heat. I see Mr. Frank across the room, debating something with a crowd of interested people.

When I step into the gallery, the first thing I see is my own portrait, hanging on the first big wall of the gallery. People around me do double takes as I step closer. I don't exactly look the same, with my white-blond hair and my lacy black cocktail dress, but they still recognize me.

The rest of the walls are filled with similar portraits, done with people young and old. Tattooed punks and old homeless men all masked with a beautiful Victorian, classical face, stripping them of the pretenses of how we might view them or judge them in their normal environment. And then there's Yates himself, a portrait of him holding up his license. I lean in close. It says Leonard Jones on the license, but the painting is still signed *Yates*.

Yates hangs near a side door, which has been propped open for air. His eyes scan the room, sweeping left to right and back again. I feel them about to hit me and my whole body tenses up. I don't know if I have the courage to see him and talk to him again. But I guess it's a little too late for that.

He edges his way through the crowd. He's got on a black shirt, black pants, and a skinny white tie.

"You came," he says. He smiles so wide, it looks painful.

He reaches for my hands. I let him take them. "Yeah." I can feel myself starting to break, even though I want to be strong. "I've missed you."

"You have no idea," Yates says. He looks around and says, "Come over here so we can talk."

He leads me through the gallery. People try to pull him away into other conversations or ask questions about his process, but he smiles them all off.

"Listen," I say when we reach the far corner. "I want to apologize for what happened the last time we talked. I was being totally selfish. You were right to be mad at me. I screwed everything up."

Yates shakes his head. "Emily, I was never mad at you. It was more like I was mad at myself. I hated letting you walk out of that room. It killed me. I've barely left my studio this whole month. I've been hanging out with your portrait."

"Really?" I've been doing the same thing with one of the sketches I did of Yates at the baseball game. I stare at it all the time.

"Yeah. When you left, I realized exactly what I was letting go of. I had this beautiful painting of this beautiful person that I was afraid to show Mr. Frank because it revealed something about who *I* really was. Or, rather, I felt like it exposed what I was holding on to. Which was basically an act. You were my muse." He smiles crookedly, knowing how funny that sounds. "I let you walk away. And it wasn't even your fault that Fiona told."

"Yeah," I say, suddenly sad. "I know it wasn't. But I've forgiven her for it. There was a lot about Fiona that I didn't know, but I understand it. It's easier to play a part sometimes than to become the you that you're really supposed to be. I get that now, but I also know I wouldn't be here today if it wasn't for her."

"Do you still talk to her?"

"No. I haven't seen her since the day she told. I've been trying to keep in touch, but she hasn't ever returned my calls or answered my letters."

"You're a good friend, Emily."

It feels so nice to hear that. "Thanks."

"How've you been? You look amazing. I love your hair." He combs a strand so it sits behind my ear.

"I've been okay. I already have senioritis."

"Have you thought much about colleges yet?" He has this hopeful look on his face. "We could be here together next year."

"I've thought about it," I say. Actually, I've thought about little else.

September

Yates and I spend the rest of the night talking in that corner, like it's just the two of us. It feels so good to see him, to be back in Philly again.

When it's time for me to catch my train, he walks me out of the gallery.

"So, can I call you?" he asks.

I say, "I'd like that."

He leans in and kisses me slow and soft on my cheek, and lets his lips stay there like he wished we could kiss forever.

The night is still young when I walk out the door, and the wind bites my bare shoulders. The noise inside the gallery pours onto the street in the way that makes your heart race. Things are happening.

Two steps later, I freeze.

On the street in front of me is pink chalk, wrapped around the shadow of a big oak tree. And all over the ground, the outlines of leaves are drawn — small delicate leaves that fell and blew away.

"Fiona!" I call out, and jog down the cobblestones. I wait for her to step out of the shadows. Only she never appears.

But it doesn't matter.

Because on the brick wall behind the tree, Fiona's traced the evolution of a single falling leaf. The same shape, repeated a million times, swirling, twirling, undulating until it hits the ground. It's absolutely stunning. She's found a new way to slow down time, to show the progress, the journey. Not just one single moment in light.

The breeze kicks up again but I feel on fire.

I know she's back.

I know I'll see her again.

About the Author

Siobhan Vivian is the acclaimed author of *The List*, *Not That Kind of Girl*, and *A Little Friendly Advice*. She currently lives in Pittsburgh. You can find her at www.siobhanvivian.com.

Smart Girls in the Real World
from Siobhan Vivian

Ruby and her friends tell each other everything . . . until secrets, lies, and boys get in the way . . .

Emily leaves the burbs for a thrilling art program in the city, but what happens when her worlds collide?

Natalie's life gets turned upside down by a school election, disloyal friends, and a very hush-hush romance.

An intense look at the rules of high school attraction—and the price that's paid for them.

Prettiest. Ugliest.

An intense look at the rules of high school attraction — and the price that's paid for them.

"I devoured *THE LIST* — it's funny, heartbreaking, suspenseful, and wise. Siobhan Vivian tells a raw, real, winning story about the perils of fitting in, the danger of labels, and how prettiness and ugliness are sometimes intertwined. It definitely makes my list as one of the best books I've read all year." — SARA SHEPARD, author of *PRETTY LITTLE LIARS*

this is teen

Want the latest updates on YA books and authors, plus the chance to win great books every month?

Join the conversation with This Is Teen!

Visit **thisisteen.com** to find out how to reach us using your favorite form of social media!

TEEN2